The Last
Game

Randa Knight

The Last Game

Copyright © 2024 by Randa Knight

For information contact :

Randa Knight

http://www.randaknightbooks.com

Editor: Jonathan Miller

iFlow Creative

bio.site/iflowcreative

Proofreader: Nadara Merrill

Nay's Notations

www.naysnotations.com

First Edition: July 2024

10 9 8 7 6 5 4 3 2 1

Prologue

Ivy—Cat's Wedding

CAT PULLS ME INTO her arms. "Thank you for everything. I don't just mean today or even this week. You... You gave me a safe place—a home at Ephemera. Without that, I have no idea where I would be."

Yeah, I did. I also told her two days after we met that she was going to be my bestie. I'm a bit bossy. That's also how Grant became a part of our circle of friends when I was six.

"Jeez, don't be so mushy. I—" I stop to compose myself and make sure I hide my guilt for not paying attention during her wedding ceremony.

"Hag, just say *I love you, bestie, and I'm forever grateful that I hired you.*"

Bitch is going to make me cry with this shit. "I hate you, and every day I regret hiring you." My voice breaks at the end, betraying me, and I pull her close and squeeze her—well, as much as I can with that fluffy tulle.

Cat pulls away, waving her hands in front of her eyes in a vain attempt to dry her tears. I let mine fall even if I shouldn't since crying will mess up my makeup. Grant blots my face with a tissue and gives me a peck on the cheek. He's the reason I was distracted during the ceremony. But I loved watching my bestie, Cat, walk down the aisle with crystals glimmering in her straight brunette hair, looking perfectly elegant in her princess dress.

It's almost as perfect as the man I've spent almost every waking moment with since we arrived. I thought it would be torture being away from Mase, my seven-year-old son, for six days, but the demands from Cat's mother and Nonna have kept me on my toes. Her sister, Sylvia, has a steady stream of wine to help.

But it's the nights with Grant that have kept me sane. His constant touches, kisses, and holding me at just the right moment are what kept me from murder charges. Oh, and those quiet moments alone in our room together. I mean, it's not really quiet since Grant pulls every orgasm from my body numerous times after he's teased me to no end. Having known him since we were kids, it's no surprise he is aware of what to do to make me quiver.

My gaze drifts from my bestie to Grant, looking sexy as hell in a black suit, white shirt, and rose-gold tie. A wink and a smirk are what he gives me before he turns his eyes to Cat.

Emma stands to my left, nudging me for not paying attention. Jesus, I'm a shit bestie. I'm missing... Shit, I have no idea what's going on. Cat and Brax are kneeling. Praying, again. I know from the rehearsal dinner last night that there are a lot of prayers in a traditional Catholic wedding ceremony. I tried keeping count, but my attention was focused elsewhere, like it is now—three rows from me. On the man being sexy AF. I'm going to hell for thinking about every way I want to jump him after the reception. How his fingers skim down my body, making me feel like a sex goddess.

Emma grinds the toe of her stiletto into my foot. I glare at her, wanting to beat her brunette ass. Damn, that hurt. Ok, it hurt just a tiny bit. Emma mouths *Pay attention* and nods to where Brax gazes into Cat's eyes as he slips the ring on her finger.

Damn. Focus. On. Cat.

In the reception line, almost forty-five minutes later, I ask Grant, "How's my makeup? We haven't done pictures yet," as he runs his finger along my jawline.

"Gorgeous." He gives me another peck on the corner of my mouth and then whispers, "But I'm a little biased." He winks, giving me his signature sexy smile that's made me melt since we were kids, and I can't help but match it. My six-year-old self didn't realize any of that. She just knew the new kid was being nice and sweet to her instead of telling her to go away.

An hour and what seems like a thousand pictures later, the wedding party arrives at Cat's family's restaurant for the reception. That doesn't mean I get to sit and relax, though. Maid of honor duties and all that. There's the wedding party dance, the toasts, the wedding party shots—oh, and in the midst of all that, Grant. He hasn't been more than thirty feet from me the entire night. Touching me. Watching me. God, why is this reception taking so long? I need that man naked and inside me.

"Come dance with me, sweetness," Grant whispers, grabbing my hand and leading me to the dance floor, where Brax and Cat can't take their eyes off each other.

It never gets old—the way his arms feel wrapped around me. I feel safe, protected, and... loved. And fuck... that makes my heart race, and not in a good way.

Grant runs his nose along the length of my neck, his breath sending signals to every cell in my body. "Thank you for this week," he says and places feather-light kisses along my neck.

I can't help but pull him closer. I need more of him. He pulls away slightly and cups my face before gently pressing his lips to mine. Our tongues intertwine just as our bodies come together. Every aspect of my body melts into him. Our kiss lasts for an eternity, and I don't want to ever stop. Grant finally breaks our kiss and runs his nose along my neck, making me yearn to feel his lips against mine again.

"Hmm... tell me this is how it's going to be when we get home. I can't imagine my life without you and Mase. Or waking up without you beside me. I've been in love with you for... most of my life." He continues to skim his mouth along my skin.

He's still talking, but I stopped listening. Why is he doing this? If he loves me—No, I can't let that happen.

So, I do what I always do—run.

Straight from his arms.

I run down the street with no idea where I'm going. Run past shops and store fronts. Running is the only thing crossing my mind—to get as far away from the man who's been my rock for decades as possible.

I run until I trip over my own feet. I cry in the middle of a city block god-knows-how-far from the restaurant. Cry for the little girl who chased after the freckle-faced new kid. Cry for the teenager who played mind games with the sexy quarterback. Cry that I completely screwed up a twenty-year friendship with someone just as important as my brother.

Chapter 1

Ivy—Present Day

"I T's all your fault! I hate you!" my not-so-adorable seven-year-old yells, hurling his pee-wee football gear down by the front door. Not waiting for my response, he runs upstairs and slams his door.

I peek through the screen door to see who dropped him off—my brother, Jax, or Grant, my brother's best friend and evidently now my ex since he refuses to talk to me. Can someone be an ex if you never really dated? That sounds like a bestie question, except the hag is on her honeymoon.

A small part of me was hoping to see a black GMC truck, but instead, Jax's blue Camaro sits in my driveway.

At first glance, Jackson and Grant appear to be complete opposites. Jackson is tall at almost six three, with perfectly gelled blond hair and green eyes, and still has the muscular tone from his days as a running back and wide receiver. While Grant is six one with dark brown, almost black hair, bright blue eyes, and a bit more muscular build than Jax.

I take out my frustration on my brother, who comes through the door.

"What the hell happened at practice?" I ask, praying it's something I can fix.

Jax's green eyes narrow as he looks at me like I'm crazy and explains in a monotone voice, "Nothing. It was a normal day. Saturday's game was moved to noon. Do you want to drive together or are you heading to Ephemera from the game?"

I throw my hands in the air, knowing my brother is pissed at me for running away from Grant. "I don't know. Does Mase even *want* me there? You heard what he said." I know I sound like a whiny baby, but I'm frustrated at myself and have no one to vent to. Jax is the first person to speak to me in days.

At this point, I would prefer to spend more time in Ephemera, my art store and co-op, than with my angry little boy. But he's still my sweet little boy, and I kinda sorta deserve his anger for pushing Grant away. He is really the only father Mase has ever known, and now he's gone.

Jax shrugs. How can he shrug it off like it's no big deal? "You'll have that. How many times did you say that to Mom?"

"Don't blow me off with *'you'll have that'* bullshit. Our mother is a controlling bitch, and the situations were totally different."

Jax leans against the wall, impatience painted across his face. "You were younger than Mase the first time you said it to her."

"How should I have reacted? She took down all the pictures of Dad after he died—like she was trying to erase him from our lives as if he didn't exist. I needed those pictures. And... it's just not the same, ok?" I glare at my brother, wanting to knock the crap out of him like I used to when we were little. Too bad he's over twice my size and a Special Forces officer.

Impatience painted across Jax's face, he says, "She cried that night, FYI. She's not always the villain you make her out to be. He say anything else? Like *why* he hates you?"

I shake my head. "Just that it's my fault and he hates me." I completely ignore the mother comments since he's mommy's good little boy and I'm the devil child. Ok, he's probably a little right, but I don't have time to deal with my mommy issues.

He nods like that explains everything. "Grant missed practice—again. I can talk to Mase, but I doubt it will do much good. You know what Mase wants, and both of you are idiots."

He heads upstairs and I grab the football gear. Normally, I would make Mase clean this up, but it gives me something to do.

When I know Jax is out of earshot, I mock him. "Both of you are idiots... Tell me something I don't already know."

I jerk Mase's pads away from his practice jersey, almost punching myself in the face. He makes it seem like I don't *want* Grant here. I miss waking up on Saturday mornings to pancakes and their voices floating up from the kitchen or watching Grant in athletic shorts showing Mase how to improve his throw.

Jax finds me loading the washer. I don't say anything when he walks in because he's on his phone.

"Yeah, well the two of you need to actually talk." He flashes me a pointed look.

He must be talking to Grant. Shows what Jax knows, I've tried calling Grant. Ass doesn't answer his phone for me. It's great how he's completely ghosted me after what happened at Cat's wedding. I know I screwed up, but it's been two weeks! Mase needs him. The man is pissing me off with these bullshit games.

I'm so lost in my thoughts I don't realize Jax hung up and is talking to me. "I'm sorry, can you repeat that?"

He shakes his head. "I'm over both your shit. Mase is going to get worse until the two of you get over yourselves. Jesus, I don't get what the issue is between you two. Big deal, he finally told you how he feels about you and Mase. How is that a big shocker? He practically lived here. I really don't understand why you ran from him." He pauses. "You've been dancing around each other for years. Honestly, probably since we were kids."

"It's… none of your business." I know my response is lame, but I can't explain my behavior. I should go over there and talk to him, but I don't. And even if Grant answered his phone, I wouldn't know what to say. I'd probably hang up without saying a word, which is also lame.

"Bullshit. How do you figure it's none of my business? *My* best friend. *My* sister. *My* business." He takes a step closer. I shouldn't antagonize him like that, especially since the right side of his jaw is twitching, indicating he's getting angry.

He slightly raises his voice, but not so much so he doesn't draw Mase's attention. "It's not my business when my best friend starts fucking my sister and living with her and my nephew? They attend one wedding in Pennsylvania together, suddenly, they're not talking. I have to sober my best friend up every night and avoid discussing the two people he loves the most. Let's not forget the angry little man upstairs because he can't see his dad."

"Grant isn't his dad." I fire back. What the hell is his problem?

"Really? Where was Grant when Mase was born?" He answers, not giving me time to respond. "Right fucking beside you. Who took turns getting up with him in the middle of the night so both of you could get more than a few hours of sleep? Changed diapers? Helped potty train him? Taught him to ride a bike? He's been there for that kid's every first. Yeah, Eli is his father, but Grant is his dad. Plus, why the hell are you building Eli to be this great guy? He was a manipulative ass…who fucking cheated on you!" He takes a breath. "Both of you need to figure this shit out. Mase needs you and Grant. I'm taking Mase Saturday night—overnight."

He slams the door behind him, leaving without letting me say a word, but I'm left with plenty of them to keep me company in the empty laundry room.

Grant—8 Years Old

I hate my room. I hate this house. I hate this town. I hate being so far away from my dad. I hate that my parents got divorced. I thought since Dad left the military, we would get to stay in one place. Not move yet again. And this time without him. Why did they have to get divorced? It ruined everything.

The only good thing is my oldest brother, Robert, is at West Point, so I won't have him pushing me around, and I get my own room—finally! No more sharing a room with Linc and all his smelly sports crap. I still have Kennedy annoying me, but isn't that what little sisters do?

To avoid having to play dolls with Kennedy, I grab my bike and explore the neighborhood. Plus, Mom told me to go ride my bike since I have an attitude right now and she doesn't want to deal with it while unpacking.

There are tall green trees and big houses, but then again, any house is big compared to the military housing I've lived in. A few houses even have flowers around the porches. I turn the corner and see three little blonde girls younger than Kennedy pulling weeds in the flowerbed surrounding the white front porch. At least Kennedy will have someone to play with. Maybe they have an older brother.

I scan for someone my age. Boys who play sports would be awesome. Turning right back toward my house, my shoulders slump from not seeing any more kids. I pedal harder so I can tell Mom she was wrong when she said there are a lot of kids in our neighborhood. Three houses from our new house, a bike similar to mine lies in the yard. I slow down as a redheaded little spitfire storms out the door. She looks a little bit older than Kennedy.

"Hey, you're the new kid, right?"

I nod. I'm used to being the new kid since we used to move around from duty station to duty station.

She points her finger at me. "Stop." She turns around, runs back into the house, and yells, "J-a-a-a-x. Come here. I have the new kid."

She has me? Dream on, kid.

A sandy-haired kid about my age walks out with the little redhead. Curiosity is the only reason I stop on the sidewalk in front of the large red-brick house. And hope.

"Sorry if my sister was being bossy. I'm Jax and bossy pants is Ivy. You like sports?"

A huge smile crosses my face. "Heck yeah. I'm Grant."

"Ivy, can you grab a football for me?"

Ivy rolls her eyes. "But then I can't play."

"Football and soccer ball?" he negotiates with her.

"Fine, but we start with soccer."

I shrug, grateful someone else likes sports and I finally found another boy. Maybe I can avoid playing Barbies and dolls for more than a few hours at a time. We head to their backyard, where there are woods connected at the left edge. That might be something fun to explore.

I kick the ball to Ivy softly like I do when I play with Kennedy, only for Ivy to lodge it back at me.

"Just 'cause I'm a girl doesn't mean I can't keep up."

This time I kick the ball back like I do with my older brothers. She gives me a huge grin.

The three of us spend the rest of the afternoon in their yard kicking the soccer ball around and throwing the football. His sister tries to climb on my back to tackle me when we toss the football around. She's a determined little thing. I kinda like her.

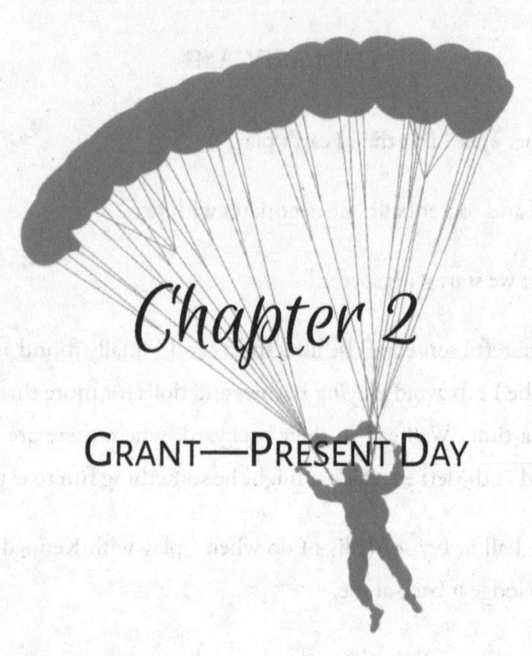

Chapter 2

Grant—Present Day

"Hey, dumbass. You missed football practice yesterday, again," Jax says, plopping into my leather recliner at my townhouse that until recently I was rarely at.

I barely lift my head off the sofa. Probably not a good sign that I'm this blitzed at almost 4 p.m. when I left work less than two hours ago. But I can't deal with my thoughts right now. If I do, I'll focus on the look she gave me when I laid my heart out for her.

She sprinted all over it. Just ran straight from my arms in the middle of a song on the dance floor. At first, I thought she went to the ladies' room to compose herself. Ivy doesn't do public displays of affection or even show it beyond the bedroom.

She was holding my hand the week leading up to Cat's wedding. She let me pull her to me during the speeches at the rehearsal. If she was within arm's reach, I was touching her. She didn't reprimand me like she usually does. Actually, she curled into each touch, even initiated a few.

I wish I could say I didn't wait for her, that I didn't search the entire restaurant for her. But I did. It's what I always fucking do. Always. Well, I guess not always. There was a time she was waiting for me. I was an arrogant ass who thought football was the only important thing. And chasing assholes away from Ivy. God, I was so stupid.

After three hours, I left. Pissed off. I grabbed my stuff from Sylvia's converted basement where we were staying and packed my bags while on hold with the airline. Two hours and three hundred dollars later, my butt was sitting in a window seat watching the clouds, wishing the night ended differently.

Maybe I should've waited longer. Maybe I should've kept my mouth shut. But I'd been telling her the entire week about how incredible she is. How beautiful and sexy she is and just about every other compliment possible to let her know how I feel about her without actually saying those three little words. Not because I needed to, but she deserves it. Instead, she fucking runs from me. Who the hell does that?

Jax kicks my leg hanging off the sofa. "Get your ass up. Little Bear has practice in thirty minutes. Shower, brush your teeth, and sober the fuck up. That kid doesn't deserve the bullshit the two of you are putting him through. My sister deserves a bit of it, but not Mase."

I mumble into the sofa about how I'm too drunk. I hear the shower starting. Fuck, I need to move before he drags my ass in there. I know that water is ice cold. We used to—ok, still—do that to our soldiers who need to sober up and fast. I stumble in the bathroom, bypassing Jax, who merely laughs at me. I adjust the water so I don't get hypothermia. Less than thirty minutes later, I'm walking out the door with him to watch Mase practice.

Being on the football field and smelling the freshly cut grass takes me back to when I played in high school and college. Watching Mase run up and down the field throwing the football fills my heart with pride, knowing I taught him how to do that. Mase launches the ball at his friend Kole. It flies from his hands with almost a spiral—ok, not at all, but I'm not telling him that. The ball slices through the air into Kole's klutzy hands.

I clap my hands. "Good job, Mase." He looks over and his face lights with a huge smile.

"I would ask why you've been so quiet, but I'm sure I know the answer," I say to Jax an hour into Mase's practice. He's barely said a word to me since kicking my butt off the sofa.

"You know me well enough to know why. If I have to spell it out, you're more of an idiot than I thought," he snaps. He then hollers words of encouragement to Mase and the other boys close to us.

"She ran. What was I supposed to do?" I ask, not taking my eyes off Mase.

"You're right, she shouldn't've run, but you know how she is. You knew she would run. It's what she does when sh—things get rough or too real for her. Unloading your feelings on the dance floor was fu—not your finest moment. She's more at fault than anyone. I'm just... frustrated." He flashes me a pointed look, and the coaches blow their whistles for the boys to take a water break.

Little Bear sprints over, flipping his chin strap and yanking his helmet off before he reaches us. His excitement bounces off him. "Dad, I did it. The spiral you taught me. I had issues gripping it the way you showed me, but I made sure to aim it at his chest. I did it!" He looks back and forth between Jax and me.

Jax hands him his water bottle. "Calm down and drink." He leans down to Mase. "That was a great throw."

Mase drinks and nods at Jax before looking at me. "Dad, are you taking me home?" he begs with those adorable green eyes. How can I say no to that?

"Sure." One last drink, then Mase darts over to the offensive team to begin their drills.

Jax watches him go. "He's sloppy with his left-hand placement."

I nod. "We also need to work on his footwork. He shouldn't need so many steps to pass the ball."

We continue our analysis until Jax leaves for our takeout. Normally, we would order enough for Mase and Ivy and eat with them. But I can't bring myself to walk in the house. Thankfully, I have enough uniforms at my house I don't need to get the rest of my clothes. If I need my blues anytime soon, I don't know what I'll do. Hersh said he won't get anything for me. I don't blame him.

Mase bolts over to me at the end of practice while I'm packing his bag. I toss his water bottle to him before he can explain why he dropped the ball two plays ago. A few large guzzles and he starts talking again.

"D-dad," he gasps, still out of breath from running so hard.

"Drink. Catch your breath. We can talk in the truck. Come on."

I toss his bag over my shoulder and throw my arm around him as we head to the truck.

"Buckle up," I instruct Mase, tossing his bag in the back seat. "That was a good practice. How much homework do you have?"

Mase rolls his eyes and looks out the window. "I dropped the ball—twice." Frustration is written all over his face. Little Bear beats himself up too much, just like his mother. My little perfectionist who hasn't realized that concept is impossible on a football field.

Backing out of the parking space, I laugh. "Little Bear, I used to drop the ball a lot. Much more than twice a practice. Don't sweat it. You're just getting started. Besides, you threw the ball what... four, five times? I dropped it every time when I was your age. You're supposed to have fun. Was it fun?"

A huge smile forms, lighting up his face.

I continue. "That's all that matters. Anything else bothering you?"

That smile instantly disappears. "What's with you and Mom? Don't tell me it's grown-up stuff or I'll understand when I get older. That's crap."

I smirk. "It's grown-up stuff that you'll understand when you get older." I watch him from the corner of my eyes. His eyes grow larger, and his mouth hangs open. I can tell he wants to rebel or backtalk. But he won't.

"Go ahead. Say what you want." I turn left on Cedar.

"That's crap. I want to know what's going on." His voice begins to rise.

"Ok. Your mom and I are not getting along. We need a time out from each other," I answer him, stopping at the light.

"That's stupid."

I glance over at him. "Was it stupid when you and your friend Randall were fighting about which Marvel superhero was the best? You started hitting each other."

I hear him sigh. "That was stupid even though I was right."

"But you still refused to talk or play with him for over a week, right?"

"Yeah."

"Well, Mom and I are arguing kinda like you and Randall were."

"I said I was sorry to Randall for hitting him and gave him one of my Pokémon cards. Even though I only kinda meant it 'cause I'm right. Iron Man *is* better than Batman. Can't you do the same?"

"I wish it was that easy, Little Bear. I don't think Pokémon cards and a half-hearted apology is going to fix this."

"That sucks since I don't get to see you. Th-that's—"

"Stupid. True, but... I honestly don't know how or what to do yet. Gimme some time to figure some stuff out, ok?"

"Mom doesn't like Pokémon, but maybe buy something else for her. She loves the cards I make for her."

"I'll figure something out."

I pull into Ivy's driveway with a pit in my stomach. I get out, grab his bag, and sling it over his shoulder. His face falls when he realizes I'm not coming in with him. This shit fucking sucks. I hate how this hurts him.

I didn't lie to him, though. I have no idea how to fix this or what to do yet. I do know that she needs to come to me—when she's ready. I'm usually the guy who makes the plan and executes it.

After I watch Mase slug up the stairs and in the house, I climb back in the truck and text Jax.

Me: I hate this shit

Jax: then fix it

> **Me: I'm getting fucked up tonight. Btw, thanks for the support**

> Jax: yw

Grant—8 Years Old

I haven't been in this small town long, but I have made some great friends, including the siblings sitting on each side of me. We shouldn't be on this rickety old dock at the Greenville Creek; it just sounded like the thing to do. We walked across town to do just that.

I have so many questions for my new friends about this town, the people, their family, and our other friend, Eli, and his family. Like why Eli is gone every weekend even though both of his parents are together, unlike mine.

Ivy hums and swings her legs back and forth, barely skimming the water with her tiny feet. "If unicorns shoot rainbows, what do horses shoot?" she randomly asks. Something she does often.

"Poop," Jax answers. He always answers every question no matter how ridiculous her question is.

"Oh." She returns to humming.

"Why does Eli leave every weekend?" I ask. "I would get it if his parents were divorced like mine, but they aren't. So... where does he go?" Eli is ok, but he's not very nice.

Jax shrugs. "They go camping and do outdoorsy stuff together... as a whole family. Every weekend. No matter what."

"No friends allowed, not even me! I'm a-dorable. I should be allowed to go with Charlie and Cassie." Ivy rolls those big brown eyes at the preposterousness of not being allowed to go.

"I have another question. I mean, you might not answer it but what-ever—"

Jax looks to his right at me. "Spit it out, Brandt. It's not like I don't answer a million questions a day with Miss-Twenty-Questions over there." He tosses a piece of grass into the water.

"Where's your dad?" I hesitate since I have no idea if I will offend them.

Jax answers quietly. "Dead." I glance at Jax. He's staring into the greenish water by our feet. Then I look at Ivy with huge brown eyes filled with tears. "He died in a car accident about three years ago."

"Sorry." What else do you say to that? I wish I wouldn't've asked. I feel like a complete jerk.

"Where's your daddy, Grant?" Ivy asks.

My dad has only visited a handful of times since we moved here. He calls every other day, but his new job keeps him busy.

"DC. I mean..." I pause trying to remember what Mom told us about why we moved here instead of closer to our dad. "He moved there right after my parents split. Mom said that it wasn't the right place for us. I don't really understand why we moved here instead of there, except she said we needed room to run and grow, not be stuck in the city. I don't get it. Dad doesn't visit us much." I explain all that even though it's a lot more than they asked for.

"Do you miss him?" Ivy asks.

"Ivy Rose, don't ask stupid questions. Of course, he misses his dad. It's his *dad*. Who wouldn't?" Jax answers as if Ivy asked the dumbest question in the world. In a way, it is.

"He did work a lot before since he was an officer in the Army. But he was home every night, and we did stuff together until right before he left the Army... and us. I don't know. It's weird. He's here but he's not. It was kinda like that before too, but he was home. But he wasn't." I shake my head since I know I'm not making any sense.

The whole thing is confusing. Neither of my parents will talk about it. My older brothers act like it's no big deal. It is. I guess it doesn't matter to Robert since he's away at a military prep school 'cause he wants to be like our dad. Linc, well, I don't know what he thinks. Linc is too busy with his new friends and ignores Ken and me.

"Why do you always wear braids?" I shake one of her braids, attempting to change the subject.

She sighs as if I'm the one who's always asking questions. "Because I'm always with Jax and he gets me all dirty and... Mother doesn't like twigs and grass and stuff in my hair." She tosses a braid behind her head.

"Why don't you hang out with your friends instead of us? I know you have friends; I've seen them." I continue my series of questions that have been bouncing around in my brain.

Another sigh of annoyance. "Mom doesn't like them and says I can't play with them. Plus, when I'm with Jax, I have fun and don't get wha-wha-wha from Mother," she mimics the teacher from Charlie Brown. Ivy Rose rolls her eyes.

Jax adds, "Our grams, Dad's mom, used to say it's cause Ivy Rose is the spittin' image of our dad. I don't think so. Maybe it's just their red hair. I don't know. But when Ivy Rose follows me around, Mother leaves her alone. No picking on her about ... well, anything." Jax smiles over at his sister, admiring the little miss dancing her toes in and out of the green creek water.

"I miss Daddy. You think he misses us?" She sniffles. "I miss his hugs. He was a great hugger." A single tear escapes each of those gorgeous brown eyes.

I wrap my arms around Ivy while she cries into my shoulder, and Jax sniffles a few times, pretending to not be affected by his sister's cries. I admit I get choked up a few times too.

Chapter 3

Ivy—Present Day

"Mo-o-o-o-o-o-m, where are my cleats?" my seven-year-old yells from his bedroom.

I'm sure he has torn the entire room up looking for those damn cleats when he left them by the back door where Grant told him to keep them. I shake my head, praying the room is cleaner than I'm imagining. Crossing the threshold of his room, I find socks thrown about from one end of the room to another. He even has one hanging from his bedside lamp. Don't ask. I doubt I want to know how that happened.

Legos are in various degrees of assembly and all over the floor along with shoes, hot wheels, little green Army men, three footballs, a soccer ball, blankets, clothes, books, and noisy character toys my brother bought him. His tablet hangs from the changer, about to fall off the edge of his dresser. He digs in his closet, tossing more clothes above his head. I adjust the tablet and the picture from last summer's fishing trip with Jax, Grant, and Mase.

"Mase, your cleats are by the back door where they're supposed to be," I remind my brown-haired bundle of energy.

He takes off down the hall without another word. I take another look at his room—his solid blue walls with white accents adorned with footballs of varying degrees. The twisted metal football I made him last year to the plastic football shapes to pictures of football stadiums are intermingled with family pictures of Masen's favorite moments. The stars of most of those photos are his two heroes, Jax and Grant. I wish Grant would come over or at least talk to Mase. It's not Little Bear's fault I have issues.

I walk around the room thinking about each picture and the moment the photo was taken. Many of them I was there for, but a few I wasn't, like the fishing trip and the handful of Carolina Panthers games they attended.

Four pictures rest on Mase's bedside table. Two, I put there—the baby picture of Mase and the one of his father in uniform. But the other two, my brother must have placed. One is from my child-hood—Grant, Eli, and Jackson standing on the riverbank, arms across each of their shoulders grinning from ear to ear.

I took that photo. I vividly remember that day. I was sixteen and thought the world of those three for graduating high school the week before. Grant left a month later for West Point Academy. Jackson left two weeks later for football camp at the University of Illinois. Eli left for basic training at the end of the summer.

The last one is Grant holding Mase minutes after he was born. Grant was with me from the moment I moved to Fayetteville. He painted Masen's nursery and put together all the baby furniture. He came with me to every doctor's appointment and lab test. He was the first person to see the rambunctious Little Bear. I miss Grant so much. I run my finger along his face, wishing I could talk to him. I need to at least apologize, but I know that's not enough.

Mase busts in. "Help me with this. I can't get it." The look of determination is pasted across his innocent face. He pulls his football pants up. How this child can pull all that football gear on yet can't tie his pants or cleats is beyond me. "Whatcha lookin' at?" he asks while I tie his pants.

"Your pictures. Uncle Jax added a few new ones in here?"

"No, I did. D—Grant helped me," my sweet boy corrects himself and watches to see my reaction to his almost mistake. I know he calls Grant Dad, but not around me. I should talk to him about that. But not when he has less than ten minutes until he needs to leave for practice.

He points at one by his window of the three at a Panthers game. Grant holds Mase in his arms while my brother leans against his best friend. Mase looks up at Grant, grinning ear to ear. He shifts his focus to one in a football frame where Mase is in his pee-wee football gear after a game. Grant is bent down beside Little Bear with their arms around each other. Again, the biggest grin on my boy's face. Masen points to his nightstand where I was looking at the two new pictures.

"I asked if I could have those. They were on Grant's table in the living room. I wanted another one. But he said I couldn't have it cause it's his favorite of you." He shrugs like it's no big deal.

"What picture did you want?" I ask, hoping he will tell me what picture is Grant's favorite. "Maybe I have a copy since I took so many pictures when I was younger."

"You were wearing a fancy dress and Da—Grant was wearing a black something. Anyway, his arms were around you and you guys were smiling. You were super pretty, Mom. I mean, you still are. You're not ugly like Donnie's mom." My boy rambles on.

"Masen Alexander, manners. You don't say things like that about people. It's rude," I attempt to reprimand him even if he's right. The woman is incredibly kind and the sweetest person I've ever met. Her inner beauty outweighs her outer beauty, but try telling that to the mean girls of the PTA or to a blunt seven-year-old.

"Little Bear, where are ya?" my brother yells from the front door.

Mase grabs his cleats and takes off. I follow, knowing my brother won't let my son in his car without saying goodbye. Plus, that kid needs to put those cleats on and have someone tie them.

I want to ask Jackson about a few things, but I'm scared to ask. Like if Grant will be at practice with them or how he's doing or anything about him. It hurts not talking to Grant. I might go upstairs and have a good cry while they're at practice instead of working in my studio. Just thinking about Grant breaks my heart, even if I did this to myself.

Over the past few years, he's become my rock. That's not true—he's always been my rock. I don't have a single childhood memory without him. Every significant moment in my life, that man has been right beside me. Until now. My gut churns at the thought of what happened at my best friend Cat's wedding and my reaction. I overreacted, but I don't know how to fix this whole messed-up situation.

Grant—9 Years Old

"Why do dragons breathe fire? I mean, wouldn't they have some pretty bad breath?" This is one of many questions that fall from sweet Ivy Rose's mouth since we entered our neighbor's woods.

Eli sighs. "Who cares? Dragons aren't real."

"I know that. I'm not stupid. But what if they were? Can you imagine how bad their breath would be?"

She continues her series of questions, I'm presuming just to annoy Eli. It's easy to do. I quietly laugh and lead us farther into the woods than we've ever been. Eli picks up his pace so he's not beside her anymore.

A gentle breeze dances across the treetops of the woods. The leaves and twigs crunch under our feet. The serene sounds of nature are around us, from the birds fluttering above to the crickets chirping, but we barely hear any of it over Ivy Rose's myriad of questions and commentary.

"Why are tomatoes fruit?" She pauses only long enough for one to believe she's waiting for another person to respond but not long enough for someone to actually answer her. Eli rolls his eyes but thankfully doesn't say a word.

Ivy Rose grabs a tree sapling branch out of her path. "It should be a vegetable because I hate them." She continues talking about other vegetables she hates and why while Eli mumbles his complaints under his breath.

I almost trip over a root. After I recover, I reach behind me to help Ivy Rose. I feel protective of her. The sun cuts through the trees and makes her red hair stand out even more than it usually does. Ivy Rose grabs a hold of a sapling to prevent from tripping over the roots and twigs, and stops talking to concentrate on her footsteps.

A few minutes later, I suddenly realize and look behind me since Ivy Rose has been unusually silent. Not even mumbling about... well, anything. "Where's Rosebud?"

Eli rolls his eyes again. "I don't get why you call her that."

Jax turns and looks around. "Leave him alone."

"Her middle name is Rose," I explain. "She's not a grown-up, so she's a rosebud. A rosebud is a flower that hasn't bloomed. My momma said Ivy Rose will be a beautiful flower once she fully blooms."

I can't stand the guy, but he's been Jax's friend since they were babies. I have to tolerate Eli, even though he's a jerk to Ivy Rose.

He glares at me like he's going to throw a punch. Normally, I know he wouldn't, but we're in the woods where no one else can see us. Eli acts one way around adults and another when it's just us.

"Whatever," he says. "Just find her so we can find this old treehouse."

We split up into different directions to find Ivy Rose, but we remain within ten feet of each other. Even though Eli complains about her, he always helps when we ask. And we always have to ask.

After we spend the next hour searching, I get attacked by a bundle of red hair with tears streaming down her angelic face.

"You lost me." She sobs in my arms, her left braid almost completely undone, dirt mixed with her tears. Grass stains and dirt cover her jeans.

"What happened? Where did you go?" I wipe away her tears, smearing the dirt on her face even more.

Between her sobs, she explains, "You left me. I tripped a-and the root, u-untied my s-shoe s-s-so I tied it. A-a-and you were g-gone. I tried to catchup b-b-but you..."

"It's ok. I'm here now," I say, pulling her into my arms while Jax ties her right shoe.

Jax brushes dirt off her clothes and pulls a few twigs from her hair. "You going to be ok, Ivy Rose?" His voice lowers as he gently pulls her remaining braid free of the hair tie. He runs his fingers through her hair, releasing the remaining twigs and leaves that were stuck in it. He looks at me and says, "She doesn't like being alone. It's one of the reasons I keep her with me."

Rosebud clings to me tighter. I remind her, "I got you. Always."

"But you left me," she says against my chest.

"Won't happen again."

"Promise, promise?"

"Promise, promise."

Two days later, Ivy Rose bounces over to me while Eli, Jax, and I are tossing the football around at the park.

Her toothy grin greets us. "This is for you so you can always find your way to me."

She hands me a green square object with a brown string. I open it to see a round compass inside. It looks just like the one my dad gave me when I was five. He was teaching me how to read land nav maps, which he uses in the Army.

I loop it around my neck since I'm wearing athletic shorts without pockets.

"Thanks."

"Don't lose it. It's special." She slurs her s's thanks to missing her two front teeth. She runs off to play with my sister, Kennedy, and two other girls from the neighborhood under the slides.

"Hey, what did she give you?" Jax hollers.

"An Army compass."

He tosses the ball at me and shakes his head. "That was Dad's. He gave it to her a month before his accident."

"Should I give it back?"

He looks over at his sister and shakes his head. "Nah, keep it. She wanted you to have it." He tosses the ball back to me.

Chapter 4

Ivy—Present Day

Ephemera is my second baby. My safe place. I pour every ounce of myself into making this place a safe haven for artists of all types, from drawing and sculpturing to ceramics and metalsmithing. Every now and again, I sell photography and various forms of graphic design in my store too.

Usually, my morning routine begins at 6 a.m. with working in my metalsmithing studio, but since my little tiff with Grant, I haven't been able to maintain my schedule. Grant used to get up with Mase, cook him breakfast, and take him to school. This whole thing is confusing. It makes it really hard to focus on... well anything.

"It's about damn time you bring your butt to work," I say to my best friend and resident artist at my store, Cat. I stand beside her at the register she's working at, blatantly ignoring my sarcasm. Instead, she's tending to the middle-aged woman buying paints. The boss in me is proud, but the bestie is irritated.

Once the transaction is complete, Cat turns around and says, "I missed you too. I heard you're having some issues." Cat studies me, probably to see if I will lie to her. In her defense, there was a time I would've. But as she has taught me, besties don't do that.

I take a deep breath and nod. "I had a mishap at your reception." I attempt to downplay being a complete chickenshit. My brother's words, not mine.

She folds her arms and her forehead crinkles slightly, showing her impatience with my half-truth. "Where's Courtney? Wasn't she supposed to be here today?"

"She quit. Two days ago, something about a 'great opportunity.' I'm pretty sure she told me, but I don't like her and I didn't care." I shrug, knowing this subject change is only temporary.

"I would ask if you chased her off, but I didn't like her either." Cat didn't like her because Courtney had a slight obsession with Brax. "Regardless, we are a cashier short today, which means we don't have anyone to fetch our food or run the register while we work in our studios. Kinda sucks."

"I hired a new girl, and Toby, the new pottery instructor, is coming in to work at nine. I mean, we don't have an intern to fetch things for us. By the way, I do know how to run things when you're not here," I say, waving my hands around the room.

"Hfff. That's... kinda true, but your personal life—that's debatable since you ran out of my reception. Hag, where were you for over four hours? Why did you leave? I was worried about you!" Cat hip checks me to help a customer who looks lost in the beads section.

This is what we do—start and stop conversations, and not just to help customers. It just happens. After I finish helping customers, I peruse each aisle looking for something to reorganize or return to their home. Cat finds me reorganizing the Sharpie display into their colors.

"Are you going to tell me why you ran that night, or do I have to guess like always?" Cat sits on the floor to sort the markers at the bottom of the display. "I can. Maybe Grant secretly works for the CIA and his cover is blown. But then *he* would run, not you."

I shake my head and quietly laugh, but I don't say anything.

"Oh, maybe Eli isn't really dead, but he had to *fake* his death to protect you and he called you that night. You went rushing off to see him? You're still deeply in love with him and couldn't wait another minute to see him?"

Giving her a look like she's completely lost her freaking mind, I keep the vulgar response I have in mind, just in case any customers wander in. She's giving me a taste of my own medicine, anyway. I used to create these elaborate stories for why she suddenly left her hometown for Fayetteville, North Carolina.

"No," I say with zero emotion. "I don't think I ever truly loved Eli. To be honest, he was just someone to make my brother mad. He left me with my... I would call her a psycho mom but she's really not. She's just more concerned with how others see *her* than anything else. You know how that feels."

"I completely understand. You saw how my mother acted. She does the same thing. That doesn't explain why you left Grant, though."

Cat stands up once she's finished with the markers while I'm pretending to still be sorting so I don't have to face my own crap.

She heads toward the register while I help Mrs. Kline, an elderly lady who is a regular of mine, find a soft yarn for a blanket she's making in her knitting club. A club I know quite well since they come in for supplies every few days. They also make hats and blankets for the babies born at our three local hospitals. Mrs. Kline updates me about two members who are having health issues.

I barely notice Toby coming in for his few hours in the store before he disappears in the pottery studio for the rest of the night.

Cat walks up with her customer service smile and matching voice. "Hi, Mrs. Kline. Did you find the yarn you need?"

"Yes, dear. I was just telling Ivy here about Mildred and Agnes."

Cat gives the elderly customer sympathetic eyes. "Oh, I know. But both have great doctors and a wonderful support system. I need to steal Ivy for a quick sec, is that ok?"

Mrs. Kline nods and wanders back to the yarn and knitting supplies.

Cat stares at me like my mother used to when I wore plaid and jeans instead of fancy dresses. Her look is filled with the expectation that I will do something to change the situation, which is doubtful. I run or hide from my problems until I'm forced to deal with them.

"Hag, office," Cat orders as if she's the boss and not me. I paint a shocked look on my face but still follow my bossy friend to *my* office. She closes the door and sits in her usual spot on the sofa in my direct view. "Enough stalling. Why did you leave? Or are you avoiding because you don't know?"

I open and close my mouth multiple times, trying to articulate how to explain my behavior at her reception. I shouldn't've left. I was the maid of honor. I slump in my leather office chair and sigh, knowing there's no logical reason for leaving that night.

Cat clasps my hand in hers. "Tell me what happened."

"Everything was gorgeous. I know I already told you this, but your family's church is beautiful with the woodworking etchings of saints in the pillars and the sculptures..."

"You're stalling—again."

Sometimes I hate having a bestie...

"I almost tripped walking down the aisle because Grant winked and smiled at me!" I shout-whisper. "How..." I stop to compose myself since everything from that night is rushing through my head at once. "Emma had to stab me with her shoes cause he was so freaking hot I couldn't focus."

"Keep going."

I take a deep breath. "It was... fabulous. Even though you were beyond beautiful, I wanted it to be over so we could leave and I could strip him down. I loved every minute... until Grant started telling me how he feels." I mumble the last part, hoping she won't make me continue, even though I know she will.

"How he's head over heels for you? Everyone with eyes can see that... but you. Why is that an issue? I know you feel the same about him. Or..."

Cat's eyes widen, and she lets go of my hand.

"What exactly did Grant say to you? You guys looked pretty chummy all week. It wasn't just him reaching for you, either. You watched his every move during the rehearsal dinner. I'm not counting the part where everyone wanted to murder my brother-in-law Lou for grabbing Emma. I swear every man in that room was about to murder Lou... Damn, that was a missed opportunity. Maybe we should've let them. Anyway, Grant was completely infatuated with you the entire night—hell the whole damn week."

I roll my neck. "Fuck. What's wrong with me? I should be ecstatic that the guy I've crushed on since... honestly, since I met him, professed his love and practically proposed."

Cat's eyes widened again. "He proposed?!"

I shush her, and she looks over her shoulder before lowering her voice and repeating herself. "He proposed?

"Well, he didn't say 'will you marry me,' but he said he can't imagine a life without me or without waking up together. Why did I start sleeping with him and letting him practically live with us? Mase is being a little shit cause all he wants is Grant, and it's my fault *he* isn't there. I gave birth to him. I'm the one who pushed him out. Let me tell you...it's never the same."

Cat hands me a bottled water from my mini fridge, and I take a large gulp to pull myself together. I'm shaking from how mortified I am.

"Keep going," Cat says after giving me a moment. "Bestie moment right here. Why would it freak you out?"

I don't normally spill my guts, but I'm angry and confused and... lost. I couldn't even decide which type of bread to use for Mase's toast this morning. And I did declare to her she's my bestie after only knowing her for a few days. I kinda owe her. I tell her what's been running through my mind.

"What if he doesn't come back? I will have to deal with Mase being mad at me for how long? What the hell is wrong with my bed? My pillows are too fluffy, and I can't get comfortable at night anymore. The blankets are either too hot or too cold." My voice turns whiny at the end, but I can't help it.

"Maybe if you had a certain Special Forces officer in your bed, it would be comfortable again?"

"He's been gone for long periods of time before and my bed didn't feel any different. *Everything* in my life feels wrong. What if I can't get anything back? Is this how my life is supposed to be? Am I just... Fuck, I need to beat or bend metal. Get out of my head. Besides, if Toby sees us in here, he will leave the sales floor for the pottery studio. "

"Toby's new, so I doubt he would do that. He actually respects the fact you're the boss. Have you actually spoken to Grant? Like, actually apologized for running out on him?" Cat questions, watching Toby hand a middle-aged brunette her newly purchased items.

I grumble low enough that I can barely hear what I said.

"What was that? A no? Call him, hag."

"Wench, I *have* been calling... He won't answer," I say, throwing my arms in the air.

She folds her arms with a knowing look. "So go *see* him. You know how to find him. His house. Mase's football practice. Hell, I bet I can find him. You're not trying."

"Duh. But he's not going to practice, either, which is why Mase is acting up. Everything is such a clusterfuck."

I stare at the small canvas that Masen created with Grant two months ago. A little green blob that's supposed to be a dinosaur throwing a football. Things like that are small treasures to me since they rarely do anything art-related, so I love it so much.

"Ok, why the hell not? Does Grant not realize how much that kid loves him? Seriously, what the hell?" Cat waves her arms around, showing how upset she is. "Do I need to go kick his ass myself cause that's beyond fucked up."

Part of me loves seeing her get riled up about my son, but another part is heartbroken that Grant not only left me but Mase too.

"I don't know what he's thinking. I wish he... he would at least be there for Mase like he always has. I can take it," I explain, trying to keep my voice from cracking. So not true, I'm just not willing to admit it yet.

"Bullshit. I would tell you to just admit it, but you're stubborn and won't listen to a damn thing I say. Can you promise me this?" She pauses.

"What?"

"While your stubborn ass is in denial, at least think about why you're freaking out. None of it has to do with Grant. So, why else are you running?"

"That's so... so wrong. This is all about Grant and only Grant. Why did he have to ruin everything?"

"He didn't. I want to call you on more of your bullshit, but the artist has been itching to paint since I haven't touched a canvas for two weeks. We are not done with this conversation. Tell me when you leave so I can leave around that time too. I'm trying to retrain myself so I can stop and start like you do. It comes in handy around kids." Cat heads toward my office door, but I stop her.

"Hold up, missy. Are you pregnant? Is that why you want to change your process?"

"No, but I'm thinking about it. I can't be manic with a kid. I figure I'll change my process, then talk Brax into it," she says, slipping out the door and then her studio.

"I'll see ya at two, then," I respond with a huge smile on my face.

Cat and Brax would be terrific parents.

Ivy—14 Years Old

Every Friday night, I'm in the same place—in the stands watching my brother and his friends on the football field. My mom is holding court at the bottom of the bleachers, talking about everything from politics to town gossip. She relishes the attention, much like the dynamic trio, Jackson, Grant, and Eli.

At least I have my friends with me—Jazmine, Ethan, and Kennedy. Occasionally, Eli's two younger sisters will hang out with me like we used to do when we were little, but that rarely happens anymore.

I hate halftime, especially right after the cheerleaders return from cheering to the opposing team, cause they always swarm me and pump me for information or tips about Grant. A few will ask about my brother. Either way, I always lie, and Kennedy fuels my lies. None of these girls are good enough for Grant, and bonus, I get the pleasure of also torturing my brother. Kennedy does it for the same reasons.

"Have you tried smacking your gum and twirling your hair while standing next to him at his locker?" I ask one of six girls. I think her name is Lacey, but I honestly don't give a shit.

"Especially if you pull it out of your mouth. Draws attention to your face." Ken winks, knowing her brother thinks it's gross and it makes him gag.

"I mean, he loves Windsong perfume," I continue. He hates it, saying it reminds him of a French whore. Like he really knows what a French prostitute smells like, but it is a saying I hear a lot.

"What else? This is good," a brunette cheerleader tells me, then calls over to her friend to join us.

"He loves to be touched. All. The. Time." Seriously, these girls must be stupid. I said the exact same thing to her last week. He snapped at her for touching his arm.

"Don't forget to run your finger down his arm," Ken adds with the same smirk as her brother.

"Love notes. The more, the better, especially with poetry," I add.

Ken says, "Oh yeah, the sweet lovey-dovey crap. He loves that. I mean, I don't but... keep that on the down low cause he doesn't want the guys to know he loves it."

I'm about to add more when Cassie, Eli's younger sister by a year, approaches. She will ruin everything and tell these idiots the truth. Then they really will have a chance with Grant. No way can I let that happen. Ken and I are having too much fun, or that's what I tell myself. Cass and Charlie always ruin everything. The little narks.

On Monday, after first period, I walk by Grant on my way to English as he opens his locker. Notes spill to the ground. It takes everything I have not to bust out laughing.

"Jesus. Really?" I hear him complain.

By lunch, Grant's in a sour mood. Jax walks up to me, quietly chuckling. I ask, "How many admiring fans just couldn't wait to touch the star stud muffin?"

"You're playing with fire, Ivy Rose." He drops his voice to a whisper only I can hear. "Don't get caught." Then he leaves for his next class.

I holler at my brother, "Wait, wait... has he choked on perfume yet?"

I laugh when Jax flips me off. I would stop, but it's too much fun. It's not like he doesn't do the same thing to me. Grant slammed Terry Promini against the lockers for telling his friends he was going to ask me out, which ended in him not doing it. Terry was hot; I definitely would've gone out with him.

I snicker again, relishing in the payback. I can't wait to tell Grant's sister.

Chapter 5

Grant—Present Day

"**W**HAT THE HELL IS wrong with you?" Jax sits beside my drunk ass—again.

I would answer him, but I'm not sure if I can formulate actual words at this point, which is sad since it's barely noon. Honestly, I'm not sure if I even stopped drinking last night. I slept but only a few hours since my brain wouldn't shut off. I drank more, hoping to forget how fucked up my life is.

I miss taking Mase to school every morning. I miss waking up wrapped around a certain redheaded beauty. It's not working. Nothing works. I still see her face as the sun breaks through the curtains of our bedroom. A bedroom I doubt I'll be allowed to see again.

I wave to the bartender for another.

Jax intercepts my order. "He'll take a coffee and so will I."

I gather all my strength to slur, "What do you want?"

"Fuck, man. You need to get your shit together. You have a school play to go to in three hours. I'll be lucky if you're sober by then." Jax pushes my whiskey away and puts the coffee cup in my hand. "Drink up. I'll be damned if I disappoint Little Bear or break my promise to him."

That gets my attention. I take a few sips. "What? Explain."

"For one, you missed his last practice. You're better than that. And he asked me to bring his dad to his play."

I finish my first cup, and the middle-aged bartender stops cleaning the bartop to refill it.

"Why would you make him a promise like that? Eli's dead." Thank fuck for that. Though I would've liked to kick his ass one last time.

Jax chuckles. "What the hell? Damn, you *are* fucked up. I said *dad*, not father or sperm donor. A dad. The guy who takes him to football practice, helps him with his homework, reads to him every night, and listens to his problems or about his day in general. You telling me that you do none of those things for my nephew?"

I clear my throat. "Well, I don't think I'll be much of a dad anymore." I take a big gulp, feeling the burn going down my throat since I didn't wait for it to cool down. "You do shit for him too"

"Shut the hell up, Brandt. You and Ivy'll work it out. Besides, I don't take him out for ice cream at his favorite restaurant before every mission or tell him about how long I'll be gone like you do. Or take care of him when he's sick."

He points his finger at me and raises his eyebrow. I hate it when he does that. That cocky look when he knows he's right and I'm wrong, especially since I'm rarely wrong.

I finish my second cup and push it toward the bartender, who's putting away glasses at each bar station. Thankfully, he notices and refills it again, along with topping off Jax's cup.

"Why would you make a promise to Little Bear like that? What if—" I stop when I notice Jax looking at pictures on his phone. The first picture is of the three of us at a Panthers football game. I feel a lump form in my throat from missing that kid so much.

"How can you say no to him?" He turns his phone to me.

I look at the corner of the room to prevent myself from... to pull myself together. I must still be drunk. That's the only logical reason for wanting to cry.

Clearing my throat, I remember this is the guy I trained in manipulation. The fucker is using it on me. "That's cold," I manage.

He smirks. "True. But I did make a promise to the kid. Your ass will be there—sober." He sniffs me. "And after a shower."

"Does your sister know I'm coming?" I take a sip, feeling the coffee kicking in. My brain is clearing up—a bit.

He rocks his head back and forth. "Sorta. Don't... Just listen. When he asked me about you and I said I would bring you, she was in the room and didn't interrupt me when I told him you will be there."

This kid is gutting me and he's not even here. I croak, trying to keep my voice steady. "What did she say?"

"It still pisses me off how she hypes Eli's punk ass up more than it was. The dick was an ass that took advantage of people." He moves his cup in a circle, waiting me out. A technique I taught him. I'm still drunk and don't have the patience.

"I meant about me, jackass, and wanting me there."

"Oh, that." He pauses. "Whatever Mase wants, more so if it will help control his outbursts. If he wants you there, he can have it."

I nod, trying to formulate what I want to say next. So many things are swirling around in my head. I could blame still being drunk, but... the more I sober up, the worse it gets. "The play's at four, right?"

"Yep." He drinks his coffee, barely looking at me.

I nod again, trying to figure out what my next move is. Obviously, I'm going to the play. I'm kinda sober. If I took a cold shower, I would sober up real fast. I'll also make a stop by Beatz, his favorite ice cream place, for a small container of ice cream. I've been a drunk asshole and missing out on shit in his life when I promised I would always be there for him no matter what. Ice cream is the least I can do.

I need more... but what? Maybe talk to Ivy and get some damn answers, but for now I'm going to focus on Little Bear. Besides, Ivy needs to be the one to come to me.

I finish off my cup and put a napkin on the top. "I need your help."

Jax gives me the biggest smile I've seen for a while. "That's why I'm here, brother."

Grant—15 Years Old

I have a love/hate relationship with summer. The obvious—no school and more time with my friends. But I also have to spend three weeks with my dad in DC and another two weeks at football camp, and then four hours for football practice that begins in July.

Today is my first day back from DC. I have two weeks until football camp begins, but at least Hersh is coming with me. So is Sumner, but I can avoid him since he's on defense. Hersh is one of my runningbacks. We have all day at the lake thanks to Linc driving us; sometimes my older brother isn't a complete jerk.

The first thing I see is Ivy Rose pulling her sundress off and revealing a tiny black bikini that barely covers—

When did she get curves like that? I was only gone three weeks! Fuck.

Blaine Henry jogs over to her and touches her shoulder. She throws her head back, laughing. Please let it be laughing at how stupid he is. I'm staring so long I get hit in the head with a football.

"Dude, what the hell? I hollered at you," Jax says as he picks up the ball.

"Sorry," I say, looking back to Ivy and... "Henry?"

Jax shrugs but watches their interaction with a scowl.

"What the hell is she wearing?" I try to control my voice, but a shriek pops out at the end.

"Yeah, we're going to have our hands full beating guys away from her. Up to helpin' me with that?" He tosses the ball at me from a shorter distance this time.

I smirk, wave for him to go long, and wave until he passes Ivy Rose, then I launch it—right at Henry. The ball makes a beeline for his head. Bullseye.

"What the hell, Grant? Why did you do that?"

Ivy Rose begins her lecture, one I've heard before. This isn't the first time I've hit someone with a football. I need to do something to get these guys away from her. Seeing them touch her is like a punch to the stomach.

I throw my hands in the air. "Sorry, I was aiming for your brother." Jax stands on the other side of her with the ball.

"Yeah, sorry, sis. You know Brandt has issues with control." Jax winks at me, knowing and hoping Ivy Rose buys our BS.

"My ass. Leave my boyfriend alone. Jerks."

"Boyfriend? Brandt, she said boyfriend."

"I know. Damn. That's unfortunate," I pause and whisper, "babe." If looks could kill, I would be dead a thousand times over. I throw my arm around Henry. "Tell me, are you our sweet Ivy Rose's boyfriend, Henry?"

Anyone else, I would feel bad about doing this to. I really did feel sorry for Patrick Vandergard. He's a nice guy who didn't stand a chance against the newest quarterback and starting running back pounding him with question after question about his intentions with Ivy Rose.

Do I think Patrick was trying to get in her pants like Henry thinks he will? No, but like I said... no one is good enough for her. Henry might be six feet two and over two hundred and fifty pounds, but he's still a player both on and off the field. Definitely, a no-go for dating our Rosebud.

Henry's eyes widen, not in fear like Vandergard since he's a junior defensive linebacker and we're freshmen offense. "So not worth it." Henry walks straight to Carly and wraps his arms around the school's resident booty call. I don't have to look at Ivy Rose to know she has a complete look of devastation across her beautiful face.

"Thanks a lot, assholes. Where's Ken?" Ivy Rose huffs, crossing her arms, which only pushes those newly formed boobs further out. My eyes take her in—the lanky, skinny legs from last summer are replaced with long ones I imagine wrapped around my waist. *Shit, where the hell did that come from?* This is my sweet Rosebud. Not any girl.

Ivy Rose pushes her brother's shoulder, then punches me in the chest before storming off. "I'll find her myself."

Chapter 6

Ivy—Present Day

MASE DROPS HIS BAG by the front door, rushes past me, and slams his door. No Jax or Grant. I look out the front window to see which one dropped him off. A black GMC pulls out—Grant's truck. At least Grant is still spending time with Mase. Part of me wants to pick his bag up and put everything away, but Grant reminds me—used to remind me—that Mase needs to do things for himself. I leave it and ensure Mase is getting ready for his shower.

Thirty minutes later, as Mase and I are sitting at the table for dinner, I ask, "Mase, tell me how practice was." I pray he gives me more than one-word answers, like he did yesterday.

Mase plays with his mashed potatoes and mumbles, "It was ok. Da—Grant and Jax talked a lot and missed my throw. He didn't see it!" Mase drops his fork and bunches his little eyebrows together.

I run my fingers through his sandy-brown hair and tell him, "They have very important jobs. I'm guessing they have a mission coming up or something. Eat up."

He mumbles under his breath so low I can't hear him.

"Excuse me?"

"Da—Grant was acting weird."

"Weird how?" I ask, desperately hoping to gain as much information about Grant as I can.

He shrugs, pretending like he doesn't care even though I know he's hurting. "I don't know. Everything. Nothing. He hugged me for a super long time before I came in the house. This is so stupid." Mase pushes his plate away.

I push it back and hand his fork to him. "Continue eating, you burned a lot of calories today."

Masen takes a few bites of his broccoli but doesn't say anything. I continue. "He's always loved football." That could still be either one of them. "Uncle Jax and he used to throw the ball around in the yard while Aunt Kennedy and I played with our dolls. Did you know she made all our baby doll clothes when we were eight?"

His little head pops up in attention, probably because this is the first time he's hearing a Grant story. I usually hype Eli up to be this great guy when in reality he was a jealous jerk.

Large tears form in his seafoam eyes, and his voice breaks. "I miss him. He was always here."

"I know. Come here." I pull Little Bear into my arms and run my fingers through his hair. "When did you start calling Grant 'Dad'?"

A shocked look crosses his cherub face. He shrugs to avoid answering me. I tilt his face up. "It's ok to talk to me about it. I know how much he means to you. When do you think he became your dad?"

My angelic boy looks up at me like I'm crazy. "Always."

Nodding and pulling him a bit closer to me, I continue. "When did you start calling him 'Dad'?"

More shrugging. I warn, "Masen."

"Last year, I think. I can't remember. He cried when I asked him." Mase lifts his head off my shoulder.

I need to hold myself together since I want to bawl my eyes out. I can imagine a freckle-faced Mase looking up to Grant asking if he can call him Dad.

A single tear escapes and trickles down his cheeks. I wipe his cheek and ask, "Why did you want to call him that?"

"Because he is," he says like I should already know this fact.

"Ok. I need more than that. Explain, please."

He shrugs again. "He does everything with me. Takes me to school. Cooks for me, teaches me more about football, we go to games together. He was there when I was born."

He gently pushes away from me and starts pacing around the table like Grant does when he's deep in thought. I didn't realize how alike those two really are, despite Grant not being his biological father.

"Oh, he taught me how to throw a spiral—that's more than Gavin's dad does, and that's his *real* dad! Dad was always here. He lived here." I can hear him getting agitated, and I wonder if I made a mistake in asking him. He looks right at me with anger in his eyes. "And *you* messed it up. Why did you have to go to that stupid wedding?"

This time there's no door that divides us. No running, no avoiding it.

"It was Cat's wedding." I stop when he tilts his head. He's giving me the same look Grant used to when we were little and I annoyed him. Honestly, I rarely angered or annoyed him, even when I was trying to.

He continues. "Now he won't even come over. It's all your fault. I want my dad back!"

And then he storms up to his room.

I have no idea how long I sit at the table. Thinking. Most parents would be pissed about their kid spouting off like that, but... I'm not so upset about that. He said... so... many... truths. I knew the moment I stopped running on that random street that it was a mistake, but I'd already screwed up. I continued to walk, thinking about why I didn't see how Grant felt about me. God. I've really fucked things up. For myself, for Mase. For Grant.

I pick up my phone and flip it around in my hand, debating who I want to call—Cat, Dee, Lizzy or... He hasn't answered a single call I've made so far. Why would he answer me now? Maybe if I text him? I need to do something to change things, even if it's just for Little Bear. He's right, he needs his dad.

Me: I fucked up.

Bestie: Duh.

Me: IDK how to fix it. Mase needs Grant.

Bestie: So does someone else...wonder what wench that is? Oh yeah, YOU! CALL HIM!

Me: Hag, I hate you.

Bestie: HAHA...yeah right. Sure you do. Let me know when you call him. Oh, BTW, call him!

Mase sneaks back into the room and begins eating his dinner. I'm so lost in thought over what Cat told me and my clusterfuck life that I don't notice him until he slurps his milk, something he learned from my brother. He doesn't say a word to me, nor does he look at me. Simply eats his food like I never feed him. He scarfs down every meal like his food will run away; he just wants to hurry up to play on his Playstation. The life of a seven-year-old.

"I'm sorry he's not here." My voice cracks and I push my phone to him. "Call Uncle Jax. See if you can stay the night this weekend." A huge smile instantly appears, and I nod to him. As Mase navigates through my phone, I add, "Speaker."

A drunk male voice answers instead. "Why does Hersh have you under annoying sister when he brags about you all the time?"

I jump in before Mase can say anything. "Get Jackson please." I hear laughter and music in the background. My bet is that they went to a bar after football practice. This is one of the guys from their squad.

"He's busy."

Another voice from the background adds, "Why do you have LT's phone?"

I hear scuffling noises like the phone was taken or fought over. I half expect to be hung up on. Instead, Grant says, "Stop being dumbasses. Here, go get a lap dance." More cheering. *Great, it's worse than I thought.*

The first voice comes back. "Oh, Cap. LT's sister is on his phone."

"What the fuck? Who answered his goddamn phone?" Grant's voice comes through more clearly than before. I wonder if he picked it up or is closer to it.

"Dad!" Masen hollers into the phone.

Grant's voice completely changes from slurred and relaxed to guarded and angry. That hurt more than Mase asking for Grant instead of me. "Hold on, Little Bear. It's noisy in here. Let me walk outside." There are a few more muffled sounds, then he says, "What's wrong? Is everything ok? Where's your mom?"

"Right here. Mase wanted to talk to you. You don't answer me, so we called Jax for a sleepover."

"Oh."

"Dad, Mom said I can come stay with you this weekend," Mase rattles off, bouncing in his seat. I actually said Jax, but I know that's where Mase will end up.

"Oh, buddy. I'm leaving tomorrow." Grant's voice fills with disappointment.

Mase looks over at me with tears in his eyes; he can't hide the hurt in his voice. "No Beatz?"

"Shit. Ivy, take me off of speaker." Grant rarely calls me by my first name only. My heart drops to my stomach. I continue to watch Mase since his mouth hangs open with furrowed brows and his green eyes filled with hurt.

"By the time I sober up and get to him, Beatz will be closed." He sounds resigned and disappointed.

"Did you know about the mission at practice?" I pray I can keep a steady voice for both myself and Mase's sake.

"Found out an hour ago."

"And you didn't—" My tone changes, and I want to rage at him for not immediately coming to Mase so they would have time for Beatz. Before I screwed up, that's what he would've done.

"I didn't think you would still let me take him. Plus, I was already drunk. I don't want him to see me like this." He's talking back to me with an anger that I'm not used to hearing.

"You ignore my phone calls."

"Ivy, I'm not going to argue with you standing outside a strip club. Put Masen back on the phone."

"Grant, I-I—"

"Put him on the phone or I'm hanging up."

"Fine." I hand the phone to Mase.

Mase speaks hesitantly. "Dad?... No, she said it was ok." He pauses. "Um... ok. Will I see you before?" Another pause. "Ok... love you." Mase hands my phone back and runs upstairs.

Glancing down at my phone, I realize that Grant hung up when Mase handed my phone back. I'm not sure if I'm upset or relieved. At least I talked to him.

An hour before Mase's bedtime, Jax, Grant, and another soldier are on my doorstep. I don't say a word, just open the door wider so Grant can tuck Mase in and let him know when he's coming back. Part of me wants to sneak up and listen in on their moment.

"Not a word," Jax warns, still reeking of booze.

I can't help myself. "A word about? You being drunk... the strip club... or the fact your mother called tonight after Mase hung up with Grant? Oh wait, maybe it's just me," I say quietly, wishing I could get drunk like they did. A girl's night might be needed soon.

"It's definitely you," Jax smirks, sitting on the sofa.

The third guy remains close to the door like he's ready to bolt. I'm sure he's surveying the collage of pictures on every wall, most of which are of Mase, although there are a few from our childhood.

I turn my attention to him. "You don't have to stand guard by my door. You can get comfortable."

His eyes move down my body in a slow perusal. I used to feel flattered by guys doing that. I'm not sure if it's this guy or what, but I'm a little creeped out.

"Cash! Look at my sister like that again and I'll tell Cap. Sit your ass down."

The guy at least looks ashamed. I disappear into the kitchen so the creepy guy—aka Cash—won't stare at me like that again. I rest my arms across the countertop and lean back slightly to stretch my back. I then take a couple of deep breaths to clear my head.

Grant, clearing his throat from the doorway of the kitchen, brings me back to the present crapshoot that's now my life.

"He's asleep."

"Thanks," I say quietly.

"No problem." He turns to leave, but I stop him.

"Can you make sure my brother is sober before you guys leave?"

"Sure, but he's not going with me."

"Oh." There's an awkward pause where neither of us moves or speaks. "Why not?"

"None of my team is going. Just me."

"Oh." Grant takes a few steps when I add, "Be careful."

"Always." And then he's gone.

Grant—16 Years Old

Why does she always have to wear low-cut dresses to Homecoming? I swear she does this shit just to screw with me. Ivy Rose runs through the living room wearing a beaded short chiffon ombre dress that barely covers her ass. How do I know what kind of dress she's wearing? My sister, Kennedy, has been talking about both of their dresses since she started designing them.

What's worse is the top wraps around her neck but bunches in the front, barely covering Rosebud's tits. And there's a fucking slit between those perfect globes, teasing me. Not only do *I* need to not touch her, but I gotta help Jax keep every other asshole from touching her too.

"Why is it taking so long for the girls to get dressed? I mean seriously, it's just Homecoming," Jax complains from the recliner.

"You know damn well it's more than that. Ken wants their outfits to be perfect so she can take photos for her portfolio. Plus—"

Madam Mayor, as we lovingly call Ivy Rose and Jax's mom, interrupts. "Girls have different societal standards than you boys. It takes time for perfection. We can't be waxed, pressed, plucked, and painted in mere minutes."

Both Jax and I cringe, and Jax says, "Mom, that sounds horrifying. Waxed and plucked? Why both? You know what... nevermind."

"Jackson, be grateful you're a guy. The girls will be ready in twenty minutes Ali is finishing Kennedy's hair. "

"M-o-o-o-m, I can't find my black shoes we just bought," Ivy Rose hollers from what I presume is her room, where my mother and sister are. Madam Mayor rushes to Ivy's room.

My mom hollers from the top of the stairs, "The girls are ready. Let them have fun in a safe, not-overly-protective way you boys treat the girls."

"I don't need these idiots to protect me, Mom. Ivy, on the other hand, maybe. I made her look smoking," Ken says, coming down the stairs right behind our mother.

I can see the top of Ivy's hair as she turns the corner. I swear she moves in slow motion like in the movies. *What in the actual fuck?* Her hair is curled and clipped back similar to my sister's. I barely notice anything but how gorgeous she looks in that dress. *Why the hell am I imaging all the ways to smear that bright red lip gloss?*

"Jesus! Where's the rest of their dresses? You know the top half where we don't have to see..." Jax trails off waving his finger in front of Ivy and Kennedy's chests. I barely glanced at my sister.

Madam Mayor answers him. "There's nothing wrong with their dresses. It is covering everything up."

"I can see her collarbone," Jax attempts to argue.

"No! Not the collarbone. How scandalous," my mother snarks and shakes her head at Jax.

"He also tries to make Ivy wear his shirt at the beach. It's really cute," Madam Mayor says to my mother. "She would be in trouble if—" She stops as her face drops, but she tries to hide it. My mother notices and pulls her into a hug. They talk quietly for a few minutes before Madam

Mayor straightens her back and does a few quick claps. "Gather up for pictures."

An hour and a million pictures later, we finally leave for the dance. The only guys we have to chase away from our sisters are the seniors who think they have the slightest chance with the girls.

"Kendrick, get the hell away from me. Don't even breathe near me. Maybe if you learn how to wear something other than gym shorts and tank tops, but also condition your hair. Until then—step away. Don't even look at Ivy or I'll gut you myself," my sassy little sister snaps at our starting defensive lineman.

Maybe I won't have to worry about my freshmen little sister as much as I thought. This isn't the first time tonight she has verbally massacred guys. I lost count ten minutes after arriving. Each time, I have to hide a proud smile.

Glancing around the auditorium, I see Eli leaning against the wall talking to Maddy Kich. Both of his sisters are huddled up with who Ivy Rose calls "the mean girls." I don't think they are mean. Maybe slightly stalkerish, but not mean.

"So, who are you going to dance with tonight?" Kennedy asks me, eyeballing one of the theatre guys. I would scare the crap out of that guy, but there's a good chance he's gay. At least, I hope so.

I shrug, watching Ivy Rose talk to her on-again-off-again friend, Jasmine. Ivy Rose grabs their friend Ethan on the dance floor. If Jasmine was a cartoon, fumes would billow from her ears. Her jaw twitches, and she balls her fists up.

"Excuse me"—I tap on Ethan's shoulder to cut in—"do you mind?"

"I do, dickhead," Ethan snaps, gripping my Rosebud tighter.

I smirk, knowing I always get what I want. "Please, Rosebud?"

She nods and pushes away from Ethan. "I'll save you a dance, ok?" she says to him. Ethan glares at me, and I give him a cocky smirk and wink to rub it in.

Pulling her into my arms, I add, "Thank you, sugarplum." I smirk, knowing that will get a rise out of her, and I don't care. I owe her for the Gloria Palmer situation *and* for sending the cheerleaders to flirt with me, popping their gum.

"Sugarplum? Seriously?"

"You're right, I can do better. How about sugar lips?"

"Why are you using sugar nicknames?" Rosebud wraps her arms around my neck.

I whisper in her ear, "Maybe I should call you Skittles—a bright hard outer shell, but a soft and sweet middle."

"I'm not soft or sweet."

"Hmmm... yes, you are. You just don't want people to see it. What about sugar pie?"

She shakes her head and rolls her eyes with a sigh. I laugh and tease her for the next four songs.

"Awwweee, look at the perfect couple," Keira, the cheerleader captain, sneers.

That's the splash of cold water I needed to remind me of who I'm dancing with. I stop dancing with her in the middle of the song and remind myself that no one is good enough of my Rosebud, not even me.

"Thanks for the dance, sweet cheeks," I smirk and head to where her brother is flirting with Leslie Gower.

"That's worse!" I hear Ivy call after me.

"Oh yeah? Well, I have a ton of sweet nicknames."

"Don't you dare!" She glares at me with those brown eyes that are yellow around the edges.

"It's on, sweet cakes." Just to be a bit of a dick, I shoot fingertip guns at her.

For the next two months, I call her every sweet term of endearment I can think of, and add in a few that the internet taught me too. She doesn't disappoint me with her reaction. Granted, I also get more cheerleaders leaving me gifts in my locker and on my car. More things I hate.

Game on, sweetheart. Game on.

Chapter 7

Ivy—Present Day

BURSTING INTO THE PAINTING studio, aka Cat's studio, while Cat is midstroke, I drop into the chair close to her easel. I shouldn't interrupt her while she's in the zone, but I'm not a good friend. I need to unload all my bullshit on someone, and since she's my bestie...

"You're right. Mira is totally crushing on Toby. I've been watching the two of them lately. I don't think he notices. Hell, does he even know sweet Mira even exists?" I jump back into a conversation Cat and I started four days ago when we were the only two working the sales floor.

Cat doesn't stop. Actually, her eyes barely leave the canvas she's working on. I walk closer and repeat myself, but louder.

"I heard you the first time. No need to shout. I'm not sure how sweet Mira is. I'm usually on opposite shifts as her." Cat blends the white at the top of the canvas with a pale blue.

After watching her for a few minutes, I blurt out, "Did I forget to tell you... no more vacations. Never again. Shit doesn't run right. And I... kinda sorta need your help." I mutter the last portion.

"Continue..." Cat lightly moves the azure blue in small circles to create the sky. I know from watching her that she's going to add three more different shades of blue, then blend it all with a dry brush to create the sky background.

"I would act all shocked, but you already told me you're retraining yourself and your process."

"Another technique I'm trying... to mimic aspects of your process—creating around other people and not going manic with my art and ignore everyone around me. Not exactly a healthy habit. If I teach myself how to control it more, then when I do have kids, it won't be so difficult to balance both... you know, like you appear to do flawlessly." Cat moves on to a slightly darker blue. I know it has a special name, but I don't know every color name like Cat does.

"You know I don't do it flawlessly. I have help, which is what I need to talk to you about." I fidget with my fingers. "I talked to Grant last night. It didn't go well," I explain, running my finger along the edge of the table near Cat's easel as she continues to dab the darker shade of blue.

"Keep going. Hand me that dry brush." She begins blending the background with the two blues and white.

I explain the phone call and how the guys came over. And by the time I've finished, Cat has moved onto the grass with four shades of green on her palette. Mira comes in with a question about one of Toby's pieces, so I go help her.

"So, how's married life?" I ask Cat after returning, watching her move the brush slowly over the canvas.

She waves her brush in the air before dipping it in the darkest green—hunter green, I believe.

"Cut the crap and don't change the subject. I take it you felt shitty cause Grant focused only on Mase and blew you off completely?"

I let out a breath and whisper, "Yeah... I-I..." I stare at the ground like it's the most fascinating thing in the world, not finishing my thought.

"Holy shit! You almost admitted it." She stops painting and faces me with utter shock across her face.

"What the hell are you talking about?" I ask, resting my hands on my hips.

"Since you're still in denial of your feelings for him, what's your next step? You can't keep going like this." She points her green-tipped brush at me.

Fuck. That's what I'm trying to figure out. "You can't tell what a hot mess I am? Seriously?" I flail my arms around, trying to make my point.

She returns to creating the grass with a slightly lighter shade of green, barely glancing at me. Honestly, between me and Dee—Cat's sister-in-law and our resident queen of dramatics—Cat barely acknowledges our diva moments.

I plop down in a nearby chair and continue. "I'm lost. I don't know what to do anymore. I can barely work in my studio without seeing his face pop in my head."

Green mixed with white is the next color combo she uses. "You freaking out isn't as bad as I thought it would be. Perhaps you would be able to work in that studio if you didn't have sex with him in there so often." She pauses to make her point. "Oh, grab my phone. I'm supposed to start taking pictures of my process for Insta. And when Brax is gone, it shows him that I'm working in a healthy way."

I snap a few pictures from five different angles. "Do you want these posted as is, or do you want to edit them? Brax is gone again?"

"Yeah, some exercise, but it's not for the company or battalion, which I thought was weird, but my brother said it's not. Post it with something about work in progress. I don't want to mess with it." Cat finishes the grass background. She won't finish the grass or the sky until the paint dries.

I edit and post the picture. Within minutes, a person likes it. I freeze at who it is—Grant.

I click on his profile and scroll through his pictures. He posted nine pictures while we were in Pennsylvania. I linger on a selfie of the two of us right before the ceremony. He'd snuck back to the bridal suite for a kiss. He snapped it right after leaving me breathless. I miss him. I screwed up so much. How or what do I do?

Cat lays her head on my shoulder and asks, "Whatcha looking at?"

"Insta. I didn't realize Grant followed you." I continue to scroll through more of his photos. Most of them are of Masen.

"Oh, I meant to ask you about that. Dee, being the super stalker that she is, realized that both your brother and Grant quit posting for almost two years. Do you know why? I think Dee cyberstalked them, but now I'm curious too."

I hand her phone back. "Show me." She scrolls back over eight years. My graduation pictures are there, but nothing until we started renovating Ephemera. "I'm presuming all their social media is the same?"

She nods.

I pull my phone out to call Jax. "My sweet brother, can you tell me why the fuck you and your bestie have two years of nothing on Insta—and all your social media?"

"What the hell are you talking about? Are you day drinking?" he snaps.

"Pfft. I wish. About eight years ago, you stopped posting. The king of self-centered selfies. Cold stopped. Why?" I demand and am slightly scared for his answer since I have a sinking feeling it has to do with me. I'm not sure what to expect, but that doesn't stop my heart from pounding.

"That's ancient history. Why is this even a conversation? It was eight years ago."

"Answer the question, asshole, or when your mother calls to tell me what a failure I am, I will tell her you don't have a girlfriend as you told her. Instead, you—"

"That's not fair." He sighs. "Eight years ago? Let me think."

"What's to think about?"

"Ivy Rose, it was almost a decade ago. Chill."

"Do you think telling me to chill will actually make me calm down?"

He laughs. "Hasn't yet, but it usually buys me a few seconds."

"Come on. You don't need a few seconds. You remember everything. Last week, you brought up how I put Icy Hot in your boxer briefs, and that was *high school*. How do you remember that but not why you stopped posting on all your social media. Twenty-five posts the day before, then bam, nothing for two years. And you both did it, which means it was a conscious decision both of you made. I want to know why."

Cat eyeballs me during my rant, though she doesn't stop painting. I'm kinda proud of her for staying focused on her work and paying attention to my hysterics. I know I'm overreacting, but this is important. I don't know why it is, and that's why I called Jax.

He speaks so softly I barely catch when he says, "Eli."

"What?"

"I can't do this on the phone. Besides, I have a drunk friend on my sofa. Wonder why that is?"

"Jackson Charles Hersh! Don't you blow me off!"

"I can't talk about this now. I have two hours to sober him up. We have a briefing." His voice is resigned and tired. I feel guilty since I'm part of the reason for that.

"Another mission? Wait, he said he had a mission without the team. What happened with that?" I need answers, and I have a sinking feeling he's not going to give them to me.

"You know how it is." He sighs and muffles the phone to talk to someone—Grant. "Sometimes things merely get pushed back and other times canceled altogether."

My heart sinks. He's not going to answer. I know I threatened to tell Mom, but we both know I won't. "I-I know when you get home. I need answers." I'm trying to hide the fear in my voice because Grant being distracted before a mission isn't a good thing.

"Depends on how long I can keep him sober. Someone shattered his heart. Honestly, he shouldn't go on this mission. But that's not up to us." Again, he talks to Grant. It sounds like he's trying to force him to drink coffee.

"Such a great brother. I love you too. Thanks for having my back and not answering my questions." I drop my voice, riddled with worry. "Please take care of him."

I wasn't being sarcastic when I told him he's a great brother, even though he didn't answer me. I did ask him out of the blue and he humored me for a few minutes.

"Always do." He hangs up.

A few seconds later, he texts.

Jax: Think about what was happening then.

Me: The last pic is from my graduation weekend at the cabin. Nothing until I moved down here

Jax: Exactly

"Well, what did he say other than you and Grant are soulmates?" Cat walks over from the sink, where she was cleaning her brushes while I was on the phone.

"He wouldn't say that," I say, side-eyeing her.

Cat stares at me like she not only doesn't believe me but I'm crazier than a crack addict on payday. I update her on my conversation with Jax.

"He's talking in riddles. I don't know what was going on eight years ago. Maybe I need Dee to cyberstalk me to remember what was going on in my own freaking life then."

Cat scans more posts on her phone. "We don't need Dee, though you should remember what you were doing shortly after you graduated."

I sat back in thought. "I mean… I did go stay at an art colony for a week, then I did a two-month-long apprenticeship with a metalsmith before I started college, which was a complete waste for me. I know it helped you, but… nah." I shake my head, trying to remember what else was going on. I can't, for the life of me, remember.

Cat flips her phone around to Eli's profile. One of the last pictures is of the two of us in my dorm room on my bed. That's a great thing to have online. "Oh shit," I say. "That's a horrible picture. I have bags under my eyes, and look at my hair. I have sex hair."

She snaps her fingers at me. "That's what you get out of that? You do not have sex hair. It is a nice picture of the two of you. Anyway… when did you start dating Eli? Shortly after you graduated?"

"Yeah."

She shows me a few more nice pictures of Eli and me. One on the beach together. Another of him kissing my cheek. "Did you notice he tagged your brother and Grant in every freaking picture of the two of you?"

"What? No." I sit beside her at the table and watch her swipe through all of Eli's photos. Some I never knew he took. A bikini pic. Sleeping in my bed. One that I'm completely ashamed about and mortified since the fucker again tagged Jax and Grant. I'm laying beside Eli—topless but my boobs are pressed against him. My cleavage is on full display.

"Oh, Jesus. All of these Grant and Jax are tagged in?! I'm half-naked in that one! How did he get by with that?!" My voice cracks since I'm moments away from tears. My brother saw these. I'm mortified. Ashamed. Embarrassed that he not only took these pictures of me but posted them where my brother... and Grant... saw them. I want to curl up and die. How am I going to look at Jax, let alone Grant?

"Insta's policy is that cleavage is allowed as long as no nipples show. It is messed up that he tagged your brother. That's freaking weird." Cat tilts her head, but we resume our sleuthing.

"I didn't know about any of this. I wasn't on social a lot back then. Oh my god, oh my *god*!" I quickly grab my phone, seeing all skin with Eli's head between my legs. All you can see is my leg and the top of his head. Maybe the picture isn't as bad as I think, but I don't want picture evidence of Eli eating me out on Insta. "Help me get to this on my phone so I can untag myself. I can't believe I ever saw anything in that motherfucker!" I'm beyond pissed at him. He posted so many intimate moments about us. Those were ours. Just for the moment.

I feel a panic attack coming. I think it's a panic attack. I'm not sure since I've never had them before. My chest and throat constrict, causing my breathing to quicken, and my palms and armpits get sweaty. I drop my phone on the table and circle the room. Pacing helps Grant, maybe it will work for me. "Shit, Grant probably saw these!"

Cat rushes over to me. "Maybe not? We can untag you in all of them if you want. It will be fine. I mean, I guess we know why Grant and Jax started their social media ban."

I half-cry-half-whine, which is completely out of character for me. I can't believe I never knew about any of those pictures. Some of them made me look like a cheese tray at a college party. Cat wraps her arms around me while I cry on the floor. I have no idea how I dropped to the floor, but here I am, crying in the middle of the painting studio with my bestie about my dead ex.

"If Eli wasn't already dead, I'd kill him myself." I feel the anger rising more and more. I can't believe he violated my trust like that.

Cat slightly laughs. "Damn. That's... morbid. I have no doubt you would do it. Still morbid."

Once I calm down, we spend the next hour going through all of Eli's photos and untagging me on the inappropriate ones. I would do it for all of them, but Mase should see how his parents were. That's his history. I can't take that away from him as my mother did me. I hate that she hid all the pictures of our father after he died.

I want to call my brother and bombard him with questions and get answers, but he said they were preparing for a mission, and I can't disrupt their mindset with my little freak-out. I need him. I need the guy he's sobering up more, but I completely fucked that up. Sometimes just a text calms me.

Me: Are you leaving from the briefing or do you have time?

Jax: 2 days if we are primary.

My breathing slows just a hair. I know when I can talk to Jax about all this later. He will know how to help me. I just wish he would help me fix this thing between Grant and me, but I'm not going to make him choose between me and his best friend.

Ivy—16 Years Old

Prom is truly a magical night. The glittering lights, the stars sparkling in the sky... I mean, I could've done better than Trevor Burke, but he's a senior and I needed to be at this prom to scare the skanks away from Grant. Since I'm just a lowly sophomore, I needed a junior or senior to manipulate. Trev is a defensive lineman, so he's not easily intimidated by Grant and Jax. Did I flirt a bit or a lot to get him to ask me? Yes, I did.

Did my brother just about flip his shit when I told him and Mother I was going to prom? Absolutely. Is it worth it to go to the prom and see Grant? Totally.

Even though Mom and I don't see eye to eye, she still took me dress shopping, including getting new shoes. Normally, Ken would make me a dress, but she can barely sketch a dress in two weeks, let alone make one. She did come with me to pick out said dress to ensure that it was fashionable since I can't be trusted to pick out anything reasonable. Her words.

Ken found a gorgeous green dress that dipped low in the back. I have to admit I'm a bit excited and scared to wear it. I adore how the dress feels on my body. I feel sexy, something I've never felt before. That scares me. Even though I lost my virginity last month, I'm not ready to have sex with Trevor.

My mom took a ton of pictures of me, Jax, and Grant, and a few with just Trevor and me. My favorite is Jax, Grant, and me all dressed up. I asked Mom to print that and hang it in my room. Perhaps I shouldn't've said that in front of Trevor, though.

Once we get to the venue, Trevor and I dance, talk, eat, and dance some more. I also dance with my brother; it's becoming a tradition that we do one dance together. I save a few for Grant too, to the dismay of our dates.

Jax bumps Grant's shoulder and shakes his head. He whispers to his date and walks to me.

Great, here it comes...

"Ivy Rose, what the hell?"

"Jesus, it's just a kiss. I didn't say a word last week when Bri sucked you o—"

Jax pinches my lips together and whispers in my ear. "Not a word, or I'll tell Mom what you did in your bedroom two nights ago."

I'm surprised he didn't intimidate him or threaten to beat the crap out of Diaz for our little make-out session.

I look up at Grant and sigh. "Ugh, fine. Just stay out of my business."

"I would say the same thing to you, but we both know you won't keep that promise. Don't bother lying to me." That is all he manages to get out before the social studies teacher, Mr. Simps, interrupts our conversation.

"Miss Hersh, do you and your brother have a problem?" Mr. Simps asks.

"No, Mr. Simps," I say as I fold my arms.

"Mr. Brandt, do you have anything to add? And where's Mr. Sumner?"

Jax shrugs. "Dancing, prolly. You know, since this is a *dance* and all."

I flash a crooked smile, knowing we're pushing our luck with Simps since I mouthed off to him yesterday during a class discussion. I pray my mouth doesn't get all of us in trouble. It's happened before. I lost count of how many times the three—ok, four, counting the time Ken and I had detention together—of us got detention.

The lack of amusement is all over his face. "Watch it, or I'll have both of you escorted out of the building." He walks back to the corner of the gym to stop a couple who's making out in the shadows.

"Trevor, come dance with me," I say, tugging his jacket sleeve.

Grant approaches and grabs my arm. "Nah, Burke is going to have a conversation with Hersh and me first."

Jax's date, Stephanie, rolls her eyes and says, "Seriously? It's not your problem. She wasn't doing anything wrong." She storms back to their table while my date glares at me.

My only response is a bored look, and Katie responds with "Whatever. Good luck blowing yourself tonight." *Like Grant cares about your skanky ass.*

"Let's go, Burke. We have a few things to discuss before you finish dancing with my *sister*." Jax glares at Trevor, who's wearing a tux with a black bow tie. He's unoriginal.

I look at the teachers on the left side of the gym before punching my idiot brother's arm, which I know does nothing, but it makes me feel better. "Why can't you idiots let me have a life?"

Trevor laughs. "Normally, you guys use the offensive line to scare guys away from her. You know that won't work with me, especially since your pretty boy ass leaves in a few months."

"We're watching you, Burke. Remember what we discussed last week." Jax glares at Trevor before returning to his date.

I look at Trevor and ask, "What did you guys discuss?"

Trevor looks over Jax's shoulder to Grant and glares. "Don't worry about it," he says to me, though he's not looking at me.

Thirty minutes later, when we return to the dance floor, Trevor whispers in my ear, "You ready to blow this place, bae?" Yeah, he calls me poop in Danish. That's all I think about every time he says it.

"Prom isn't over. Where would we go?" I ask with a sinking feeling.

He gives me a smarmy, crooked smile that creeps me out. "We have our *own* after party to attend, if you catch my drift." He pulls me closer, rubbing his dick against me while we're on the dance floor.

"I'm sorry, it's so loud I must've heard you wrong."

Letting go of one of my hands, he reaches inside his suit coat and exposes a hotel room card slightly so only I can see it.

"I said, it's time for our after prom," he says as he guides me to the double doors leading to the hotel lobby.

I hear my brother and Grant talking in the distance, and the rest of offensive line can't be far behind. Sadly, this wouldn't be the first time those two have bullied my dates, even if this asshat deserves it. I'm not giving them satisfaction.

"You presumptuous ass. Why the hell would I go back to a hotel room with you?" I grit my teeth, trying to keep my temper in check. I twirl around to face him, barely noticing our classmates trying to squeeze around us since I stopped just outside the double doors.

"Bae, that dress screams 'fuck me.' You didn't wear that for it not to land on the floor." There's that smarmy smile again. He grabs my arm and walks us to his car as he says in my ear, "Besides, after what Diaz said about you ... and that sweet pussy and how that mouth of yours blew him. So, let's go." How did I miss his sleezy factor before?

I ball my fist up just like Jax taught me and punch him. I hear a female gasp along with a few *Damns*. Great, I knew this would draw a crowd.

"You bitch! You fucking punched me."

I hear people moving closer and hope none of them are teachers but keep my focus on the asshat in front of me.

"I never said I was going to fuck you, asshole, nor did I even hint at it. Just because I wear a sexy dress doesn't mean I'm gonna take it off for you. DON'T YOU EVER PRESUME SHIT." I have a lot more to say, but Grant pulls me back before I can punch the douche again. Grant has both my arms pinned, and he lifts me a few inches from the ground. Probably to prevent me from kicking or charging at the dick with ears.

"Walk away, man, or I'll let my sister finish you off."

"She's fucking crazy," Trevor says a few feet away before speeding away.

"You ok, sweetheart?" Grant says in my ear while still clutching me tight against him. Probably to make sure I don't get away since I've been squirming and fighting his grip.

"I want to murder that asshole." I stop fighting Grant's hold on me.

"I know, but I'm pretty sure you gave him a black eye. Good job. Hersh and I need to know if you're ok. He didn't touch you, did he?"

I shake my head. "Never gave him a chance."

"Good girl. Want to dance with me?"

"What about your date?"

That's when my brother decides to enter the conversation. "She yelled at him when I noticed you left. She gave him an ultimatum. You know how he loves that. Sure yyou're,ok?" he says with worry etched across his face.

When I nod, Jax holds his arms out for me. There's nothing better than a Jax hug. It heals my heart every time. Grant dances with me for the rest of the night. A perfect ending.

Chapter 8

GRANT—PRESENT DAY

STANDING ON THE SIDELINES at the middle school football field, Jax and I watch Mase run his warmup drills. Little Bear looks over every few minutes, probably to ensure I'm still here. I royally screwed up with him. I need to figure out how to make it up to him. I forgot the most important thing—being his dad.

While watching Little Bear, Jax mentions, "I received a phone call before we left."

He waits for my response.

"I'm presuming you're about to lecture me about Ivy Rose," I say, not taking my eyes off Mase.

"Nope. Eli's parents."

That shit gets my attention. I look over at him. "What did they want?"

"His baby sister noticed Ivy Rose untagged herself from some pics. Out of curiosity, the sister... Shit, I can't remember her name for the life of me... Cassie, Casey, Carrie?" He waves a dismissive hand in the air. "Fuck it, who cares. She went on Ivy's Insta. His mom straight up asked me if Mase is yours or Eli's."

Jax returned his eyes to the field in time to see Mase throw the ball to another kid.

I breathe a chuckle as I look back to the field. "He *should've* been mine."

"Probably *would've* been if someone wasn't a scared bitch." He whispers the last part to me since we are at a school function. "You going to fix this crap with Ivy? I get that she screwed up... royally."

I sigh. "I don't know what to do. I'm outta ideas with her. The only thing I haven't tried is..."

"Properly date her, maybe."

"Like she would allow that." I shake my head at the same time Mase drops the ball. His little face falls. "It's alright, buddy. Keep going," I holler as I clap to encourage him. The coach has them take a water break. Mase drags his feet coming over. His little face scrunched up in disappointment and frustration as he rips his helmet off. I walk over to him and wrap my arms around him. "What's the issue, Little Bear?"

"I dropped the ball," he says, his eyes not leaving the ground.

"Hey..." I tilt his chin up so he looks at me. Jax hands me Masen's water bottle. "Drink up. Don't be so hard on yourself. Have fun. Everyone drops the ball at some point. You're alright." I ruffle his hair.

He nods and answers after a drink. "Thanks, Dad." He takes another swig, grabs his helmet, and jogs back to the team.

"Eli's parents are going to be a problem." I fold my arms and watch Mase.

Jax grunts next to me. "Probably. I'm more concerned about my sister. You're starting to get your shit together, but she's still spinning. For once, I can't fix it. Though if we're being honest, I rarely fixed anything... You always beat me to it." Jax claps his hands when the offense holds the defensive team at bay.

I chuckle, remembering the schemes we pulled off to keep guys away from my sweet Ivy Rose. I was too young and stupid to realize how much I truly loved that girl. I probably always have.

I pat Jax on the shoulder. "For once, I'm out of plans. If you come up with one, I'm all ears. I tried showing her by helping around the house and with Mase. I straight up told her at Cat's reception. Those blew up in my face. This time... she needs to come to me."

"Actually, only one blew up. In her eyes, you helping raise Mase and helping her with the house was subtle. I don't know how that's subtle, but Ivy's weird. Why does she need to come to you?"

"You mean other than she ran from me?"

"Obviously. I know there's another reason."

I look back to the field to see Mase run another play. "She needs it more than me. You know she doesn't do anything unless it's something she wants or needs."

"You want to make sure she needs you."

"Nah, she doesn't need me."

Jax busts out in a full-belly laugh. "Yeah, right. How often have the two of you been apart since we met?"

"When I was at West Point and she refused to talk to me during my last year."

Mase runs the ball down the field, dodging around a defensive lineman and another before getting tackled forty yards past the line of scrimmage. The head coach resets them back on the fifty. Each team meets with their coach for the new play.

"Besides, with all this tension right now, how the hell am I supposed to ask her out? She would say no. That contradicts her coming to me."

"Try. If she says no, we move to plan B."

"You have a plan B?" I look over at my friend. He's smirking, and I chuckle. "Of course, you do."

"Ask her." He claps and walks over to the offensive coach.

"I still think it's a horrible plan and that she needs to come to me."

"Ask her," Jax says.

I remain silent even though I feel in my heart that she needs to come to me, but I'm not going to argue with my friend. Am I going to follow through with his plan? Absolutely. Do I think it will work? Nope.

Ivy—18 Years Old

I love coming up to this cabin. Grant's dad bought it a few years before they moved down the street from us. The decor reminds me of my grandma's house with the mismatched furniture and wall decorations that look old enough to be in a museum. I begged both my mom and Grant's if we could spend a week here after my graduation. Then I wasn't sure if I would be alone or if my brother and his friends would join me.

I'm annoyed that I have no idea if my own brother is coming to my graduation. Granted, he did recently transfer from the University of Illinois to West Point on a football scholarship. But they get breaks between semesters, right? Or time off?

I open the fridge just to slam it shut. I'm not hungry. Just bored. I've never been home from school this early. We only had to show up for graduation rehearsal and were dismissed. I have no idea what to do. I would go over to my friend Jazmine's, but she said she was heading to her boyfriend's house. Probably to have sex since both of their parents are still at work. I'm still fidgeting in the kitchen when I hear the front door open.

"Her car's here. I bet she's in her room or something like that…" I hear my brother say. To whom, I have no idea, but I hope and pray it's Grant. I've missed those guys.

I run to the living room and jump on Jackson, who barely sees me before catching me.

"Damn! I missed you too. Ack… I need air, Ivy Rose."

I hang on to him for much longer than I need to. He's only come home twice a year since he left. I suppose I would do the same. I don't want to be here with my perfectionist mother who thinks we have to be just as perfect as the facade she puts on.

I finally release him so I can punch him. "Why haven't you come home more? Life is… boring. I have a new hobby that of course pisses Mother off. Sooo, I love it." I pull Jax's shirt sleeve to lead him to the garage when another familiar voice speaks.

"What am I, chopped liver? I don't get a hug?" Grant asks, holding his arms open for me. I freeze for a second before jumping on him. Thankfully, he catches me.

"Oh my god! I'm so happy to see you guys. How long are you here? Can you come with me to the cabin after my ceremony, or do you have to go back?" I rapid-fire in the crook of Grant's neck. I'm going to hold him as long as he'll let me. I'm a little surprised he's still holding me.

"Rosebud, we have a week. Plenty of time to catch up," Grant answers. I sit up in his arms, but he still doesn't let me go. We stare into each other's eyes for what seems like an eternity but is probably only a few seconds before my brother spoils the moment.

"You said it's in the garage, right?" Jax points to the opposite side of the house, where the garage door is connected to the living room. Grant sadly puts me down but slings his arm over my shoulder as we join Jax in the garage.

"I reorganized the garage, as you can see." I point to the wall of drawers and tools hanging on hooks. "I organized all of Dad's tools and added a few more. Did you know he already had an anvil and the vise?" I explain, along with how I transformed the garage and my latest three-day necklace project.

I show them the wood table with my hammers, pliers, drills, tabletop bench press, and a multipurpose vise block attached to the side of the table. I pull my latest project out of the set of drawers lining the wall.

"How did you get into this?" Jax asks, picking up the needle-nosed pliers hanging on the wall.

"Ken. Her necklace broke and we... we spent all night fixing it," I explain, knowing they won't understand.

"It was just a necklace. She could've just bought another one," Grant points out.

I raise my eyebrows. "No. It was her *footprint* necklace."

Grant nods as he makes an acknowledging sound in his throat. That necklace, he knows, was the last thing their father gave Kennedy before their parents were divorced.

"Did you know there's a metalsmithing shop in town? That metalsmiths are also jewelry makers... Well, many of them are."

The boys shake their heads and mumbled they didn't know.

"Me neither. We also stumbled into an artisan shop during a shopping trip with your mom." I look pointedly at Grant. "That's what gave us the idea that we could fix the necklace ourselves. FYI... we didn't. We went back to the shop. I made the cute middle-aged guy show me how he fixed it. He gave us a flyer for classes they teach, and I've been going ever since. I want to learn how to use a forge and welders, but he said I'm not ready for that." My heart swells as I explain the best thing that ever happened to me.

"Good to hear that you ditched Jaz and are spending more time with Ken," Jax says with his back to me, still inspecting all the tools hanging up.

"That's what you got out of all that? I take it back; I didn't miss you. Ass. By the way, BethAnn keeps asking about you. Evidently, she's *still* hung up on you—two years later. My question is why? No way could you or your—"

"Is Ken taking these classes too?" Grant interrupts.

"You know how she loves fashion. She figures she can create a jewelry line to go along with her clothes. It's kinda cool. She does miss a few classes since she started modeling. She has a photo shoot this weekend, which ticked off your mom. The wannabe stepmom... who keeps inserting herself into Kennedy's life, thinking that's the way to your dad." I continue without waiting for his response. "Anyway, she signed Ken up for it without telling your mom." I pick up a drill bit that I must've forgotten to put away earlier. "So, I'm sure you already know all about that drama since it's your family."

Grant nods. "I do. I also know that my mom has been taking you on her traveling adventures."

I shrug. Ali, his mom, has always included me in things, but usually it was because Jax went with Grant or Ken asked for me to come. "It's fun, and it gets me away from here and the microscope. No way will Mother complain about me hanging out with the high school Spanish teacher or the Senator's ex—Sorry, I've been spending too much time in here alone. I can't shut up today. I'm so happy you guys are here." I steal another hug from Grant and then Jax.

"Rosebud, I'd love to keep listening to you chatter on, but I should go see my mom. Ken already left with the wannabe mummy dearest, right?"

"Yeah, she left this morning. Your mom was pissed since the office called her class and interrupted her lesson to get permission for Ken to leave. Heads up"—I point my finger at him—"you might get an earful about that."

He kisses my head. "Thanks for the heads up. See ya tomorrow, Rosebud."

Chapter 9

Ivy—Present Day

Monday, the only day I don't have to rush around getting homework done, prepare dinner, and attend football practice all before bed. I know it's odd to say, but I used to love Mondays. It was the only evening we didn't have anything planned. No sports. No teaching metalsmithing. No working my beloved art store. I relish that time. Grant used to help Mase with his homework while I cooked dinner. After dinner, we would either do a game night or movie night. Of course, Jax used to arrive the moment food was done.

Mondays look a bit different now. My son doesn't bounce into the car. He drags his feet and barely looks at me.

"How was school?" I close his car door while he buckles up.

"Fine." He stares out the side window.

I sigh. "Movie night sound good? Or game night?" I attempt to be excited when I know my little guy is mad. I was hoping his anger would lessen, but it appears to be getting worse. Mase doesn't answer.

"I don't know... I hear a certain streaming service calling our names... one with mouse ears? Oh, I picked up a new board game." I lean over a bit without my eyes leaving the road and whisper, "It has zombies?"

No response.

"Come on, Mase. I'm trying here," I beg while maneuvering through pick-up traffic.

He turns and faces me. Eyebrows furrowed, pinched mouth, and clenched jaw. The same look Grant wears when he's pissed. "Last Monday, you let me go with Uncle Jax."

"I want to spend time with you. Jax has to work late since your dad left this morning for a mission. I know this isn't ideal, but..." I stop, feeling my voice about to crack.

Mase stares at me like I kicked his puppy. "When will Dad be home?"

I roll my eyes, hoping he doesn't see my frustration. "You know the answer to that."

His little face falls. "Can we watch football instead of a movie?"

I give my little guy a small smile to reassure him. "Sure." Of course, the Carolina Panthers are playing on Monday Night Football.

Grant—20 Years Old—At the Cabin Two Days Later

Jax and I relax in the chairs on the back deck that overlooks the small lake and a forest. "Why the hell is Sumner here? I thought we ditched his ass when we graduated?" My scowl tightens with my disdain.

Jax laughs. "Sumner *still* pisses you off that much? Ivy invited him. Evidently, they've been writing… like actual snail-mail letters and email since we left, which is slightly fucked up. She's only sent me a few cards. No way should that little shit get more crap from my sister than me." His voice is filled with sarcasm, and he sips his beer.

"I need to be drunk the rest of the time we're here just to tolerate his ass. Why wasn't he here for her graduation if they are so tight?" I get up and pace the length of the deck, something I do when I'm thinking or trying to process.

Jax smirks and takes another swig. "He couldn't start his leave until yesterday, and he drove straight from Fort Sill."

"He drove? Eli Sumner, the selfish prick… drove almost nineteen hours? No guy does that for a friend." I stop, look at the lake view, and continue my analysis… and pacing.

"And he's going to be here a week longer than us." Jax continues to throw more information at me.

"The fuck? And your mom is ok with her being here alone with fucking *Sumner*?" My voice fills with shock over the stupidity I'm hearing.

"I didn't ask." Jax watches me pace. "Although, I personally find this fucking hilarious."

I open my mouth to respond when Ivy Rose comes out with Sumner trailing behind her. I wish I could say I didn't notice how the cut-off shorts accentuate her legs or how the tank top with her bikini strap tied around her neck hugs her curves.

"Why don't you guys have your swim trunks on?" Ivy claps her hands, trying to get us to move faster.

Jax answers, pointing his beer at her. "Chill, Ivy Rose. We're relaxing a bit. We're on leave."

"Thought I said we were swimming when Eli got here. Why the hell are you drinking already? Go. Change."

Of course we jump right up and do as we are told, though Jax keeps pushing it by arguing with her about which pair of trunks he wants to wear. I turn around in the kitchen to see Sumner stepping into her personal space, but she steps away. That puts a smile on my face and a bounce in my step.

Once we reach the beach, Ivy sets up a blanket, and I set the cooler where she tells me. Eli makes a big deal about taking his shirt off since he lost weight and gained muscle while at Fort Sill. Jax kicks the entire corner up of the blanket Ivy just set up.

"What the hell? Not cool!" Rosebud complains, focusing on fixing the blanket instead of Eli's mini strip tease.

Jax flashes a mischievous smile to show his trick worked. I bend down to brush the sand off the blanket while Jax nudges Eli into the water.

She offers me one of her sweet smiles. "Thanks. He's such a jerk sometimes."

"Come on, let's get wet." I pull my shirt off and toss it on the blanket. A smirk appears when I notice her checking me out and biting her lip.

"Chop chop, Rosebud. Strip." I stare into those dark green eyes filled with... longing? Maybe? Why do I hope I'm right?

She pulls her shirt off in one movement. It seems like she's moving in slow motion pulling her cut-offs down. Her fingers flick her fly open, and her thumbs hook on each side of her hips to shimmy them down.

"Damn," I whisper once she's out of earshot and halfway to the water.

I take off after her. In a matter of seconds, she's in my arms, squealing for me to put her down. Jumping in the still freezing water until it's waist level, I drop on my back, bringing us both under. And releasing her so she can rise to the surface on her own.

A huge splash of water hits my face the moment I surface, "Damn you, Grant!" she shouts and attempts to swim away, knowing I'm going to chase her because I always do.

My hands itch to be on her again. I grab her and pull us under again. When I surface, she swims away, then dives under me so she can jump on my back. We continue our cat and mouse game for the better part of the afternoon, completely ignoring everyone and everything else. Just like we used to when we were kids, except Jax used to help me dunk her. I couldn't care less about Sumner. He comes near us a few times, but I quickly grab Ivy to twirl her back under, intertwining our arms and legs.

When I surface, she's halfway to the shoreline. "I need a drink," she hollers as she walks the remainder of the way. I lie back and float through the cool, fresh water.

"I would ask what you're doing, but..." Jax trails off and watches Sumner chase after Ivy.

"Just promise me that you're not playing games with Eli like you used to. You promised you would always protect her. She's not a pawn in your bullshit games."

He treads water beside me. Part of me wants to watch Ivy get out of the water, but I know Eli is right beside her. Am I only doing this to fuck with him? But then again, Ivy and I have been playing water games for years. Who am I kidding? This is more than that. I need to figure out what the hell I'm doing and what I want.

Jax and I swim around for another hour before heading back up, finding Ivy in the kitchen sauteing asparagus and mushrooms. The cabin is filled with smells of rosemary, thyme, and chicken, and my stomach rumbles. I didn't realize I was hungry until I inhaled those delicious aromas.

Jax groans, "Oh, you're killing me, Ivy. I'm starving." He walks over to talk to her while I go shower.

We eat and start drinking. Sumner is at least smart enough to keep his distance from me. Sadly, he's stuck-up Ivy's ass. After our fourth drink, Ivy's phone rings.

"Hey, Ken. How's it going?... Ok, hold on." She walks out toward the bedrooms.

Sumner leans back in his seat. "How's West Point?"

I want to roll my eyes, but he's not worth the effort. "Like you give a shit."

"Brandt, believe it or not, I do give a shit. We've been friends since what... nine?" He takes a large gulp of his beer.

Jax watches us from his place at the end of the table. My response is kinder than what's running through my head. "Eight, asshat."

"So, I heard you have a girlfriend. Think she's the one? Gonna propose?" He raises his glass to me before taking a drink.

I laugh at how preposterous that is. And I need to have a talk with my mother about sharing my social life. I hear the front door slam shut and say, "Oh, hell no. She's just someone to fill the time."

Eli asks, "Still looking for the one, then?"

Jax laughs. "We all know he found her a long time ago."

A wicked smile creeps across Eli's face. "What if she found someone else while you were gone?"

The smile is wiped from Jax's face, and he shoots a deadly look toward Sumner. "I would know that. I know everything about her, even when she lost her virginity to Diaz."

"Sure ya do, Hersh." Eli drags out the first word sarcastically and tosses his empty beer bottle in the trash. "Gonna hit the hay. Got an early morning hike." He winks at me and smirks. Then his expression drops in disbelief. "Wait, *that's* why we beat the shit out of him? I thought we did that cause Diaz hit on Brandt's girl the week before."

Jax laughs. "Brandt didn't give a shit about Marcy or any other girl but one. Think about it. If he did, why wait a week?" Jax taps the side of his head with his beer bottle.

Eli looks like he swallowed a lemon and walks out the front door instead of to his room.

"He's going to be a problem," I say, watching the door.

"Yeah, but we need to let it play out." Jax also intently watches the door.

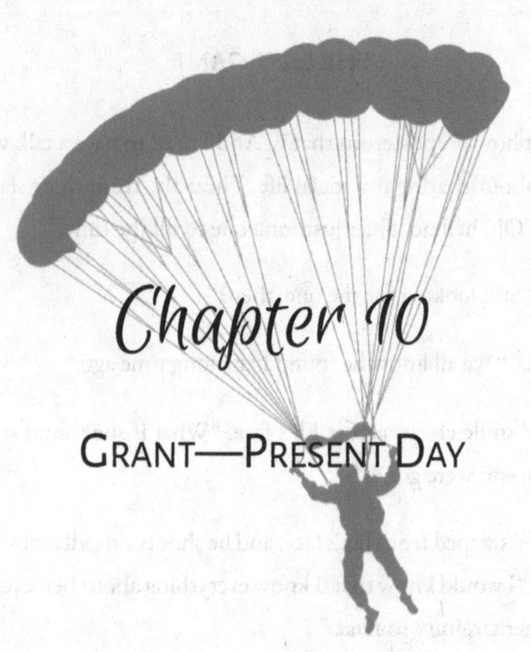

Chapter 10

Grant—Present Day

I PULL MY SHIRT off and toss it in the hamper. I'm still not used to being in my own apartment for so long, especially after a mission. At least this mission was a short one.

Glancing around my bedroom, I focus on the pictures sitting on each bedside table. The most recent one sits to the right—it's a selfie I took during our movie marathon. Mase fell asleep on my lap with Ivy leaning her head against my shoulder. Right beside it is my favorite picture—Ivy in a green cocktail dress, her hair curled and flowing down her back. My arms are wrapped around her in a tux. My senior prom. The one I should've taken her to as my date. The night I almost confessed how much I love her. Almost. I wonder what we would be today if I had. Married? Would Mase *really* be mine?

Maybe I should put away some of these photos, but that would break my heart more than it already is. Besides, if I did that, my place would be pretty bare. I have more photos on my dresser and scattered throughout the townhouse. My walls have more pictures of Mase, Ivy, Jax, and me than decorative shit. In fact, Ivy hung that up too. The only thing I picked out is my sofa. Fuck, that's not true since Ivy was with me when I bought it. I probably bought the one she thought looked good in here.

I finish changing into athletic shorts and a T-shirt, making my way to the kitchen so I can cook for one. Another thing I haven't done in about eight years.

Jax walks in as I pull a package of chicken out of the fridge, the corner of his mouth curling up. "Good, you're sober."

I shake my head with a chuckle. "Yeah, well, I figured getting drunk every day for a month is a bit much. What's up?"

"Honestly? Figured you'd already be shitfaced. Being the awesome friend I am, I was going to kick your ass, then sober ya up. Buuuut... what's the plan for the night?"

I shrug. "Any ideas?"

"That doesn't involve my sister or nephew? Not really. You haven't noticed how often I was over there before all this shit went down?"

"I did. I knew you would tell me when you were ready." I stare at him, waiting. It would give me something else to focus on besides Ivy and Mase.

"Still not. How pissed would Ivy be if I kidnapped Little Bear?" Jax leans against the door jamb.

I pull out bell peppers and tomatoes for the pasta dish. "I mean, it's your funeral, man." I drizzle olive oil in the skillet.

"What did we used to do before?"

"Party too much and do stupid shit." I begin to sauté the chicken breasts. "Maybe..." I stop because just thinking about it hurts. "Maybe we need to"—I take a deep breath and look over at him—"start dating again."

Jax's eyes widen and his jaw slacks. "What?" he whispers.

I flip the chicken and glance over my shoulder at Jax. "I don't think we're going to work it out. Hell, we're still not talking. I don't think she's going to come to me."

"You guys have always had a weird, fucked-up relationship. But"—he pauses, probably to figure out the best way to phrase what he wants to say—"you've never really been *together*. You practically lived with her and Mase and had this friends-with-benefits thing"—he cringes—"but you've never actually dated. You know, get dressed up, wine and dine. At this point, just call her."

I give him a *what-the-fuck* look and calmly ask, "Why the fuck should I call her? She ran from me. I told you; she needs to come to me." I check to see if the chicken is ready to be flipped. "Besides, who am I kidding? I won't date. I'll say I will... maybe even go on a date, but...

I'll…" I don't want to verbalize how much I belong to Ivy even though I'm still angry and hurt about her leaving me.

"I love my sister, but she can be selfish—"

"Don't. We need a distraction. A mission would be fantastic right now, especially overseas."

"I'm sure you can find one. But I'm not sure if I want to go overseas. Those usually turn into longer deployments, and I don't want to be away from Mase that long since he's acting out."

I flip the chicken and add the veggies. "I miss that kid."

A huge smile crosses Jax's face. He's up to something. "I have an idea. You may not like it."

"Jesus, Hersh. How many times in my life have I heard that? Every time, I do it. No matter how idiotic it is."

"The downside, Mase might act out even more. But Ivy will pull her head out of her ass."

"Just tell me." I toss the veggies around in the pan and add butter and cream.

"You date. We know you won't actually do it, but she doesn't need to know that."

"She?"

"Ivy. Little Bear will tell her. It will be obvious if I tell her. That kid will be pissed that you went on a single date with someone other than his mom. We will have our hands full with him. We'll have to help Ivy control his outbursts, and damn, man... you won't have time for those dates anymore cause you're too busy trying to help handle Mase." His smile grows.

"That's... low and manipulative."

He rubs his chin. "One thing I know about Ivy is she has a huge jealous streak. She may not admit it, but she's always claimed you as hers. Remember when she used to chase girls away from you? The lies she used to tell? I used to think it was odd that you never stopped her."

"It was a game. She wanted to see how fast she could get rid of a girl, and I would threaten anyone who looked at her." I shrug, pretending like our game wasn't more than it was.

"Sure." He drawls the word. "Are you game?"

"To manipulating and breaking your nephew's heart?" There's got to be more than what he's telling me cause he would never willingly hurt Mase. This will definitely do that and then some.

He sighs. "I know, but it won't work if we tell him the plan. What if he slips and says something to Ivy? He's seven. The kid is a wildcard. Can't take a chance with this mission."

I want to laugh at how serious he's taking this. "I don't like this plan, and if it's too much for Mase... I'll end this or tell him."

"So, it's ok to play with my sister's heart but not the kid's?"

I pull the sauce off the burner and start the pasta. "Pretty much."

"Good."

Grant—21 Years Old

I almost regret coming home, but we have two weeks before the next semester begins. Plus, Ivy begged us when she found out we had the time. After two days in our childhood homes, we packed up my truck and headed for the cabin. Of course, Sumner showed up this morning. The one person I was hoping to be absent. Kennedy and Ivy Rose left a few hours after us since they had to help our mothers at the mayor's luncheon.

Sitting on the back deck with Hersh, I sip my beer when Sumner sits down. I glare at him for being here... for doing what I was too scared to do—date Ivy Rose.

It doesn't take long for him to notice. "What the hell is your issue, Brandt?" Sumner asks.

"I don't have an issue, just wondering why you're here," I respond.

"I came to spend time with my girl." His voice fills with pride, like he's bragging. "You think you get to come home and everyone will bow down to you like when we were in high school? Guess what? No one gives a shit about who your daddy is." Eli spits, complete with pointing his finger at me. I want to laugh at his comment since he always hides behind his father, but I let it go.

Instead, I yawn, knowing it will piss him off more. I'm tired of his crap already, and I've been around the cocky asshole for less than five minutes. Sumner's always been an arrogant jerk since his dad owns half the town.

"People didn't bow down because of who my dad is. People did that because they thought I was the next Peyton Manning. You have anything else to say?" I look over at Hersh, who is relaxing in my mom's glider.

"Sumner, nice to see you," Hersh says. "I heard you've been home for a while, yet you haven't come up to see your best friends? Awfully suspicious."

"Or has a certain *annoyance* kept you busy?" I add, remembering the names he used to call Rosebud when we were kids.

"Annoyance?" Eli looks at Hersh, then me. The dumbass can't figure out who I'm talking about.

"Isn't that what you called Ivy Rose when we were little. Why pursue her now?" I lean back in the Adirondack chair.

"Why not? Do I need a reason for dating a hot college girl? You're just pissed that I fucked her first," Eli says with an arrogant smirk.

My fist connects with his cheek without any thought, knocking him out of his chair. He licks the corner of his mouth. No way in hell is anyone going to talk about Rosebud like that. "Stay the fuck away from her!"

Hersh continues drinking his beer but is intently watching us, probably hoping we'll finally work this shit out. No way in hell I'll ever deal with this idiot's shit again.

The cocky fucker laughs. "I can't. Just like you can't."

"We're done."

He shrugs. "Fine. Not my fault. You had your chance, but you were too chickenshit to try. Face it, Brandt. You're just pissed that she's not yours anymore to follow you around like a puppy. Hang on your every word." He knows he's winning by getting under my skin, something that has never happened before. "She's mine."

My fist connects with his mouth this time, sending blood trickling down his chin. Maybe it will shut him the fuck up. "She deserves better than your bitch ass." I pick him up and punch him again in the same spot, feeling my knuckle swelling.

Eli spits blood on the newly stained boards that my father spent a week on for my mother, even though they were divorced. "Awwww, is the golden boy upset that he doesn't get what he wants, and Daddy can't get it for him?" I swear he has a hard-on for my dad, though I'm pretty sure it's just because he's jealous my dad is a state senator.

I shove Sumner farther to the opposite side of the deck. "Do you want me to kick your ass? How are you going to explain that when you get back to base? If you don't shut the fuck up, I will, all the way back to Fort Sill."

Hersh drags me away from Sumner, probably because he knows I'm seconds away from committing a felony. "Hey, assholes, did you forget why we are up here? It's Ivy's day and to relax for a few weeks. Don't fuck it up. I've had enough of your pissing contest over the years. The girls will be here any minute. Ivy just texted me that they are on Washington Boulevard."

"What the hell, Jax! He shouldn't be near her."

Jax gives me a hard look. "Her birthday wish was for all of us to be here." He waits until I look away before he addresses Sumner. "Eli, go wipe your face and clean your blood off the deck." The moment Sumner is gone, he shoves me. "Get your shit together, Grant!"

I lean against the railing, gripping it to prevent from hitting something. "You're just going to let that happen?"

Jax looks through the sliding glass door Sumner just walked through and says, "What do you want me to do? Force her? She can date whoever she wants to now. We're not in high school anymore."

I look out into the water. He's right. I know he's right. But the thought of them together just...

"It's probably just a phase," Jax says, sitting down with a grunt. "She doesn't want *him*. She just doesn't realize it yet. Remember when we told her she couldn't date that pothead, Gavin? She stayed with him just to spite us. Don't push her or this crap will last longer than we want. Besides, nothing has happened between them."

I cut my eyes over to him. "How do *you* know?"

He watches my reaction since I'm still seething. When I see his calm look, I realize. "The diary?"

He nods once and grabs his drink again. "Never lies. And don't lecture me on still reading it when you used to read it with me. That's how I found out she didn't give a shit about Gavin. Plus, she knows I read it."

I turn to him. "What?!"

Jax nods. "She even leaves me notes in it. Reminding me not to kill the punk bitch that dumped her or for touching her in any way but platonic. It's a thing now."

"This is bullshit," I say, looking back toward the wall I was scowling at. "We both know he's not good for her."

I start pacing the deck, hoping to pull myself together before Ivy Rose gets here. I have to admit to myself I feel better knowing that nothing has happened between them. I don't know if I'd be able to stomach the thought of Eli and Ivy together.

Chapter 11

Ivy—Present Day

"T HANK YOU FOR SHOPPING Ephemera. Have a great day."

I wish my mood matched my customer service voice or the pretentious smile I have plastered on my face. That's what I need to do. Fake it till I make it. Or that's what I've been telling myself. I've been faking it for a month, and nothing is getting better. Jax only stops by to pick Mase up for practice, and I haven't seen or heard from Grant since before he left on their last mission. Thankfully, for Mase's sake, that last mission was less than a week long.

I reorganize the shelf behind the registers since the baskets were moved and papers scattered about. I have issues dealing with clutter and disorganization, which I've been told is weird since I'm a creative person.

"Hey, Ivy. How's it going today?" Toby greets me while he holds the door open for a familiar brunette with brown eyes and an olive complexion. I remain frozen like I've seen a ghost. I forgot how much she looks like her brother. I just stare at her, completely speechless.

She looks around my store. Examining every inch of my pride and joy—from the canvases hanging along the wall by my office to the photography hanging along the back wall above the windows, showcasing the studios and classrooms down to my office on the opposite side of the store. A step closer takes her toward the clay works that Toby and the two other potters have on display.

Her eyes return to me, standing awkwardly waiting for... I have no idea what, but standing with my former friend slash ex-boyfriend's sister is... weird and slightly awkward. She finally says, "Ivy."

As soon as I hear her voice, I find my nerve. "Cassie. What brings you this far south of the Ohio River?" I attempt to keep my friendly customer service voice going to cover the concern about why she's here.

"I can't come visit an old friend?" Cassie walks closer, studying my jewelry display case between the registers.

I laugh. "No offense, but we were never close enough for visits... and I haven't heard from you since..." I trail off, not wanting to say Eli's name. I still want to beat Eli's ass for those pictures.

She nods. "True. I never did understand why Elijah started dating you. You were complete opposites... maybe that was the appeal. Nice place." Her eyes continue to survey the community board to the left of register two. I'm sure Cassie is internally judging every inch of my store, trying to find a flaw. She strives on perfection and expects it from everyone else too, which is why we drifted apart as friends when we started middle school.

"Pfft... of course you wouldn't. This is all mine," I say with pride. I don't have the energy to defend my second baby to little miss... but thankfully, my internal reverie is broken when Mira talks to a customer about building a homemade kite.

"I'm sure it is," she adds, shifting her attention to my office. "Do you have a minute for us to talk?"

"We're talking." I smile at a customer passing by while Toby rings up a mother and daughter.

"Please."

I roll my eyes and sigh. "Come on." The last place I want to be is in my office, where I have numerous pictures of Masen. I don't want her to see anything pertaining to my son. Instead, I lead her down the hall into my metalsmithing classroom, passing Cat working in her studio.

Cassie continues her assessment of the long wooden slab tables with different stations at the end of each.

I pick up the three pairs of pliers lying on the countertop and put them in the top drawer. "Talk. You obviously have something on your mind."

"Your son. Is he Grant's or my brother's?"

I laugh. I shouldn't, but this is typical of the Sumner family. They always think they are above everyone else and expect others to cave to their will.

"I'm sure you already know the answer, so why ask me? I guarantee your mother has already spoken with Madam Mayor. Tell me what you want."

I'm surprised my mother didn't call me to reprimand me about the Sumner family asking questions since even she can't stand them. Even though I clash with my mom, she will do whatever it takes to protect us, which is why she sent me to my brother when we found out I was pregnant. The Sumners tend to manipulate others. They are not above bribes or blackmailing people to get what they want. Hence, my mother forcing me to leave our hometown and her coldness to me that night.

"To see him. We have a right." Cassie folds her arms.

"We?"

She nods. "My family and I. He's our family too."

"So, let me get this straight. You come into my store, insult me, and demand to see my son without a word from any of you for over eight years?"

Cassie smirks like she knows something I don't. "You never told us about him. We have rights. We're trying to be nice about this. Don't force us."

"You think threats will convince me to let you see him? Really?" Nothing changes with her. Always bullying people to get her way.

Cassie sighs. "You're right. Occupational hazard. I'm used to bossing people around."

"Cass, you've *always* bossed people around. I'm not convinced any of you should be *near* my son." I lean against the front countertop that runs the length of the room.

Cassie runs her finger along the end of the table. "He's the last part of Elijah. We just want a chance to get to know him." Her voice softens. "He looks just like him."

"I know."

She looks over at me. "You didn't ask how I found out."

I shrug. "My mother has a big mouth, and I post a shit ton of pictures on social media. I'm proud of that kid."

"He plays football like Elijah."

I shake my head. "No, like Jackson and Grant. He's a quarterback, not a linebacker."

"Can we at least meet him, please?"

The last thing I want is for them to meet my sweet boy, but Mase should know his father's family. I'll have guilt for the rest of my life if I keep this from him.

"Let me check his schedule. He's a busy kid."

"Thank you," Cassie says with satisfaction and leaves.

I burst into Cat's studio the minute Cassie closes the storefront door.

"Hag, this is next-level bullshit. You need to tell me what to do. None of this thinking about my actions. Because that bitch just threatened to take my son!" Cat continued to paint ignoring my hysterics until the last part.

She freezes midstroke and demands. "What the hell? Explain. Try to keep your shit together long enough for me to understand who is trying to take Mase which I find hard to believe.

I take a deep breath and spend the next hour retelling the event first to Cat who resumes painting ten minutes into my rant, then over the phone with my brother. My heart breaks over not being able to tell Grant. I wonder if he'd even pick up the phone anyway.

Ivy—20 Years Old

Eli should be here in a few hours. I should be excited about that, yet I'm slightly pissed and a bit nauseous. I just want to hide in the metalsmithing studio within the art building or... well, I would say study or read, but I just took my last final. Only one paper left to write and my semester is done.

Why am I like this? I know I should be jumping for joy, but I'd rather do pretty much anything but spend the entire weekend at a hotel with Eli. I shouldn't feel like this. He's my boyfriend, and I haven't seen him in three months. Tons of texting, Facetiming, sexting, and emails. Why. Am. I. Like. This? I should break up with him. Yeah, definitely. Maybe even this weekend. My stomach rolls, but I keep my breakfast down.

It's not like he's the most supportive boyfriend. We never do anything I want or that I even like. Hell, we don't even talk about me—at all. I could have another secret boyfriend and he wouldn't know. I doubt he even knows what my major is. Plus, I have a feeling in the pit of my stomach that I'm not the only girl he's dating, even though we had a conversation over a year ago about being exclusive.

Spending the next two hours revising and submitting my last paper of the semester makes the time fly. I don't realize that Eli should've texted me by now. He usually calls when he lands. I check the time—1:45 p.m. Should I call him? But what if he's just stuck in traffic or his plane was delayed? I don't want him to snap at me or start our long weekend off on the wrong foot.

I slam my textbook close and shove my book, note cards, notebook, and colored pens in my backpack. It takes about fifteen minutes to get back to my dorm. Hopefully, he calls before I get there. Maybe a stop by Mr. Smoothie, the smoothie shop, is in order.

Right after I place my order at the bright orange counter, a nasally voice emanates from my pocket.

"It's your mother! Answer your phone!" I step to the side to wait for my smoothie and answer my phone. "Hello, Mother. How can—"

"My sweet girl, what are you doing?" She's being too nice. Someone important must be with her. The last time she called me pet names was when Grant's dad was in her office.

"Just getting a smoothie, then heading to my dorm. Eli should be calling soon."

She sniffles. "Baby girl. Where are you?"

Is she crying?

"Mr. Smoothie waiting for my smoothie. Why, what happened?... Are you crying?"

My mother has cried four times in my life. I can hear it in her voice. My thoughts immediately go to Jax and Grant. I try to remember the last time I spoke with my brother. Right before taking my psych exam—two days ago. A lot can happen in two days.

It could be Grant. He graduates from West Point, what... this week? God, I used to know everything about him, and I don't know when he graduates. Maybe I should call him. Definitely calling my brother after I find out why my mother is crying. I don't realize she's spent this time just crying in my ear.

"Mom? Please tell me what's going on, you're scaring me. You never cry unless..." My voice breaks trying not to think who could've died.

"It's Eli... H-he isn't coming..." she trails off. "H-he was in an accident." She pauses. I'm not sure if she's really upset or if it's for dramatic effect. "There was a huge accident on the freeway just outside of Chicago... and his car was involved."

She describes more, but my brain can't process it. She says everything but that he's dead. I focus on the fact he was in Chicago. He was supposed to be in Oklahoma—where his military base is. Not in some big city.

I interrupt my mother. "Why the hell was he in Chicago?"

There's silence on the other end. Quietly and with very little emotion, she answers. "I don't know. I'm booking you a flight home, and I'll pick you up. Are you ok to email your professors? Or did you finish everything?"

I feel like my brain is moving in slow motion. It takes me a minute to answer her. "Submitted my last paper a few minutes ago. Everything is done." I walk out of the building, not registering the smoothie girl calling for me to pick up my drink. "Text me the info." All emotions drain from my body.

Not a single tear. I feel numb, like this isn't happening. I'm in someone else's body, watching myself. I should be devastated. My boyfriend of two years is dead. Not from his job in the Army, but a fucking Prius. At least, I think that's what my mother said.

I call the one person I've counted on my entire life. The one person who is my rock. He's also someone I haven't spoken to since a year after my high school graduation. Yeah, not my finest moment.

After three rings, I start talking to the ringer. "Come on, pick up. Please answer."

The second I hear his deep voice, my nerves are slightly calmer. "Sweetcakes? Tell me what's going on." Grant's voice is filled with happiness and a touch of shock, like he's excited to hear from me even after all this time.

I walk aimlessly around campus, only half paying attention to where I'm going.

"Grant..." My voice comes out in more of a wine than I expect. My mouth can't formulate words yet. I blow out a deep breath. "Something bad happened."

"How bad? Lose my jersey bad or wreck Robert's Mustang bad?" I can hear his smile through the phone. I realize how much I miss talking to Grant.

The first tear falls as I take a left to the cobblestone path that leads from the library to the art building. I swipe the subsequent tears away. I can't break down yet.

"I don't know... Robbie's Mustang wasn't that bad." I try to downplay our joyride in an attempt to feel something—anything.

"Sweetness, you totaled my brother's brand-new car by sideswiping a tree and putting scrapes and dents down the entire right side of the car. I was grounded for three months." He's laughing the entire time.

"I mean, Robbie got a nicer car."

"You have a bad memory. He ended up with a beater from the used car lot on Jackson Street. He's still pissed about that and brings it up all the time. Is this bad thing something I can talk you through or something I need to help you fix?"

I chuckle and then remember my reason for calling. "Well, this is worse than that. Nothing can fix this." My voice changes to a serious tone. Or maybe I slip back into that void space.

His voice does the same. "Ok. What happened?"

"Eli is dead," I say like I'm explaining the weather.

"What?!"

"Yeah, he was in a car accident. Mom is getting me a ticket home. I should be back in Michigan either tonight or tomorrow." Why am I still not feeling anything about his death? Well... except nausea and a touch of lightheadedness. But I'm sure that's stress from the semester and... what is wrong with me? A few more tears fall as I continue talking to Grant.

"I'll be home shortly. I have some phone calls to make and then I'll text you my flight info. I'll bring Jax too. Are you ok?"

I pass the make-out trees—a cluster of six trees and bushes that give students the perfect cover, an indicator I'm two buildings away from the metalsmithing studio, where I can bang on metal to let my frustrations out. I continue to walk because I know the moment I stop moving I will fall apart. I can't do that until I reach my mother's house.

"I have a few green amethyst stones I was thinking about making a few necklaces with." I blurt out what's on my mind, which is probably sad... not healthy. My boyfriend is dead, and I'm thinking about necklaces.

"Feelings, Rosebud." He uses a slightly stern voice.

I shrug, even though he can't see me. "I have none. I feel nothing. What is wrong with me?" I whine, pulling the door open to the Ann Blaise Memorial Art Building.

"When did you hear about Eli?"

I look at my phone to see how long it's been since my mother called me. Grant will want an estimation, though anyone else, he would require precision. "Almost forty-five minutes ago." I grab the compass necklace around my neck and move it side to side for comfort. My sweet sixteen present from Grant.

"Stop beating yourself up. You're still in shock. I've gotta let you go so I can get things taken care of to be there with you, ok? I'll call you a little later. Text me your flight info."

"As soon as I get it, I'll forward it to you."

We say our goodbyes, and I check my messages since my phone beeped while I was talking. I hope Mom found me a later flight so I have time to make at least one necklace.

Mother: Your itinerary is in your email. Your flight leaves from the Eastern Iowa Airport at 6:45 pm. I paid for an extra bag since the semester is over and you will probably need to bring everything home.

Normally, I wait until the last minute to pack everything, but I have all my stuff in two oversized bags ready to leave when my weekend with Eli ended. Guess I'd better grab my stuff and head to the airport.

I open my email and forward the info to Grant via text. My mother hasn't figured out that she can text my flight info, but this is the same woman who still handwrites letters to people every week.

I barely remember my flight home. My mother picks me up. I don't remember ever hugging her for so long in my entire life. I needed it.

"Let's go, baby. Ali is picking Jackson and Grant up, and Kennedy is waiting for you at the house." She wipes my tears and tilts my face so I look at her. "I love you, and we will get through this."

I nod with tears still flowing. My head swirls with all the memories of Eli—from our childhood to last month when we were together at the hotel—as I walk with my mother, who has all my luggage. When did she do that?

Kennedy doesn't let my mother stop the car before she yanks my door open and pulls me into her arms where I stay until Grant and Jax arrive. Grant holds me all night while I cry.

Chapter 12

GRANT—PRESENT DAY

Normally, I love watching Little Bear play—even more so when it's his last game of the season. This one is going to be difficult. At least Hersh gave me the heads up on why Mase begged me to be here. After the strip club phone call, I always answer my phone from Ivy Rose, just in case it's Mase again. Though, now, Mase is the only one to call me. Not gonna lie, I'm a little disappointed by that.

Climbing out of my truck at the middle school football field, Jax asks, "You ready for this? She needs both of us today. Don't let them get to you."

I nod. "Yeah."

"She might not admit it, but she's gonna need you today. You know how the Sumners are."

Again, I nod, and my mind drifts back to the time I found out about Eli and Ivy. Now more than ever, I wish I'd killed him.

"We'll get through this," Jax says

I step onto the grass, remembering how it felt to practice in the morning light when the dew glistened. My uniform would be soaked from a mixture of sweat and dew.

Little Bear paces in front of his mother as she tries to tighten his pants. "Mase, stand still," she says with a hint of exasperation.

He looks up and sees Jax and me. "Dad!"

"Not so fast, mister. Pants first."

"But—"

"No, today is not the day, buddy. I need you..." She trails off since her voice starts to break. She has to be a nervous wreck. Every cell in my body wants to reach out to her—hold her.

She finishes fixing his pants as we approach them. Mase wraps his arms around my waist like he hasn't seen me for months when it was just two days ago at practice.

"Hey, what's wrong?" I toss his hair with my fingers.

He looks at his mom, then Jax, then me. "I-I don't want to meet these people after my game. I just want to play and get pizza like we used to," Mase says to my chest.

I take a knee so I'm eye level with him. "Sorry, Little Bear. Sometimes we gotta do things we don't want to. Besides, they're your family too."

Ivy brushes her fingertips along the side of his hair. "I get you don't want to do this, but they are your d—" She stops and begs for help with those chocolate eyes I used to get lost in. "Eli and his family are a part of you, and you deserve to meet them. At least once, then you can decide if you want them in your life or not."

Mase slumps his shoulders. Jax drops his hand on Mase's shoulder. "Come on, buddy. Why don't we see if the concession stand is open? I'll get you cocoa."

Ivy takes a few calming breaths, watching Jax and Mase walk to the white shack at the end of the field. I want to reach out and pull her to me—hold her, make everything melt away. That's not us anymore. She made it clear she doesn't want that anymore.

"I'm sorry. I—" Ivy begins to say.

"Ivy!"

We both turn as another football mom named Lanie approaches, and the two start an excited discussion about what they will do with all their free time since football is over after today. Ivy seems too eager to jump into a commentary on the latest romance novel—a Navy SEAL rescuing a girl from a stalker.

I feel a small smile appear knowing she's still reading her favorite books. I should walk away and join Jax with Mase, but... I just can't move. I listen to all the details about the Navy SEAL and his heroine, which takes me back to when Ivy used to tell me all about her latest reads while we were lying together in bed. My heart aches.

Once she's done talking to Lanie, Ivy turns her attention back to me. "I know we are both about to be bombarded by other people here in a minute... but there are a few things I want to say to you. I... I... Can we sit down sometime so we can talk? A-and... I'm sorry I ran out that night. I should've—"

I see Cassie with her sister, Charlotte, and their parents coming toward us. I nod to Ivy and give her a relieved smile. "We'll talk later." I point behind her with my eyes and nod my head toward them. She nods and takes another deep breath.

"You got this, Rosebud." I squeeze her arm to reassure her. I don't blame her for feeling the way she does. I know what it's like dealing with the Sumners.

A small, nervous smile is all she has time to give me before Cassie begins talking. "Grant. Why am I not surprised to see you?"

I press my lips together. "Cass. Charlie. How've you been?"

Charlotte is still an inch or so shorter than Cass with blonde streaks and a curvier shape than her lithe sister. Hopefully, she's still the friendly one.

Charlie raises her eyebrows and lifts the corner of her mouth. "Could be better."

"I feel that." I watch Mase and Jax joking around.

"Where's the kid?" Mr. Sumner barks impatiently.

Ivy rolls her lips inward to prevent from snapping all over Dick Sumner in front of all the football families. The corner of her eyes crinkle slightly, indicating her irritation, but she paints her customer service face on to answer him. "*Mase* is getting cocoa with his uncle. You will meet him after the game. He doesn't need the distraction right now."

Evelyn Sumner hasn't changed much—same blonde bob cut meticulously styled, very little makeup, and her typical khaki pants and one of her many, *many* bird shirts. Today's shirt is white with bright pink and orange tropical birds flying below the collar. Hersh and I used to make jokes about those bird shirts and make bets about how outlandish they would get until my mother found out and made us volunteer to work for Dick as penance.

Evelyn speaks up in a soft voice. "Richard, you remember how important this game was to Eli?"

Her husband nods and heaves a sigh.

Charlie speaks up brightly. "Why don't we get situated for his game, then? Ivy, do you mind if we sit with you guys?"

Ivy's brow twitches. "Sure."

I whisper in her ear, "Do you want me to stay with you?" Her eyes fill with hurt and pain as she shakes her head, and I continue, "Alright, I'll be right over there. Text me if you need me." She nods, rolling her lips inward—again.

"Dad! They have cocoa with Lucky Charms marshmallows! How cool is that?" Mase runs into my arms right as the whistles blow from the coaches, indicating the team should gather.

"Grab your helmet, let's go." I ruffle his hair and smile at him. Jax points his head to the coaches while Charlie's gaze never leaves Jax.

When we get a few feet away, I lean in toward Jax. "I don't like leaving her alone with them."

Jax looks over his shoulder to see Ivy situating her lawn chair and small cooler. "She's sitting beside Lena. That is one football mom I would never mess with. She'll help Ivy if things get heated. Besides, if we change anything, Mase will get suspicious and... Ivy needs this to go well just in case Dick tries something underhanded later. Ivy can say she tried."

Jax looks down at Mase, who takes off running to the middle of the sidelines.

"I need two parent volunteers for chain gang!"

I look over at the head coach as he hollers his request, facing the audience. Of course, Jax raises his hand.

Five minutes into the game, Mase glances at me from the sidelines since the defense is on the field. I cheer along with everyone else when Everret, one of the cornerbacks, tackles the opposing runningback. I watch Mase talk just as animatedly as his mother to his teammates. I look back at Ivy. She's standing, watching the next play begin. Two whistles blow—flag on the play. While the officials explain the flag, I text Ivy.

Me: You doing ok?

Rosebud: They haven't spoken to me. I can tell you everything about Leonard's health issues, including how his dick is "malfunctioning."

Me: *puking emoji* Glad you're not sharing that info with me.

Rosebud: Guess it's better than the glares from tricky Dick.

Me: Glares are better than his barbed jabs. Let me know if you need a break from them.

I walk over to check on her ten minutes later. "Ladies." I pause, making eye contact with both of them. "How's it going?"

She looks over at the Sumners and says, "About the same. Things have changed for you, though."

"I suppose it has. Ivy, you want something warm to drink?" I ask, hoping to give her a small break since I could feel the icy tension when I walked up.

She nods and smiles. "Sure. Oh, wait. Mase is on the field. You better get up there. If he can't see you... you know what happens."

I shake my head. "He can wait. He does just fine when I'm on missions or deployed. He—"

"He wants to show off for his dad on his last game. Get up there so he can." It's the first smile I've seen on her face since... Cat's reception.

I can't help but smile back and nod, knowing she's probably right. "I'll be back in a few."

Grant—22 Years Old

Standing beside the two most important people in my life as I watch our childhood friend be lowered into the ground is surreal. We played, fought, and laughed together since I was eight. Eli and I rarely saw eye to eye on... well, anything really, but he was still one of my closest friends, or "frenemy" as Kennedy calls it. Eli and I loved to compete against each other more than anything.

My heart breaks for Ivy Rose because Eli's family is completely ignoring her. Not one of them has said a word to her since she arrived. Honestly, the only people Mr. Sumner has spoken to is me, Madam Mayor—aka Ivy and Jax's mom, Margaret, and my father.

The preacher from the First Presbyterian church drones on about love, loss, and our place in this world. I continue to watch Ivy Rose with tears streaming down her freckled face. Jax stands on her other side, occasionally rubbing her back. Margaret stands beside Jax. My mom, sister, and I are behind them. I want to wrap Ivy Rose up and take away all her pain. My sister, Kennedy, who is four inches taller than Ivy Rose, encases Ivy in her arms and whispers in her ear, causing a faint smile. Ken looks up at me and winks.

The ceremony is barely over when both our mothers shoo us into the mayor's black Suburban.

"But I was going to talk to them." Ivy Rose stops and looks over at Eli's sisters and parents standing in front of the lowered casket, his mom crying so hard her shoulders shake. One of the sisters is trying to pull their mom away from the lowered casket.

Madam Mayor shakes her head. "Not right now, baby girl." Ivy Rose looks at my mother, who also shakes her head, before Ivy Rose allows the mothers to drape their arms around her and lead her to the SUV.

The five of us return to the Hersh home, where our mothers continue to flutter around Ivy Rose. Jax and I sit in the living room, watching and waiting for Rosebud to snap at them. Thus far, nothing. Kennedy sits beside Ivy, holding her as tears continue to stream down Ivy Rose's face. Kennedy whispers in Ivy's ear, and the girls walk out to the back deck.

"Brandt, let's go." Jax nods his head to the deck.

When we walk through the kitchen, the mothers are talking quietly in the back corner. That can't be good news, especially for Ivy.

The moment I walk out, Ivy Rose rushes into my arms, wrapping her arms around me and burying her face in my chest.

"I got you, sweet pea," I whisper, knowing she hates the fake name I gave her in high school. Anything to get her to smile at this moment.

Instead, she gives me a weak punch. "I hate you."

"Awwwee, did you guys hear that? Rosebud loves me." I tighten my grip on her, pretending to give her a bear hug to push her even farther.

Kennedy rolls her eyes. "Can't you be nice for one day?"

I rest my head on top of Ivy's. "Of course I can. I just choose not to. Besides, if I didn't give her shit... that would hurt her feelings. I think she's dealt with enough of that. Don't you?"

"That's true." Rosebud grants us with a watery laugh. Her smile doesn't reach her eyes, but at least it's a smile.

"Plus, I have to pack as much as I can since I'm leaving in the morning." I look down at Ivy. "I was accepted into Ranger School, and training starts Monday. I will need letters... so many letters from you. I need to make sure you're doing ok. I'll call when I can." My heart breaks for her because I just want to hold her and take away all the pain. All I have are lame jokes.

"You better call me if I'm sending so many letters," she says between silent sobs. "What time are you leaving?"

"I have to be at the airport Sunday at 7:30 p.m."

She nods and looks over at Ken. "Ken and I will take you."

Kennedy smiles and wraps Ivy Rose in her arms. "I love you, my friend. Definitely." The girls start crying again.

Ivy gives her a watery response. "Back at you. I love all you guys. Thank you for being with me."

All of us hug her. We stand there in a group hug for who knows how long... until my mom takes a picture of us and tells us to come inside so they can feed us, yet again.

Chapter 13

Ivy—Present Day

"**W**HY DID YOU SEND him away?" I hear Lena whisper to me. She never watches the game when the offense is on the field, which is why I miss so many of Mase's plays. Lena's son, Chuck, is a defensive tackle.

"I didn't," I say back. "Mase really does like to show off for Grant. He looks for Grant when he's on and off the field."

Lena clicks her tongue, looks beside me. "I want to say so many things right now. You asked me to behave"—she motions with her head to our visitors— "cause of them."

I smile. "We'll talk about it another time."

"I expect a phone call in a few days. If not, then Chuck will stop by for a playdate."

The crowd cheers. I stand up—Mase runs the ball down the field, he dodges around a pudgy linebacker. He then takes two steps left to avoid being tackled by another linebacker. A few more steps to avoid the safety. He has no one to stop him from the endzone. Five. Ten. Fifteen. Twenty yards.

Holy crap! I'm screaming my head off for Mase to keep going. The safety begins gaining on him. The little shit tackles my baby on the goal line. But it was a low tackle—Mase's upper body crosses the endzone. Touchdown!!!

I cheer with everyone around us. People are looking at me and giving me high fives. They know he's my son.

After a few moments, I talk into Lena's ear so she can hear me over the noise.

"I told you sending Grant to the sideline would help. Mase will try to do that again as much as possible today."

Lena just shakes her head with a laugh. "He should stay over there for the whole game, then!"

Charlie pulls me into an excited hug. Over her shoulder, I watch the conversion play. Brian, the center, hikes the ball to Mase. He hands it off to Bernie, the left runningback. Bernie runs to the open pocket near the left edge of the endzone. He makes one point.

Cassie leans over. "Wait... shouldn't that've been two points?"

I shake my head. "This is pee-wee. They complete a two-point conversion, but it only counts as one. A touchdown is six points, plus a completed point makes it seven. In a game, the boys won't throw the ball, only run it. And no special teams. After each play, the referee will place the ball on the fifty-yard line instead of having a conversion kick."

"Oh." Her voice changes to disappointment.

"Any other rules that are different than high school ball?" Charlie asks from the seat beside me.

I pause to think while watching Mase come off the field with the rest of the offense. His teammates are patting him on top of his helmet and celebrating with him. "Not that come to mind. The point at this level is for them to learn the basic rules and have fun. Mase knows how to throw, but they won't do that for two more years. He keeps beating himself up because he's a little perfectionist."

I watch Mase look at Grant, and a beaming smile develops the moment Grant gives him a thumbs up. Grant turns and heads my way. My heartbeat picks up pace just seeing him. Damn, he looks good. Not at all how Jax described him or how he looked three weeks ago when he came to tuck Mase in.

"Mom!" Mase calls. Six moms look over and answer him, which causes a laugh in the crowd.

"Landon forgot his water," Mase says to me.

I nod and grab a water from the cooler. Grant lifts a hand in the air, indicating he wants me to toss the bottle. I toss it underhand to him so he can run it over to the boys. He talks to Mase for a few minutes, ruffles his hair, then walks to me.

"Come on, sweets, let's go get a warm drink." I look at Lena, who's pretending not to hear anything and is now watching the game as Chuck is on the field.

Charlie pops up out of her seat as we are walking away. "I didn't know they had a concession stand."

Wrapping his arm around me, I look up at him in surprise. It's the first time he's touched me since the reception. I lean up and whisper, "Sweets?"

"It's better than babe."

"Fair," I say, nodding a bit. "What's up?" I ask suspiciously.

He hesitates and lowers his voice. "I don't like how Cassie has been eyeing me like I'm a medium-rare porterhouse. I figured we could do each other a favor. If you want to go back to whatever after today, fine."

I chuckle a bit. I had noticed that earlier, and I can't help but feel relieved that he's not interested in her. I clear my throat in hopes that it won't crack. "I don't. I-I..."

Charlie catches up to us, rattling on about how great Mase was with that last play. I'm so focused on Grant that Charlie's voice, the referee whistle, and every other sound on this field melts away. Grant places a kiss on my forehead, and I wish I could say it didn't send tingles throughout my body. Even if it's just for the moment, I feel my heart dance. God, I was such an idiot for running from him.

When we step up to place our order, Grant slips his hand to my lower back. It takes everything in me to focus on ordering my hot chocolate while Grant gets a coffee.

He turns to Charlotte. "Charlie, what are you ordering?"

"I'm getting the whole family," she says, holding up cash.

"It's fine. Just tell me what they want. You know I'm not going to take no for an answer. Coffee or cocoa?"

She huffs. "Coffee for everyone but me. Thank you."

He pays one of the parents volunteering the stand and starts handing drinks out among the three of us. "So, I see your dad is still a grumpy ass. Is he mad that Mase isn't a linebacker or because we are not doing what he wanted?"

Charlie gives us a small smile and blows on her cocoa. "Both. You know he likes getting what he wants. Where do you think Cass got it from?"

"She still pisses you off?" I dodge around a toddler running from another toddler.

She nods and looks over at us. "There's a reason I live in Ohio and not Michigan."

The crowd gets quieter with a few "Nos," and the opposite side of the field starts cheering. The other team must have made a big play. I glance up at the scoreboard—still 7-0.

When we get back to our seats, we pass out drinks, and I settle in beside Lena to watch the rest of the first half. Neither Mr. nor Mrs. Sumner say anything. I know I shouldn't want a thanks for the coffee, but is it too much to ask for politeness? They should at least say it to Charlotte.

Grant returns to the sidelines when Mase hits the field. He hovers over Mase until shortly before halftime.

All whistles blow, indicating the kids' five-minute break with their family before getting a pep talk from the coaches. Mase flips his chin strap and jogs straight to Grant. Together, they make their way to me. Mase points to the field. I love how he openly shows his feelings. There's no mistake how happy football makes him. I know his eyes are sparkling, and a smile bigger than Mount Everest washes across his face. Even after they join us, all he talks about is the game. How Chuck tackled a kid the size of a high schooler and how far Mase ran.

"Drink your water. You only have a few minutes," I remind him.

He only has time for one drink when Jax walks up. Before Mase can talk, Jax holds up a hand. "Not a word till you finish that bottle. You were on the field for eight plays. Drink."

Mase heaves an annoyed sigh. "Fine." He downs the bottle. "Dad, are you coming with us for pizza?"

Mr. Sumner jumps in. "Pizza?"

My adorable, sweat-drenched little boy looks over and nods. "After every game, we get pizza. After the last game, the whole team goes out."

"I was going to take everyone for seafood," Mr. Sumner gruffs, folding his arms.

Mase's gaze moves from me to Grant to his grandfather and back to Grant. "Today is super important, and you want to meet me a-and all, but football and pizza every Saturday is me. We can do both? Dad, what did you call it... wait, compromise." He points his finger at Grant just like Grant does when he makes a point.

Jax slaps his forehead while Grant has a small smirk. I'm shocked. How the heck does this kid know about compromise?

Cassie smiles, and all eyes go to Mr. Sumner. Cassie says, "I like this kid. He knows what he wants and isn't afraid to go after it."

"Depends," Mr. Sumner leans forward in his lawn chair.

Mase holds his ground, looking the old man in the eye. "On what?"

Mr. Sumner lifts his brows with a serious look on his face. "Can you complete another touchdown?"

The confident smile returns. "Pfft. Yeah." He answers like that was the dumbest question in the world.

"Make that touchdown"—a smirk forms on Mr. Sumner's mouth—"and we'll talk."

Mase looks at Grant, and that cocky smile on his face widens.

The coaches blow their whistles to round the boys up. I wish I could say the game was uneventful, but it was a rollercoaster. We were close to the endzone, but we lost the ball after failing to get another down.

The opposing team, the Wildcats, scored the first time they got the ball, but Mase did a fake and ran the ball himself for another touchdown. It kept going like that the entire game and ended with a score of 28-21.

With the game finished, Mase runs to Grant and jumps in his arms with his helmet still on, something he rarely does.

Charlie looks at her father and says, "It looks like we're eating pizza tonight?" Dick shakes his head. I'm betting he's trying to figure out how to change Mase's mind.

That's when my boy walks up, with Grant and Jax following him. "That we are. I made another touchdown." Mase grins.

"Nice hand-offs to your running backs, Little Bear," Jax says.

Dick stands, pats Mase on the shoulder, and asks, "How far away is this pizza place?"

Ivy—20 Years Old

"Ivy, for the love of all that's holy—change your clothes! Sweatpants and a tank top are not suitable to wear beyond your bedroom, especially since I need your help with this luncheon," my mother nags.

It's been two weeks since Eli—since she called me home. I still get choked up about it. What I haven't told anyone yet is I'm not crying because I'm sad. It's the guilt. I'm riddled with it. Guilty for wanting to break up with him. Guilty for not being sad. Guilty for being relieved that I didn't have to break up with him now.

Sadly, I'm stuck here with my ambitious mother, who has her hand in everything in this town. I mean, it makes sense that she does with being the mayor and all, but it's exhausting putting on the facade that we have this perfect life. I just can't right now.

God, and all the looks of pity. *That poor thing lost her boyfriend. It's so sad, he was so young. They had their whole life ahead of them.* I have to pretend he was a faithful, loving boyfriend. If not, the gossip mill will go running straight to Dick. I don't have the energy to deal with his crap, let alone what he would attempt to do to my mother's political career.

Rolling my eyes, I pretend I didn't hear her. Maybe she'll leave without me.

"Ivy Rose Hersh! Get your ass dressed!"

She actually shouts at me from my bedroom doorway. Something or someone has ticked her off, probably me. Her hair is dark blonde and curled under in her usual pixie cut. She's not in her usual power suit. Instead, she's wearing an A-line blue and white floral dress with matching white cardigan and the white pearls Daddy bought her as a wedding gift. She wears those pearls at least once a week.

I pull my face out of my pillow and whine, "Why do *I* have to go?"

She walks to me and places her hand on my head. "You need to leave this room," she says in a softer voice. "What will people think? Eli wouldn't want you to do this. He'd want you to get up, get dressed, and attend this luncheon with me. Wear the pink dress and white sandals."

I almost laugh. She didn't know Eli at *all*. He damn sure wouldn't want me to go to the luncheon. All the mayor's friends and family dressed nice at a public setting? Nah, Eli liked to hide our relationship from everyone but Jax and Grant. Those three didn't think I noticed how hostile their relationship became the past few years. The snarky jabs and barbs at each other, especially between Grant and Eli.

She remains by my bed for an uncomfortable pause. Looking to the left, I see she's still there, staring impatiently at me.

Huffing, I stomp to the bathroom. Part of me wants to jump right back into bed, but I know from experience that she's waiting to hear the shower and will return every ten minutes until I'm dressed to her satisfaction.

After stepping into the shower, I bolt right back out when I feel my breakfast and late-night snack coming back up. The next few moments are spent dry heaving until tears form. Shaking with tears streaming down my face, I crawl back into the shower and attempt to figure out why I threw up so violently. Maybe all this stress is getting to me more than I thought. I've been nauseous for the past couple of weeks.

My delightful mother knocks on the bathroom door. "Ivyyy, you ok? Just checking on you."

"Just finishing up," I lie, praying she doesn't come in to make sure I'm not lying to her.

I hustle to finish my shower and get dressed before her next check in. Seriously, why did I throw up like that? Why do I feel better? I reach under the sink for my hair dryer, knocking over an unopened box of tampons in the process. *How long has it been since I used those? Fuck!* That box should've been half empty. Damn it, I should be going to get another box, but instead...

"Son of a bitch," I whisper. I need to go to the pharmacy... now. But nooo... I have a luncheon to attend. *Thanks, Mother.*

After shaking hands at the ladies' luncheon, consuming small sandwiches, and drinking stale coffee for over four hours, I finally get to the pharmacy. I'm sweating bullets walking—ok, sneaking—into my own home with three Walgreens bags. I thought for sure that I was busted when I realized Tamara would be my cashier. The gossip in this town is unreal. Boss level. I wouldn't be surprised if everyone knew what I bought before I walked out of the store. But I'm a master of distraction—thank you very much. All I had to do was mention my beloved big brother, who Tamara graduated with and has had a crush on, and I was home free.

Now, I just have to pee on the stick. Easy-peasy. Why am I sitting on the toilet eating a Slim Jim and not peeing?

Because...

I can't...

I can't pee! I don't have to. Or was I nervous about the answer on the stick?

I turn the water on. I've heard that helps. I listen to the water gush for a few moments. Nothing. Drink the water. I waddle across the room with my pants around my ankles, picking up the tiny mouthwash cup my mom keeps in every bathroom, and drink five tiny cups of water. Nothing. Damn it.

Googling how to force yourself to pee is not recommended. What the hell is a perineum? I'm not tickling or stimulating it. No way. I can dip my hands in water. Letting the cool water run down my fingers is relaxing until the water gets colder, freezing my fingertips. Still, no pee sensation. Relax. Yeah, right. Not happening. I need to know whether or not I have a bun in the oven or if my birth control is making my body wacky again. Not the first time that's happened. Thank you very much mother-fucking-nature.

The front door slams. Great, Mom's home. So much for getting answers. I leave everything on the bathroom floor, pull up my big girl pants—literally—and greet my mother.

"Can you help me with this?" She has a huge plastic tote that she's dragging across the entryway.

Grabbing the handle, I tug a little, thinking it's all papers like before. This is heavy. It barely moves. "What is this?"

Mom sighs. "I honestly don't know. It's supposed to be all the documents to organize the Fourth of July Jubilee, but you know how Old Man Peterson is. I'm a bit scared to open it. It doesn't feel like just papers."

"Did he add rocks to it, just to mess with you? That sounds like something he would do since you beat him every election."

Mom nods and opens the lid once we get it to the sofa. I have to pull the sofa to the tote, that's how heavy this crap is. "How did you get this out of your SUV?"

She smiles. "I talked his nephew Kyle into following me and unloading it onto the porch."

"You should've had him bring it in."

Mom scowls at me like I asked her to wear black jeans before Labor Day. "Why on earth would I do that? Then I would have to offer him a drink, and neither of us wants to spend any time with that man."

I nod. She's right. That dude creeps me out. I pop open the lid, pulling out red tulle, a graduation banner, an IOU from Mavis Everly for... Lord, I hope I read that wrong... for sex?! Mavis is ninety-one! "Gross!" I drop the note and pick up a stack of papers.

"I knew he was a perv," Mom adds, picking up another stack of papers.

None of these papers have anything to do with the Jubilee. Three more IOUs from elderly women asking for all types of sexual favors and a pie. Two flyers for the American Legion Breakfast from two years ago and other miscellaneous junk. The more we dig, the more I think this tote is just to mess with my mother. I'm starting to think there really are rocks at the bottom.

"I'm going to change. Do you still have my lotion?" Mother asks.

"Bathroom." I continue digging, trying to find something that will help us with the Jubilee Mr. Peterson has been organizing for the last thirty years. But none of these papers are useful.

My mother clears her throat and drops a pregnancy test box on the stack of papers I'm still sorting through. *Shit!*

"Explain."

I haven't heard that level of anger for a few years. Mostly when I was sneaking back in the house after she'd grounded me.

"Umm..." I fumble for an excuse—*any* excuse. When I can't think of anything, I settle on the truth. "I have an unopened box of tampons, and this morning I threw up. With everything that happened with... Eli... I hadn't even realized how long it's been. I should've used them by now, or at least opened them." I do everything I can to avoid looking at her.

"Go take it, now." She gives me her impatient voice like when I used to badger her to let me play with Cassie and Charlie.

My shoulders slump the same way they did when I stole Linc's car when I was sixteen.

"I tried earlier. I couldn't pee."

"Try again."

Her eyes are filled with complete disappointment, even though we don't even know if I'm pregnant or not.

I get up and try to pee—again. This time, I return successfully with the white stick in my hand. I toss it at her. I should've waited for the results, but I know what it will say.

"Damn it, Ivy. How the hell am I going to face this town with my unwed daughter waltzing around pregnant? How will that look?"

"I don't know, Mother. Like a woman who got pregnant by her long-term boyfriend?"

Mother rolls her eyes at me, her voice becoming icy. "And who will believe that since he's dead? The speculation will be insane. People will wonder, *Is it Eli's or isn't it? How many times did she cheat on him? How often?* You'll be a trollop by the end of the week. That's not adding Slick Dick's commentary into it all."

Tears stream down my face. I know my mother is concerned about what others think, but I always thought she would have my back if I ever needed her. Guess I was wrong. I want to run to my room and hide from her, but my feet refuse to move.

"You better hope to God that your brother takes pity on you cause you can't stay here."

I look up at her in complete shock. The resolve in her eyes is something I've never seen before. I suddenly understand how and why she was elected as the mayor.

My voice comes out watery as I ask, "What?"

"You heard me, missy. You might want to call him and pray he helps you." She goes to her room, slamming the door.

Throwing myself on the sofa, I cry into the cushions. After a few minutes, I get control of my emotions, remembering that my own mother just kicked me out and I need to make a plan, starting with calling my brother.

The tears return, blurring my vision when I pick up my phone to call Jax. One ring. Two..."Jax... I need your help..." I explain everything, including how our mother kicked me out.

"Fuck. You know Dick will try to take the kid from you, right?" Jax responds.

"Seriously? I just found out like less than fifteen minutes ago, and I have to fight to keep this kid already? What a fucking crock." The more I think about this, the more it pisses me off.

"Come down here for a little bit. I'm sure you could use a break from Mom, and we can figure shit out. Besides, it's been forever since I've seen you. Plus, Grant is at my base now. And North Carolina is nice and warm."

"Ugh. I'm not running away from this. I don't care about the rumor mill and their bullshit."

Until five minutes ago, I would've already been at the airport to see my brother just so I wouldn't have to attend the Gourd show this weekend with Mother. Anger courses through my veins knowing that I have to leave my hometown because of Mother, the gossip mill, and now Dick. Total bullshit. Though, I won't have any of those issues where Jax is.

"I'm not saying you are. You're visiting your brother, who misses you dearly."

"Ass."

"Awwwe, I love you too. Put Mom on the phone so I can talk her into booking you a flight. I have a three bedroom off base. You'll have your own room. Don't make me call Brandt to talk you into this. At least come for a few weeks. Please, sis. I promise everything will work out."

He begs, something he rarely does. Maybe if I was thinking clearly, I would question his persistence.

"Fine." I head to Mother's bedroom and hand my phone off to her without saying a word and go to my room.

Pulling out my two large suitcases, I begin to pack as much as I can. I'm not coming back here with my mother being a bitch like that. I need her to be supportive like she's always been. Not kick me out when I screw up. It was a pretty big screw-up getting knocked up by Eli, but still. I'm not going to cry... at least not until I get on the plane.

So not how I pictured my life going.

Chapter 14

GRANT—PRESENT DAY

I TURN LEFT DOWN Oak and listen to Mase rattle on about his friends and school, something I'm going to miss while I'm gone. Thankfully, I only have this mission and then I'm taking leave to visit my sister for a few days. I would stay with her longer, but I hate being away from Little Bear.

"... and Anna told Mrs. Fitch that she used her mom's horn to become a unicorn," Mase explains.

I look over at him when I stop. "Wait, what? Her mom's horn?"

"Yeah, Anna said it was purple, and if she hit the button on the bottom, the horn moves," Mase informs me like *I'm* the idiot.

I look at him confused for a sec, trying to figure out what the hell they found with a button on it that makes it move in their mother's room. Did they find a Christmas present or someth—Wait...

"What?" Mase asks.

I look ahead as the light turns green. "Nothing."

I try to keep a straight face, but I can't. For some reason, I can see a seven-year-old girl wearing her mother's vibrator on her head. I crack up.

"Whaaat?!" Mase asks again. "What's so funny?"

I come down from my laughing fit. "Ahhh... I'll tell you when you're older."

Making another right turn on Maple, Mase's voice fills with disappointment. "We're going to Beatz? How long will you be gone?"

"Should be about three weeks, but could be closer to a month," I say, pulling into the parking lot of the strip mall Beatz is in.

Mase takes his time climbing out of the truck, and we head in.

"What are you getting, bud?" I ask.

"Superman in a waffle cone."

Beatz has bright yellow walls, red bench seats, and blue tables. Yellow, blue, red, and mint green dots decorate the walls.

"Waffle cup," I correct him, knowing he won't eat his ice cream fast enough for a regular waffle cone. We'll have a melted mess in no time.

Mase rolls his eyes. "Fine… with sprinkles." I nod and try to figure out what I want as the blue-haired teen welcomes us.

I place our order while Mase watches the teen scoop our ice cream and make the waffle bowls with complete fascination as if he's never watched the workers make his food before.

"Don't forget my sprinkles." Mase points to his ice cream, which only has one of three scoops in the waffle cup.

The teen responds, "I got it, kid." She finishes scooping his red and blue swirled ice cream then adds the multicolored sprinkles, pausing to see if he wants more. Mase nods, and she adds another sprinkling of sprinkles before handing it over the glass case protecting the ice cream.

I spend the next hour listening to Mase rattle on about his friends at school. I love these little moments with him. I hate that I have to leave him for who knows how long. This is my consolation prize. The smile on my kid's face eating ice cream and hearing about all the little things happening in his life.

Grant—23 Years Old

"Rosebud, what color do you want in each studio?" I ask, standing in the nearly empty building Ivy Rose just bought to house her art store. We've spent the last week cleaning and emptying the miscellaneous things so we can begin remodeling and designing.

"I think we should go with a neutral color for the main studio and let the products and artists work give those pops of color. I want *my* studio to have light tan walls. The pottery studio should have pale terra cotta. I want each studio to showcase what it is a bit. The paint studio we can do pretty much anything with, same with the matching classroom." Ivy Rose waves her hands and points at each room she's thinking about.

It took the contractors two weeks to put the dividing walls up between each studio and classroom and install the plumbing and cleaning sinks. Now, we are ready for the painting before bringing in the large pieces like shelving, display cases, registers with counters, etc. That's not counting the types of equipment we need for each studio and classroom. I never realized how much went into running a store.

We've come a long way in the three months since picking Ivy Rose up from the airport with her two large suitcases. I figured she just had to get out of our small town—I didn't expect her to tell me she's pregnant with fucktard's baby. What a kick to the balls. I should've manned up and told her how I felt about her years ago. Maybe she'd be carrying *my* baby. Focusing on the past doesn't help with the present. She's here and living in our apartment.

"I still think we should hire someone to paint all this for us." Jax walks in the door, still in uniform. I'm not cause Ivy Rose had a doctor's appointment that I took her to. I may not be that kid's father, but she's always been mine to take care of and now her baby.

"I agree, plus it will take forever with Jax and I painting in the evenings and weekends," I explain, pointing at the empty studios and class-rooms.

"I can help too. Just because—"

Jax and I interrupt her simultaneously. "Hell no" from me and "You've lost your mind" from him.

"Paint fumes are dangerous. No. Either we hire someone or Grant and I do it. No arguments. Don't make me pull the Mom card. I will call her for this." Jax is not hiding his frustrations since this isn't the first time she's tried to do something herself.

Ivy Rose huffs. "Fine. I don't have the money to hire someone."

"Sis, do you really think we would let you do any of this alone? We have money to help you. Let us. If you want professionals to paint, I'll pay for it."

Ivy opens her mouth to protest, but Jax lifts a hand. "Consider it my grand opening gift."

Ivy huffs again. "Thanks."

"Make the call."

"How was your appointment?"

Ivy reaches into her purse for her phone. "Grant recorded part of the baby's heartbeat on his phone. We have pictures. It's a boy for you idiots to corrupt. We need to discuss baby names tonight."

"Come on, let's get some food in you and prop up those feet," I tell her since her eyes are getting heavy.

I know she loves and hates how much I hover over her, but I need to take care of both of them. Maybe because I lost over a year with her. Or maybe because I wish things were different. I don't quite understand why I feel this way, but I do. They are mine. This is my second chance. I just don't know how to move Ivy and I out of the friendzone and into... more.

Chapter 15

Ivy—Present Day

"I vy!" Jax hollers from what sounds like the front door. "Ivy!"

I drop my laundry back in the basket and call down to him, "Up here," before making my way down since there's something alarming in his voice. Desperation? Fear? I need to figure it out.

"Where's Masen?" His mouth is slightly pinched, with worry lines across his forehead. I've seen this look before. Whatever this is, it's not good.

"His room, playing video games. What's going on? You're kinda scaring me," I say, grabbing his arm to force him to look at me.

Jax takes a deep breath. "I need you to pack a bag. We have a flight to catch in two hours."

"Ok, where are we going in such a rush?"

"Bethesda."

Shit. Fuck. Damn. I close my eyes, praying for it not to be my greatest fear becoming a reality.

"I need you to say it." My voice cracks at the end, knowing what he's about to tell me. I feel in my soul that something happened to Grant.

"Grant is in ICU at Walter Reed. Ali and the Senator want us at the hospital. The doctors say he should've woken up days ago. There's no reason why he's not waking up. Ali thinks if he hears Mase or you, he'll wake up. We need to leave ASAP."

"Oh god... Oh my god!"

Jax says all of this with very little emotion, but I know he's worried and scared. I want to fall apart and cry, but I need to get to Grant. My mind goes to everything that happened between us. God, I've wasted so much time trying to figure out how to fix things that I haven't done a damn thing.

"W-what happened?"

"We can talk on the way." Jax's phone rings. He points upstairs as he answers it. "Talk to me." He walks to the back of the house.

I stand numb for a few minutes before running up to my room. So many things are racing through my head, but I keep reminding myself that I need to focus on packing, then getting to Grant. *Shit. What will I do if something happens to him?*

We didn't get a chance to talk before he left. I have so many things to tell him. I need to apologize to him. Tell him what an idiot I was for leaving him at Cat's wedding. I need him to forgive me and… and… we need to fix *us*. Now I might never get the chance. And that scares the *fuck* out of me.

Suitcases are in the hall closet. I rush out to grab them and return to my room. I have no idea how long we will be there. I also have no idea what I'm grabbing out of my dresser and closet. I toss Grant's shirt and shorts.

Four deep breaths and a few head shakes before I'm ready to tell Mase what's going on. "Hey, Mase, can you pause your game for a quick sec?"

"Sure. Did I hear Jax a few minutes ago? I beat this level and want to tell him." A huge smile filled with pride crosses his cherub face.

"Yes, he's downstairs on the phone. I'm sure he'll be up here soon." *Shit this is hard. How the hell did Jax do this with a straight face?* I take another deep breath. "Something happened. I don't know the details, but Dad is hurt. We need to…" I stop.

Mase's green eyes fill with fear. "Where is he? How bad is he hurt?"

"He's in Maryland. Jax is here to get us. I need you to pack some clothes. Jax'll tell us what happened on the way."

Mase runs to Jax when he hears him coming up the stairs and rattles off question after question about Grant. I have the same questions: How bad is he hurt, where is he hurt, how did this happen, what happened, how soon can I see him?

Jax picks Mase up and brings him back into his room. "Shut off your game. Grab some clothes and your tablet. Little Bear… he's hurt pretty bad." Jax pauses, probably pulling himself together. I'm in awe of my brother for keeping his shit together. "Your dad needs to see you to help him get better. Let's finish packing so you can cheer him up, ok? Don't forget socks and underwear." He then turns to me. "You packed?"

I have no words but merely nod. My thoughts come in spurts.

Toiletries. I forgot toiletries. I rush into the bathroom to discover all of them are in bottles too large to take on the plane, so I grab my brush and makeup.

Work. I won't be at work tomorrow.

With shaky hands, I text Cat.

> **Me: Grant is in ICU in Bethesda. Can you cover for me at the store?**

> **Bestie: HOLY SHIT! Yes, of course. Are you ok? I'm presuming you're going there?**

> **Me: Yes, leaving in a few hours. I'm not ok. I don't know what I am. I'll call you later tonight.**

I drop the last of my things into the suitcase where Jax has added Mase's clothes. He has also packed Mase a backpack full of things to keep him occupied. At least someone is thinking clearly.

The drive to the airport is a complete blur. My mind goes through every memory I've ever had with Grant. Every smile he has given me. Every touch we've ever had. When a lone tear escapes, Jax wipes it away from the back seat of the Uber with Mase situated between us. He looks down at Mase, then up to me.

We talk without saying a word. An eyebrow raise for *Keep your shit together for Mase.*

If I fall apart, so will Mase.

I can't wait any longer to find out more about Grant. I clear my throat. "Tell me what you know so far."

Jax hands Mase his Switch with headphones before beginning. "There was an explosion. He has a severe concussion that led to some slight brain swelling, broken leg and arm. He also has some second-degree burns and some cuts. Thankfully he was far enough away it didn't do more. The swelling is completely gone, which is why they are worried he's not waking up." Jax leans his head back.

"How long has he been in the hospital?"

"Almost a week at Reed... Well, I'm not sure if it's Reed anymore since that hospital is merging with the National Naval Medical Center, so

I have no idea what the hospital is called now. Maybe it's still called Walter Reed, but either way, he's in Bethesda."

"I don't care what the hospital is called as long as he's getting the best care possible."

Jax and I spend the flight focusing on Mase and how to keep him distracted. Jax does answer a few of Mase's questions about Grant. Thankfully, my brother sugarcoats it and doesn't give Mase a lot of information. Mase reads a few chapters from his Percy Jackson book while I attempt to read a military romance on my Kindle, but I can't focus. My thoughts stay on Grant. I picture him lying in that hospital bed, never waking up. My throat tightens, and my nose stings with tears and sobs that threaten to come out.

I barely remember leaving the plane or entering the naval base, let alone the hospital itself.

I will never forget the look on the Senator's face. His pale face, purple circles under his eyes, deep worry lines across his forehead, straight mouth. One arm wraps around Kennedy, and the other hand holds Ali's. In the corner sits Grant's eldest brother, Robert, with his wife.

Linc, the second oldest, comes up behind us with coffees. "Hey, Ivy." He passes the coffees out to his siblings and then comes and wraps his arms around me, holding me tight. Kennedy does the same.

Ali looks up and smiles. "There's our Little Bear. Come give Mimi some love." Mase runs right into her arms, clenching tightly like she holds everything in his world.

Grant's father, Mitch, or as we mockingly call him "the Senator," looks over at Jax, "Thank you for bringing them."

My brother nods and sits down beside Robert and across from Ali.

Mase finally releases Ali and jumps into Kennedy's lap. "Oh geez, bud. You are getting way too big for this." She adjusts him so he's sitting sideways in her lap, almost disappearing under him. Kennedy wipes the tears from Mase's face. "Go give Pops some love too."

Mase gives Kennedy one more hug before climbing into the Senator's lap for a hug. Mase pulls back and looks at his grandfather. "Can I see my dad now?"

"Masen!" I reprimand him.

"What? I love everyone, but we came to see Dad."

Robert chuckles from the corner. Linc grins, and Kennedy rolls her lips inward to prevent from laughing.

Linc whispers to Kennedy and me so their parents can't hear him. "That kid acts exactly like our brother."

"Why don't we go talk to the nurse and see if he's ready for visitors?" Mitch tells Mase.

Mase and his Pops walk hand in hand to the nurse station twenty feet away by a locked door. I realize we are the only ones in the waiting room. The walls are tan with solid blue loveseats lining the two walls, and across from each set of loveseat is matching seating. There are four pictures hanging on two of the walls of bald eagles, each in various forms of flight.

Ali wraps me in her arms once Mase and Mitch walk through the door I previously thought was locked. Part of me wants to break down and cry in her arms, but I know if I do, I won't be able to stop. I need to keep it together for Mase.

"You can let it out, sweet girl," Ali says, practically reading my mind.

I shake my head and loosen my grip on her. All I can manage is a whisper. "Later. After Mase is asleep. I can't do anything until I see him."

"Let's go. You know that little boy of yours will not leave my son's side." She looks at the rest of her children. "I'll be back in a few. Make sure the child bride stays the hell away."

"Do I even want to ask?" I whisper to Ali when we get to the door.

Oddly, she doesn't check in with the nurse like Mitch did. I'm sure Ali's jab was directed at Mitch's latest girlfriend. Why do they all think he's going to marry them?

Ivy's 25th Birthday

I haven't had a birthday party since my sweet sixteen, and I have no idea why my brother thought it would be a good idea. I like parties, but I just wanted a few people over with a bonfire and maybe a few drinks after Masen went to bed.

It has turned into a huge party with almost fifty people, including the single dad, Dan, from Mase's Pre-K. I'm not entirely complaining about Dan being here. We had a nice time when we went on a date last Friday night, and he's not bad-looking. I mean, yes, he has a slight dad bod—the complete opposite of Grant. Dan has a sincere smile, *unlike* Grant, who's smile looks like he's up to something. Dan is perfectly fine. And maybe he's the one to break my dry spell. Because nice guys do that, right?

Mase runs out the door, chasing his friend Kole with a nerf sword. Why do I have a feeling that child is hyped up on sugar? *Pick and choose your battles, Ivy. He's laughing and having fun, even if it's an hour past his bedtime.*

The front door opens, and Grant walks in wearing jeans and a soft gray shirt, both of which hug his muscular body. I gasp. Jax and I didn't think Grant would be back until next week.

He picks up my son as he runs past. "Hey, Little Bear. How was everything while I was gone?"

"Grant!" Mase hollers.

Standing in the doorway of the kitchen, I watch my five-year-old rattle off everything that's happened in the past two weeks, even though Grant has been gone for just over three months.

"Mom! Grant's back." Mase has a huge smile that makes his green eyes sparkle.

Grant walks to me still holding Mase. "Hey, beautiful. Aren't you a sight for sore eyes." He uses the same line every time he returns from a mission or deployment. He leans over to give me a peck on the cheek.

To follow his return routine, I say, "Hey, handsome. Glad you're home." Grant winks at me to finish the little game.

"Does this mean we can go to the zoo now? Mom said we could but not till you come back... cause you would be upset that we saw your friends without you," Mase says so quickly I swear he's not breathing.

"My friends?" Grant asks, probably questioning whether he should even ask. I roll my lips inward, knowing what's coming.

"Yeah, Mom said your friends... the baboons. Did you know baboons throw poop at each other?" Mase says, giggling.

Grant puts Mase down and tells him, "Go play with your friends." Then, to me, he says, "My friends are baboons, huh?" Grant questions, taking a step closer to me.

"Pretty much. I mean, a few are dogs... who need to be put down," I tease him.

"Really? You know, your *brother* is one of those friends."

I shrug. "He's the one that needs to be put down."

Mase runs back in. "Soooo, the zoo?"

"We're talking about it, Little Bear. Go play, I'll let you know when," Grant tells him with a soft, caring smile on his face.

"Yes! Come on, Kole. Uncle Jax has fireworks!"

I groan. "Why does my brother do this to me? He knows I hate fireworks, yet every opportunity he has, he sets them off."

"Maybe for the same reason Kennedy used to tell cheerleaders to pop their disgusting gum at me or why we used to move everything in Robert's room a half an inch," he says, brushing my auburn hair behind my ear. "Come on, Rosebud. Let's toast to your quarter century birthday by the fire and get drunk."

The backyard has lawn chairs surrounding the firepit, along with tables lining the side of the house. Kids are running around with glowsticks and sprinklers. If I was a stranger walking in, I'd swear this is a Fourth of July celebration instead of my birthday party.

Grant hands me a Jack Daniels wine cooler, knowing it's my favorite flavor, and I immediately start drinking it. Anyone else, I would've checked the label before touching it.

Slinging his arm over my shoulder, Grant kisses my forehead and says, "Come relax with me."

A few minutes after snuggling together on the outdoor loveseat, I remember Dan. I'm a horrible person for completely forgetting about him. "Oh, I almost forgot. Dan. I should go find him." I peck Grant on the cheek and attempt to dash back inside.

But Grant grabs my wrist and asks, "Who the hell is Dan?"

"I met him at Mase's school. He picks up his son at the same time I get Mase."

"So, this guy is picking chicks up at the school pick-up?"

I throw my hands in the air. "Seriously? We've been on a few dates and... hopefully, he helps me end my dry spell."

Grant clinches his jaw but plasters a fake smile. "I gotta meet this guy. Go, let's see who you deem worthy enough to break your nearly six-year dry spell."

I playfully slap his arm. "It hasn't been that long."

Grant stops by the sliding glass door. "What? You go on one, maybe two dates and you're home by nine p.m. I have so many questions beginning with"—he lowers his voice—"when was the last time you had sex? But first, this Dan guy." Again, he clenches his jaw. Yeah, Grant is pissed.

"How do you know what I do during your deployments and missions?" I walk away and look around for Dan, who is walking out of the living room.

Dan walks up with a soft smile on his face. He says, "I hope it was ok to let the boys play video games in here."

"I'm surprised they're still awake, but then Jax gave them sparklers and set off fireworks. Four little ones, wide awake."

Dan chuckles, ruffling his son's hair.

"Grant!" Mase drops his controller and runs to Grant like this is the first time seeing him, but Mase does that quite often—yelling and running to Grant even though he saw him two hours ago.

"Hey, Little Bear." Grant picks Mase up and they hug each other, again.

"Can we play that game you play with Uncle Jax, please?" Mase sticks his bottom lip out, complete with those sad puppy dog eyes.

"No can do, buddy. That game is too violent for you. Besides, you're playing with your friends. Spend time with them. I'll be here in the morning. I'll do whatever you want, ok?" Grant barely glances at me, then his gaze watches Dan's reaction.

Mase nods and picks his controller up, returning to his game and friends. Grant turns toward me when Masen says, "You're making pancakes in the morning, right?"

Grant's gaze locks with mine as he responds, "Nah, *we're* making pancakes, remember? I wasn't gone that long; how could you forget that I need my helper?"

Mase shrugs and answers, "Mom tries, but they're done when I get up. Uncle Jax buys them from the girl he smiles at a lot."

I clarify, "He picks it up from the diner."

Grant nods, throws his arm around me, and says, "Let's get the birthday girl another drink."

"Dan, do you want something to drink?" I ask, realizing he's barely said anything since Grant entered the room.

"Nah, we're going to head out after they finish this game." Dan waves at me less than thirty minutes later and leaves. I guess he wasn't as interested in me as I thought, or maybe Jax and Grant "talked" to him. Either way, that was a bust.

A few hours later, Mase finally crashes on the sofa with a controller in his hand. I don't realize that everyone left until Jax shuts off the gaming system and television.

"Looks like you had a nice birthday," Jax says, dropping into an oversized chair.

"Yeah, thank you for all this, even if you did it as an excuse to get drunk and avoid talking about she-who-shall-not-be-named." I lean back on the sofa, letting the booze further relax me.

Jax fell for his girlfriend... well, ex-girlfriend, Janessa, who broke up with him shortly after his last mission. He's been attempting to hide how crushed he is about it. Grant comes and drops on the sofa beside me, watching Jax calm himself down.

Looking at the ceiling, Jax tells us, "I'll take Little Bear to bed and crash in his room."

"Let me get him. You can still crash with him if you want," Grant says, picking Mase up and helping Jax upstairs. I hear the two of them quietly talking and take a few happy breaths.

Grant returns and wraps me in his arms. "Did you have a good birthday?"

"For the most part, yes," I answer, realizing Grant is giving me a curious look and his gaze tells me to explain more. "Dan left with just a wave. I was hoping he would break my dry spell."

"He had no intention of having sex with you... at least not tonight. Come on, he showed up to an adult birthday party in khakis and a polo like it's casual Friday. And he brought his kid."

"Mase and Kyle are friends," I attempt to rationalize.

"Even if he did come without his son, a guy like that would leave you frustrated. Yes, the dry spell is over, but can he give you multiple orgasms that each one leaves your body feeling like Jell-O and you crave more?"

I roll my eyes. "That only happens in the novels I read. Very few guys can actually pull it off, but I was thinking about trying to find out if he could."

"He couldn't." Grant leans back on the sofa, resting his head on the top.

I shouldn't ask cause he's going to piss me off. I know it. "What makes you such an expert?"

Grant leans over, gazing into my eyes as he says, "I know you."

Maybe if I go into explicit detail about what I want and need, he'll change the subject. "You don't know anything about that part of me. I haven't been properly fucked in years. I miss passionate kisses, the weight of a man on me, orgasms that are not self-inflicted. And that's just the basics. I really want someone who can throw me on the bed and isn't afraid I'll break. I want something that might leave a mark in the morning. Something that I'm literally walking weird in the morning for how hard he pounded into me."

"I've told you before... all you have to do is ask," he says like none of that fazes him.

"What? No, you've said that about the things around the house. My vagina isn't like the leaky faucet." I can't believe him! Oddly, a part of me wants this from him. A huge part. *What would sex with Grant be like?*

"One, you didn't tell me about the faucet. That will be fixed tomorrow. Two... I haven't given you your birthday present," Grant says, leaning close to me. He rests one hand on my neck and my hair while the other rests on my hip.

"You gave me the compass keychain," I whisper, afraid I'm dreaming.

"You really think that was your present? It's not. Tell me why did we stop the birthday kisses again?"

"I-I can't remember," I lie.

"I'm bringing it back," he says against my lips before brushing on mine so lightly that if I wasn't looking at him, I wouldn't believe he kissed me.

His tongue swipes along my lower lip, begging for access. The moment my lips open for him, he devours me. He goes from soft and tender, like he's searching for something... to demanding and desperate. Pulling me closer with each swipe of his tongue, Grant moves my head back to deepen the kiss.

I grip his neck before diving my fingers through his silky dark hair. He slows the kiss down but doesn't break it. Taking his time. Enjoying this moment. I'm trying to memorize every groan and gasp along with how he tastes and how his touch feels. I want to cement this moment into my memory.

He breaks the kiss, only to move down my neck as one hand glides down my shoulder, sending shivers through my whole body. Grant makes his way back to my lips, but this kiss isn't like before. The soft eases into more passionate. This is consuming.

He moves his hands up and down my body, gripping me closer to him, like he's afraid I'll disappear. Slipping his hand between my shirt, I decide to mimic his movements. I've always wanted to touch his rippling abs and contoured chest.

Inch by inch, I move my hand under his shirt. The moment I touch his skin, he gasps but continues assaulting my mouth with his. I flatten my hand against his stomach as he groans against my lips, further encouraging me to keep touching him. My fingers continue to explore, circling his nipple before lightly flicking it.

Grant breaks the kiss to pull my shirt off, cupping my breasts in his hands before freeing one and sucking the nipple in his mouth, sending warm waves straight to my vagina. He switches sides, wrapping my legs around his waist. I can feel every glorious inch of him against my warmth. I want more. Need more.

Desperately, I push his shirt up. A cocky smirk appears on his face, and he does that guy thing where he pulls it off with one finger, tossing it across the room. I move my hands from the bottom of his abs over his chest. He shivers every time I touch his nipples. Roaming across his shoulders and down his arms, I want to keep exploring, but he breaks my reverie.

"Tell me we're finishing this," he pleads in a gravelly voice I've never heard before as his unhooks my bra, tossing it over his shoulder. He kisses around each nipple without pulling it into his mouth until I'm about to lose patience with him. Swiping his tongue along the top of the nipple before pulling it into his mouth, he sends another shockwave of pleasure through my entire body.

"You better."

He stares at me with lust-filled eyes for what seems like an eternity but is actually only a second or two. He wraps his muscular arms around me, picking me up with him as he stands. "Wrap your legs around me." After I circle my legs around his waist, he jogs up to my room, dropping me on the bed, then locking my bedroom door. "Last chance to change your mind."

I shake my head, unable to formulate actual words.

"Get naked," he demands, flipping the fly on his jeans and pulling them down along with his boxer briefs. I take the remainder of my clothes off faster than I've ever moved before. "Fuuuuck, you are absolutely perfect."

He grabs my ankles, pulling me closer to him at the end of the bed as he kisses up one leg and then the other. Flicking and playing with my tits, he runs his nose along my inner thigh before he ever so slowly licks where I need him most. I've never wanted a man to tongue fuck me so much in my life. Grant, of course has to be the best.

"You are the best thing I've ever tasted, my sweet, sweet rose." He groans, causing me to be even more turned on. I can feel the waves coming stronger and stronger with each flick of his tongue when he adds a finger—and it pushes me over the edge.

"Mmmm, my sweetness... we're just getting started." He slides two fingers into me while sucking on my clit, and I swear I see spots. He uses his other hand to push me back down on the bed while I chase my euphoric high.

Grant languidly kisses my lips and says, "I need to be inside you more than my next breath." The blissful stretch of him causes both of us to groan.

"Move... I need you to move."

"Gimme a sec." I'm so absorbed in him that I barely notice his voice crack. "Fuck, you feel incredible," he says, giving me a punishing kiss that matches his hip movements. It only takes a few slamming strokes before I feel those tingling waves building. I never want this to end.

I move my hands down his back to grip his ass, using them to tell him where his hips need to move. He has other plans as he lifts my ass up ever so slightly, adjusting the angle so his dick continuously hits my G-spot with every damn stroke, causing the biggest orgasm of my life. I swear I stopped breathing and passed out for a few seconds. Grant follows my lead a few seconds later.

Chapter 16

GRANT—PRESENT DAY

I DON'T WANT TO open my eyes. Everything hurts. Hell, even my hair hurts. The steady beeping beside me is concerning. Then everything comes back. The explosion, the sounds, being thrown airborne. Everything. *Shit!* My team. I moan, or maybe it just feels like I'm moaning.

I have to still be dreaming because I hear Mase calling me. "Dad. Wake up. Pops! Dad moaned."

He sounds like he's right here. But that's impossible. If the beeping is real, that means I'm in the hospital. *Shit. Maybe I should wake up so I can tell the nurse or someone to give me something for the pain.*

Mase is still talking, but I can't hear what he's saying. There's a soft touch to my face and a faint smell of roses. Fingers gently massaging my hair. My sweet Ivy. I'm definitely dreaming. If I am, I don't want to wake up.

Her lips are right beside my ear. "Grant Alexander, wake up so I can see those gorgeous blue eyes that make me melt... Plus, you're scaring the shit out of your son. He needs his dad. Please wake up..." Her voice cracks. "I need you too." Her voice is riddled with worry.

No way would Ivy say that unless she thought I was dying or... Am I dead? No. The pain in my head, leg, and arm tell me otherwise. Fuck, the pain is intense. Sleeping will make it go away. I drift back into the darkness.

I fall back to sleep. I hear my sister's voice and Robert's. Shit. I must be pretty messed up if he's here. The pain overwhelms me again and pulls me back under. The room is quiet except for the beeping and a hum, both coming from my left side. There's something else on my left side... a soft body.

Leaning into its warmth, I realize it's Ivy. I must be dreaming again, but if so, I'm going to make this a great dream. Having Ivy in my arms one more time. The sweet roses fill my lungs, reminding me of the mornings I used to wake up with her. I try to lift my right arm to wrap around her only to realize it's too heavy. Maybe I should wake up and figure out why I can't move my arm, but Ivy feels so good.

I doze off, feeling the pain dissipate as I do. Ivy isn't beside me. I can't hear Mase rattling on. I try to readjust my stiff body.

"Captain." I hear a voice I've never heard before. "I need you to hold still for a minute, then I'll help you resituate, ok?" I'm presuming it's my nurse since her voice has no emotion.

I whisper, hopefully loud enough she can hear me. "Ivy?"

"She went to the cafeteria for lunch with a few of your siblings. They should be back shortly after I finish checking everything. I'm going to turn down the lights to make it a little easier to open your eyes. I'll let the doctors know you woke up." She leaves.

"Shit."

"You do look like shit, little brother," Robert says from the foot of my bed.

I try to swallow, but the dryness in my throat makes it painful. "Fuck you... hand me... my water... please."

It takes a lot of energy just to talk. Robert brings the straw to my lips so I can take a few sips. I lean back, feeling every ounce of pain.

"How are you feeling?" Robert asks, his voice gentler.

"In pain," I say with a bit of a whimper.

"Whatever painkiller they're giving me... it's not working. I feel everything."

"They took you off of painkillers four days ago."

Four days?! "That would explain some of my dreams. Did I hear…" I pause to catch my breath, and Robert holds the straw to my mouth as three doctors come in. They poke, prod, and grill me with questions. Grill probably isn't right, but it feels like that since talking is painful.

"What happened?" I ask after they finish.

"There was an explosion, Captain. The surgeons removed the shrapnel from your calf with minimal damage to your muscle tissue, but the impact broke your fibula and caused two hairline fractures here and here." The middle-aged Major points to a spot a few inches from my wrist and another in the middle of my forearm. "Both on your radius. Plus all the cuts and scrapes. We'll need to run some more tests soon. I'd like another CAT scan since you're awake. If you or your wife have any questions, the nurses can page me."

Seems my family lied to get Ivy and Mase up here to see me. Ivy and Mase walk in at the end of the doctor's directions.

"Ma'am"—he nods—"let me know if you have any questions since he's awake."

"Pain meds?"

"Already ordered." The Major leaves, but a nurse continues to type into the computer beside my bed.

"Dad!" Mase hands what he was holding to his mother and starts running to me.

But the brunette nurse stops him. "Hold on, buddy. I need your dad to take some medicine first, ok?"

My son stands at the foot of my bed, bouncing. I can see how anxious he is from how much he's fidgeting and the fact that he's twisting his mouth from side to side, like his mother does when she's getting frustrated and impatient. The nurse leaves and returns with a small cup of pills. It takes me a lot longer than I want to get all the damn pills down, but each sip of water sooths my sore throat. I hand the empty cup back to the nurse, and she refills it and has me take a few more sips.

My anxious Little Bear asks, "Now?"

The nurse nods. "Be gentle. He just woke up and is in a lot of pain. Let me type in this last thing, and I'll help you up to him. Can you be careful with your dad's casts and all his tubes and wires? Captain, if you remain stable and your scans come back with positive news, you'll be moved to a regular room."

Mase's eyes fill with worry, fear, and love. "Yes, ma'am." I nod my acknowledgment to the nurse.

The nurse types into the computer, then lowers my side rail while she holds her hand out to help Mase up. He doesn't need it. He crawls right into my arms where he clenches me tighter than ever.

I wrap my left arm around him and bury my face in his little neck. Cling to him and will myself not to cry. Time stands still while I hold him. My hospital gown absorbs his grateful tears as his little body slightly shakes from his sobs. I know if I look around the room, my mom and sister are also crying. Ivy is probably hiding behind either Jax or one of my brothers so no one can see her tears.

Running my good hand along the length of Mase's back, not only to comfort him but to help ground me, Little Bear begins to calm down, but he doesn't let go. He rests his head on my good shoulder and watches me.

"You scared me." He sniffles.

"I know, buddy. Me too." I attempt to squeeze him.

With a cracked voice, Ken adds, "He scared all of us."

"Are you going to be, ok?" Mase asks uncertainly.

"Eventually," I answer.

He nods and pulls me closer to him, squeezing my chest. He returns to watching me for a bit before his green eyes droop and he begins to fall asleep on me. I kiss the top of his head and join him.

A different nurse wakes me when she takes my vitals. "You need to eat, Captain," the young nurse says. "Let's move your son to the sofa."

Mase tightens his grip on me, and I squeeze him back. "He stays right here until he decides to get up." I know I shouldn't get grouchy with her, but I need him as much as he needs me. Nothing will take him away from me.

"You need to eat. Maybe your wife can hold him beside you while you—"

"Just bring my food here and don't tell my wife what she's going to do, Lieutenant. My son is going to stay right here until he decides otherwise." I glare at the nurse for wanting to move my son.

"Grant," my father warns as the nurse leaves.

"I'm not apologizing. Where's Ken?"

"On the phone with her boss," Linc answers with a grateful smile. "Glad to see our asshole brother is back. I almost missed you."

"Lincoln!" our mother reprimands.

Linc smirks and shrugs. "I'll be back, little brother. I'm going to check on Ken."

"Thanks, Linc. Tell her she can go home. I'm fine." He nods and chuckles at my comment.

My mother quietly reprimands me. "You are not fine. You are anything but fine. You were in a coma for days. Stop acting like a petulant child and let everyone take care of you." I would argue with her, but I have been a jerk and I know better than to cross my mother.

Ten minutes later, a male nurse brings my food. "Do you want help readjusting your bed and your son?"

"Nah, my wife will help me." I watch Ivy's eye fly up and her mouth open slightly. Robert coughs to hide his laugh. Jax quietly chuckles as

Ivy links our fingers together and squeezes. I return the gesture, trying not to get my hopes up.

It takes Ivy, my mom, Linc, and my dad to help me readjust the bed and Mase before I'm comfortable enough to eat. Ivy angles my food tray diagonally so I don't have to force Mase to move.

"Don't even think about trying to feed yourself left-handed with our son laying on you," Ivy snaps, taking my fork out of my hand.

My mom pecks me on the cheek. "I love you. I wish I could ask you to not scare us like that again, but…" She trails off, knowing how dangerous my job is, and changes the subject. "Son, we're going to grab some lunch. Ivy, what would you like?" my mom asks, moving to the foot of my bed.

"A salad is fine."

I look at Ivy. "You hate salads." My focus shifts to my mom. "Get her a burger—"

"I've been sitting around here not doing much so… I feel blah."

I finish Ivy's order. "A yogurt and fruit instead of fries."

The rest of my family head to the cafeteria, Jax following them, leaving me alone with Ivy and a sleeping Masen.

Ivy pushes the chair closer to my bed then must decide against it since she sits down and immediately gets back up. "Your mom and dad asked Jax to bring us—"

I jump in so she doesn't have to verbalize that my parents lied to get her and Mase in here. I don't want any hospital staff to accidentally overhear us. "Don't apologize. I'm grateful…" I tail off and lean my head back since it's so quiet. I'm suddenly exhausted and want to sleep.

"Grant, open your mouth. You need to eat something before going back to sleep." Ivy has a forkful of green beans at my mouth.

I comply, watching her feed me. It stirs up every ounce of love and affection I have for her that scares me more than the explosion did. I can easily see myself falling… Would it be falling if I never stopped loving her?

"Stop thinking. Just relax and let me take care of you for once," she says softly after giving me a bite of what I think is supposed to be meatloaf.

I turn my face away. "Whatever that is, I'm not eating it."

"Yes, you are. You need—"

"Ivy Rose," I warn and give her a stern look that used to intimidate her, and she used to cave.

She mimics my look. "Grant Alexander. I've been around you for too long for that to work on me anymore." She scoops up a fork of mashed potatoes and holds it near my mouth.

I want to be an asshole and say something snarky or maybe even mean for the shit she's put me through after the wedding. But she dropped everything, packed Masen up, and flew here for me. Now she's feeding me and even hiding that disgusting meatloaf behind the mashed potatoes like I can't see that crap. Yet I don't say a word. I'm a little scared to say much because everything has been so weird and awkward. I fucking hate that shit.

"Part of me wants to talk about us but… it also doesn't seem like the right time… or place." Ivy switches to a spoon for my pudding.

"Talk. It's not like I can get up and walk away. Besides, I hate how things have been. We've never…" I stop to ensure I'm phrasing this properly. "We've never had this weird, awkwardness between us," I say, opening my mouth to say more, but Ivy shoves a spoonful of pudding in.

"I wish I knew how to fix all this. I shouldn't've—" Ivy begins, but Masen wakes up.

"Hey, buddy, have a nice nap?" I ruffle his hair, and he responds with a big squeeze.

"I'm hungry." Mase sits up, rubbing his eyes.

I look over at Ivy. "Take him down to get some food so I can sleep for a few minutes before everyone comes back." I don't wait for her response before I lean back and close my eyes.

Grant—24 Years Old

Last night with Ivy Rose was more than I ever dreamed possible. Believe me, I've had numerous dreams about what it would be like—nothing compares to reality.

I only take a few moments watching her sleep and how her gorgeous red hair splays over the pillow and my arm. I want to touch every mark I left on her creamy skin, from the love bites on her chest to my beard burns on her neck and face. Instead, I watch her sleep. As much as I love holding her in my arms, I know my girl; the moment she wakes up, she's going to freak out. I brush a light kiss on her lips before I reluctantly climb out of bed.

I would go for a run, but it's already after eight a.m., which means Little Bear will be up soon, even though he didn't crash until well after midnight. He is going to be extremely grumpy today, but so will his momma since I barely let her sleep.

After popping a K-Cup in the coffee machine, I refill the machine with water when I remember Ivy told me about the leaky faucet. After grabbing my coffee, I get my tools from the laundry room. It takes no time to fix the faucet, but I hear another drip, which means there's a leak under the sink too.

As I'm finishing up, I feel a nudge against my leg. Much too heavy and silent to be Mase. I know who it is even with my back halfway in the cabinet. "Morning, Rosebud."

"How did you know it was me?"

I answer her while finishing tightening the coupling. "Who else would nudge me? Little Bear would be on the other side of this cabinet... in the cabinet. And your brother would kick my leg or step on me."

"Oh."

Tossing my tool in the tool bag, I run the water to ensure I fixed both leaks, also giving her time to figure out what she wants to say.

"Soooo, last night..." She trails off, just like I knew she would. I have a feeling she's worried about how it will change our little family dynamic. If I had my way, I would move in here and make her mine, something I've thought about a lot over the years but been too scared to do. I can't come out and tell her or she'll run from me. Maybe I can ease her into it.

I want to tell her how incredible last night was. How it was beyond every dream or fantasy I've ever had, but... that will scare her off too. I shift gears a bit. "The sink is fixed."

"I don't give a damn about the sink." She huffs.

"Like I said last night"—I grunt as I ease out from under the sink—"if you need *anything*... I mean *anything*, call me." I stare into those gorgeous brown eyes to ensure she understands the full meaning of what I'm saying. I stand and add a quick peck to her lips as Mase barges into the kitchen.

"Are we making pancakes?" he asks, climbing onto the barstool by Ivy.

"Of course, what flavor today?" I smile at the little boy I would do anything for.

"Blueberry!"

"Let's get everything out and get started." I open the fridge to pull all the cold ingredients out, then head to the cabinets for the dry stuff as Mase pulls the bowls and the pan out from the bottom cabinets. We spend the morning eating, talking, and playing.

Two days later, Ivy calls me.

"I need *anything*," she says quietly and uncertain.

Smiling, I tell her, "I'll be right over."

Chapter 17

IVY—PRESENT DAY

I T'S BEEN THREE DAYS since Grant woke up and two days since he moved out of ICU. Linc went home the night after Grant woke up, but not before profusely lecturing me about taking care of him, as if I wouldn't. He knows better than that.

Me: Why are men stubborn and stupid?

Bestie: Grant or his brothers?

Me: Why would I text to complain about Linc and Robbie? Grant! He's a stubborn ass. He's hurt so I'm giving him … some grace.

Bestie: How pragmatic of you. Maybe he's just acting like his "wife" who has yet to tell him how she feels.

> Me: I hate you, hag. I never should've told you that.

> Bestie: Hmm… go be with your man and help him heal. I expect an update after Mase goes to bed.

> Me; Duh. Tell Brax to expect another midnight phone call.

Hell, with so many people still here, Grant does very little for himself, which actually is annoying him. I've seen his jaw clench and twitch a few too many times today. Grant almost kicked Kennedy out to get her to go home. She flew out this morning, promising to come visit in a few days when he goes home. That leaves Grant's parents, who have said they are not leaving until he does, and Robert.

"Robbie, why are you still here?" Grant asks, ignoring Jax on the phone and his mother whispering to his father.

It's odd his oldest brother is still here without his wife. Robert has barely been able to use the restroom without Mallory asking twenty questions, and that began shortly after they started dating, yet Mallory went home the day after Mase and I arrived. She wasn't here when Grant woke up. I haven't even heard him on the phone with her, just him checking in with his office since he's a state congressman.

Robert tilts his hands, which is like my throwing my hands in the air. "I can't be here for my brother?"

"I told everyone to go home. Besides, they're going to release me as soon as we—"

His mother interrupts. "Figure out where you're going to stay while you're recovering. You need someone to help take care of you, and what better place than with Ivy and Mase?"

"I'm not going to burden Ivy with having to take care of me on top of everything else she has to do."

"Why would you think you're a burden to her?" Robert asks.

"She does a lot... the store, mentoring artists, raising Mase, that's a lot," Grant tells them.

Ali jumps in. "She has Cat to help her with the store, there are many other artists who mentor including Cat, and Mase... Who doesn't help with that adorable little one?" she ends with a huge smile.

Mitch speaks, barely glancing up from his phone. "Where else will you go? Your townhouse is two floors with all the bedrooms and bathrooms upstairs. You can't function like that."

"I don't feel right asking Ivy to take care of me when..."

"You're fighting? Arguing? Whatever you want to call your BS?" Jax comments from the corner of the room, sliding his phone in his pocket.

"May I say something?" I stop eavesdropping outside the door and jump in the conversation. "Since you're all volunteering me and everything."

All eyes turn to me. I look at Grant, who looks annoyed. I've never seen him so helpless. "It's not a bother, Grant. I think you should stay with us."

Mase climbs into Mitch's lap, causing the Senator to stop looking at his phone and focus on Mase.

Grant looks over at him. "Masen, what the hell, bud? You want Pops instead of me?"

Mitch's smile stretches, lighting up his whole face. Mase rolls his eyes. "Dad, I'm going to see you a lot now. I don't know when I'll see Pops again."

Grant looks at the two of them, then over at me. "Alright."

Mase looks over to Grant like he's a moron and is not only interrupting but annoying him. "Because Mom and Mimi will win. You told me not to argue with Mom. Yet Mimi told you to do something and you're being a baby."

Mitch looks at his son with a twinkle in his eyes, trying to keep from laughing. Mase grabs Mitch's phone.

It takes everything in me not to bust out laughing.

Robert whispers, "Damn."

Grant just stares at his father and Mase watching football videos on Mitch's phone.

He nods. "I'll stay with you. Everybody happy now?"

"Actually, *yes*," his mother says. "I'll go let the doctor know."

I sit on his bedside and take a hold of one of his hands. He looks over and breathes a sigh through his nose. Then his smile returns.

"Thanks."

I nod, a smile taking over my face as well. I have to swallow to maintain my composure and not cry. Again.

"You're welcome."

Two days later, we're back home with Grant in the downstairs gue-stroom and Ali in the other room beside Mase's. Robert didn't leave until we did. Mitch came with us the first two nights, sleeping at Grant's place on base.

That first morning, I found Mase curled up with Grant in the recliner, watching ESPN with the captions and no sound.

Grant—25 Years Old

A long, exhausting mission is over, and I just want to sleep. I pull my cap over my face, prop my legs across the bus seats, and finally relax for the first time in weeks. I hear my six-man squad talking amongst themselves about what they are going to do once our debriefing is over. A few of them are heckling Hersh about the last time he took them all out for drinks and the girl he turned down. A few more ribs on the new guy for... well, being a FNG—fucking new guy.

"That girl didn't want me. She wanted my uniform and rank. Don't be stupid enough to get caught up in that trap, LT," Hersh lectures. "Make sure she wants you for the ugly fuckers that you are, like Cap."

Asshole. Why does he have to drag me into this?

"Cap has a girl? Thought he was... like a monk or something," one of my guys adds.

"I swore he was gay," another adds.

The speculation gets worse among them about why I never flirt or even look at women when we go out for drinks. I love how they continue to talk about me like I'm not here. They know I'm not asleep, even though that's what I'm trying to do.

Hersh kicks my foot, hoping I'll jump into the conversation. I'm enjoying their preposterous theories about me, even if they're keeping me awake.

"If he was gay, he would be all over this." That one made me chuckle. They argue about who I would fuck if I was gay. Idiots.

"Can you fuckers not see I'm trying to sleep?"

"He's not gay and far from being a monk. Just pining over a girl he's been in love with since he was... what, sixteen?" Hersh questions, airing my past for our entire squad. He's going to regret that.

"Something like that," I mutter, trying to stay comfortable and remain completely still even though the bus shifts for the sharp turns.

Hersh is wrong, I've always been in love with Ivy Rose. I just didn't realize it until she was fourteen and taking an interest in boys. I wanted to be the only one to kiss, touch, and do everything in-between with her. But my teen self was an arrogant self-centered jock who didn't realize what he had until West Point.

"Cap, if you can't close, I can help ya out," one guy says.

Another adds, "Sure you will, McGill. Help the girl out of her panties."

I sit up with a sigh, stuffing my cover in my pocket. "You assholes have no clue." Hersh silently laughs behind his hand. I shake my head. "Closing isn't the problem. It's keeping her. None of you know anything about that, especially you, Hersh."

The group hollers at the dig I throw at my best friend.

"Ouch, man. What the hell did I do to you?" Hersh asks.

"Didn't keep the peanut gallery quiet so I can sleep and dragged my past up. You know I can't be tired when I get home. You know that more than anyone," I add, lean back, and watch the guys chatter about. Luckily, only two of them are paying attention.

"What's wrong? Not getting enough?" Hersh smirks.

"First, who is on this bus? We've been gone for five months and eight days. And two, I get plenty. Ask your sister." A huge smile crosses my face because I know he won't respond to that.

The group hollers again, louder this time. They grab each other and laugh.

"Oh damn! Cap burned LT," McGill hollers.

"Not funny. Not funny at all," Hersh deadpans.

"Hey, you opened that can. Deal with it. Besides, you know one of the first things I'm going to do is sink myself into—"

"Okaaaaaay! Shit man!" Hersh squeezes his eyes closed and holds up a hand. "Damn. Stop, just stop. My nephew sleeps in that house, and don't even tell me what you do with my sister..." He trails off, trying to figure out what he wants to say. That's why I went there. Serves him right.

The group hollers a third time, this time chanting my name. I smile as I close my eyes again.

"Wait, wait, wait," Daizic says. "Cap, thought you were pining over a woman since you were a kid. Or are you just messing with LT about screwing his sister?"

"Yes and no. His sister is—"

Hersh jumps in. "Who he's too chicken shit to tell that he loves her. He practically lives with her and my nephew, who worships the ground

Brandt walks on. Another thing that's bullshit, but what can I do?" Hersh kicks my leg.

I can't help but laugh. "You forgot a part."

"What part is that?"

I debate whether I want to say this nicely because we're discussing my Rosebud or be an asshole to Hersh for not letting me sleep and dragging my personal life into the team's gossip.

"How I get to fuck your sister senseless every night we're home. The 'my sister' jokes are hilarious when you're fucking said sister. Plus, how many times have you made 'mom jokes' about the bimbos my dad dates? Or about my sister and what you would like to do with her?"

"For one, I ignore that part of your relationship with her. And two, your sister is a model"—he looks at the guys— "a legit New York runway model. I mean, who wouldn't make those jokes? Plus, I would never actually touch Ken. She's too young." He pretends to have noble intentions when he's far from noble.

"Kennedy is a year younger than your sister. You're right, you wouldn't touch her. Her IQ is too high compared to the women you usually take home." I shrug.

The squad listens to our bickering. I should be nicer to him, but I'm sleep deprived and just wanted a nap before heading into debriefings.

He shrugs, not caring how true the statement is. "They don't need intelligence. Only two things. Nice tits and"—he flashes a shit-eating grin complete with sexual innuendo about what he's not say-ing—"well…"

The sad truth is he doesn't mean a damn word out of his mouth. He hates the type of women he's been with, which is why he quit taking them home. He only flirts when members of our squad are around. He wants more but is stuck.

That's also where Masen comes in. Hersh spends all his free time with his nephew to distract himself from being lonely. That's the thing about being friends with someone since you were eight. You know everything about them and then some.

Just like he knows how I really feel about his sister and what I wouldn't give to never leave her house. I don't want to drop in every so often. I want to wake up next to her for the rest of my life. But my Ivy Rose—my Rosebud—won't have any of that. She's scared to let me in. Slowly, I've been showing her.

Chapter 18

Grant—Present Day

THIS IS ABSOLUTE TORTURE. Almost the worst torture I've ever endured. Not the worst physically—that prize goes to the Belize mission. But emotionally... yeah, being this close to Ivy Rose and not being able to touch her is killing me. Although part of this torture is self-imposed. I could make a move and tell her I want more, but I want her to come to me.

Every time I hobble into the kitchen, I see the time I laid my sweet Rosebud across the kitchen island. I come back to the living room and remember being balls deep in her against the wall or when she scratched the hell out of my back on the living room rug. Every inch of this place has a memory.

"What the hell are you doing?" my mother asks like she can't see me grabbing a coffee cup. She takes it from me and shoos me back to the living room.

I almost collide with Ivy coming down the stairs. She chuckles and gives me a knowing look. "She kick you out of the kitchen again?"

I lean on my crutch. "I can do things for myself. A cup of coffee isn't difficult."

"Hmmm, but how were you going to take that to the table?" Ivy folds her arms and taps her finger.

My patience is running thin because neither of them will let me do shit. It's like they think I forgot how to live or something. Thankfully, I have a physical therapy appointment today, so I can get out of the house for a while.

Ivy wraps an arm around me and guides me back to my maroon recliner—a piece of furniture I used to love. It was the first thing Ivy let me bring into her home.

Mom stands behind Ivy, waiting for me to get comfortable. My foot keeps slipping off the footrest, allowing me to look down Ivy's V-neck T-shirt, and she picks my foot up and gently rests it on the pillow.

"I'm going to take Mase to school, then I'll be back to take you to your appointment... unless Ivy wants to take you."

"No, you can take me, Ma," I respond, and my mother merely nods before heading upstairs. I need the distance from Ivy.

I avoid looking at Ivy, knowing I hurt her feelings by insisting Mom take me instead of her. But my feelings are fucked up the way it is by being this close to her. No way can I start depending on her more than I already am.

"You good?" Ivy asks.

I sip my coffee. "Go to work, Ivy." I keep all emotion out of my voice. I'm not purposefully being a dick; it's just the way to protect myself now.

Instead, Ivy slams her purse beside me. "That's it."

Mase runs up and kisses us both. Ivy says, "Love you, have a good day at school."

"Love you. Bye, Mom. Bye, Dad."

The biggest smile covers Mase's face. If I wasn't so irritated from not thinking about Ivy naked, I would muster more than a small smile back and ask Mase about why he's so happy.

The moment the front door shuts, Ivy's attention shifts to me. "First, this Ivy shit needs to stop. You said you hated how awkward it is between us. Or were you just saying shit cause you almost died?"

"I didn't almost die. I broke my arm and leg. It's no big deal. In a few weeks, I'll be back to work and out of your hair." My impatience seeps into my voice, unintentionally.

"You are not in my hair. It's the least I can do for all the times you've helped me. Hell, there were moments when I barely made it out of bed. You pulled me out of some deep shit. I'm trying to…" A tear falls and her voice cracks. "Shit."

"You don't owe me anything."

She wipes her face and continues. "Yes, I do. I ran away from you for a dumb fucking reason… an-n-d… you've been so fucking sweet about it. I mean, not entirely since you abandoned Mase for a bit, but you got your head out of your ass and started acting like his dad again. So thanks for that."

I want to say something, but I can tell from her breathing that she's not done.

"Why haven't you yelled at me or some shit for what I did? That was shitty of me."

"You apologized."

"Really? *Really*, Grant? One apology for running out of your arms in the middle of a fantastic week… God, that place was so romantic. Perfect for Cat. Damn it, I'm getting off topic. You should be pissed at me."

"I was. Why do you think I was drunk for almost a month? I felt like I lost you, Mase, and the little family we were building. I loved every minute of our lives before the wedding. It got better that week in Pennsylvania, so I told you how I felt. I got swept up in love and romance and forgot about how you run when you're scared. I don't know, maybe I was hopeful I alleviated that fear."

"Well, you didn't."

"Obviously." I pull her into my lap and hold her, which I shouldn't do, but I hate seeing her in pain for any reason.

She curls up, wraps her arms around me... and cries. Her cries only last a few minutes, but she doesn't loosen her grip around my torso and her face remains at the crook of my neck. I lightly rub her back with my good arm. A half hour later, my mother returns and points upstairs.

When Ivy sits up a bit, she rests her forehead against mine. I breathe in her soft rose scent. It's always been my favorite smell. She's known that since I was twelve.

"Shit, you're going to be late. Sorry." Climbing off me, Ivy turns and adds, "Stop calling me Ivy. You've never done that before. It hurts. I want my friend back. Maybe find that guy. I miss him." She pecks me on the cheek and rushes out the door.

I grab my phone and tell the one person who's always had my six, "I have a plan and need your help."

Chapter 19

Ivy—Present Day

W ALKING STRAIGHT INTO THE painting studio, Cat makes a long black line—probably the outline of Brax's body since she tends to sketch him when he's gone.

"I almost kissed him." I spread out on the floor by her feet.

Cat's eyes don't budge from her canvas. "I hope you're talking about Grant, or we will have words."

"Of course, who else would I kiss?"

"Tell me what happened. Did *you* almost kiss *him*, or the other way around?"

"I almost kissed him when I wanted to rip him a new ass for calling me Ivy. Oh, and I apologized to him, again." I lift my head to see her reaction—I can't. I can only see her jeans and black T-shirt.

"Ok, that's a bit to unpack. First, it *is* your name."

"He never calls me that. It's always Ivy Rose, Rosebud, or sweetie, sweetness… something like that." I wave my hands in the air, looking up at the wood cross beams.

"What're you going to do about it?"

"I cried in his arms."

After I explain everything that happened this morning, Cat sighs and turns around. "Why are you on the floor? You know what, I don't care. FYI, the floor is gross. Why do you keep torturing yourself? Just tell him you're in love with him. And you need to do more than apologize. Explain things out to him."

"This is the cleanest floor out of the four studios, thanks to you. It's been… what, three months since your wedding? What if he's changed his mind? He can't stand to be around me. He's trapped at my house."

"Stop! We both know he's not trapped. If he wanted to leave, he'd tell Ali to take him to his townhouse or he'd go home with her. From what I understand, Grant has been in love with you forever. Why would that change now? I don't get why this is even a problem since you told us during girls' night that you've been in love with him since you were twelve. Just tell him. Explain what was running through your neurotic brain." Cat taps her foot against my jean clad leg.

"I can't."

Cat looks up and mumbles under her breath, probably wondering why we are besties. "I'm going to regret this, but why not?"

"If I say it, it will happen."

"Hag, quit being so cryptic. What will happen?"

I sit up and lean my forehead against my knees. "I have this fear."

"I mean, don't we all? But seriously, tell me about your particular fear. Also, get off the floor, you're grossing me out." Cat scrunches her face in disgust. I get up just to appease her.

"I'm scared if I tell him, he'll die... you know, like my dad did... like Eli did." I watch every movement Cat makes.

Her blue eyes stare straight at me. "Nothing about Eli and your father are the same. I question whether you even loved Eli cause you barely talk about him."

I sigh, knowing she's right. I never truly loved Eli. I liked the idea of someone who would love me.

"There's something I've never told anyone about Eli." I lift my head to see Cat put her brushes and palette on the table. She sits beside me and nods for me to continue. "He cheated on me. He was on his way to see me, but he was coming from the wrong direction. But I knew in my heart he was lying. That morning, I wished he wouldn't make it to me. The crash happened two hours later. I-I..."

Cat pulls me into her arms. "Don't you dare say that accident was your fault. Accidents happen. Everything happens for a reason. If my parents would've been supportive and caring, I would still be in Pennsylvania, and I'd have never met the craziest, most neurotic bestie in the world or married the man of my dreams. I one thousand percent believe that bad shit happens to us for a reason. I would go through it all over again for you and Brax."

I hug her tighter. "That was the sappiest shit ever. I am a fucking amazing bestie."

"I never pegged you for someone to put up with a cheater."

"I was actually going to break up with him. It wasn't just that I suspected him of cheating. I mean, that was a huge thing, but it was one of many reasons. We had nothing in common. He was so fucking selfish. He knew nothing about me. I still think he never knew what my major was."

"So, what are you going to do about Grant?"

I lean back in my chair. "I have no clue. I want to climb him like a spider monkey, but he's hurt."

"You have time. You need to talk things out. Lay everything on the table for him."

"What if he doesn't want me? It'll be weird."

Cat pulls us up and dusts imaginary dirt off her jeans. "Oh, I almost forgot. A customer called asking if you do custom jewelry orders. He said he'll call back tomorrow since I didn't know if you did that or not."

"It depends on what he wants. I mean, I'm not a jewelry store. I can't get certain types of stones, but I do custom orders all the time. The order form is by the store phone. Make sure you get his number in case I have any questions."

I spend the next two hours making earrings for the display case, thinking about everything Cat said. She's right, I do need to talk to him and make things right. But how? This isn't like my novels and then I can just write a hit rock song dumping all feelings out there because I can't say them to his face. Maybe I need to lay off of the rockstar troupes.

Chapter 20

Grant—Present Day

"**S**ON, WHAT'S THE PLAN for the day?" my mother asks as she hands me another cup of coffee.

It's irritating dealing with my mother right now. What kind of question is that? She knows damn well I can't go anywhere even if I wanted to. I shouldn't be grouchy, especially to my mother, who would do anything for me and my siblings. Hell, she would do anything for Ivy and Mase too.

I put my crutch against the island and lean against the opposite countertop to face her. "Thought about sitting my ass in the recliner and moping about how I can't ask Ivy out for a date. So, my whole plan to win her back is going nowhere."

"Oh, that all? I thought you were a man of action, not a pouty little bitch." She heads into the living room and picks up one Ivy's romance novels.

I can't believe she called me a bitch! I take another sip of my coffee so I don't spill it hobbling into the living room.

"What the hell? How am I a bitch? I can't believe you called me that," I say, setting my coffee on the table beside my oversized recliner and dropping myself into it.

She answers without looking up from the book. "Pouting is a bitch move. Do something. Even when you were kids, you flirted and played these stupid games, chasing other people away. You never stopped doing that. You haven't made one comment about her tiny sleep shorts or tank tops. The two of you have never done things traditionally. Why would you start now?"

I noticed her sleep attire—immediately. Thankfully, I'm usually already at the table when Ivy Rose struts around in those tiny fucking shorts that I want to rip off her.

"I've never been on an official date with her. Where we get dressed up and..." I trail off, realizing that dream is months in the distance.

"Why can't you have a date here at the house? Order some food, or"—her eyes light up—"I can make my famous chicken enchiladas. Then I can take Mase to play some ski-ball or something to give you guys some privacy."

I have to admit, that sounds like a damn good idea. "You would do that?" I ask, picking up my coffee.

"In a heartbeat. You two need a night alone so you can talk. Go back to your roots, son." She checks the clock on her phone. "If I'm going to make you my enchiladas, I need to run to the store. You want me to grab you anything?"

I smirk. "Can you pick up some roses and stuff for strawberry short-cake?"

She gives me a proud smile and nods. "That's my boy. I can do that. I'll also pick up a small bag of pink Starburst."

I give my mom a small smile for remembering my favorite candy.

A few hours later, my mom arrives with armfuls of groceries and a chattery seven-year-old.

"Dad, Mimi said we can have a movie night," he says, dropping his backpack by the front door. "I want to watch *Spider-Man*, but she said it should be your choice since you're hurt."

I point to his backpack. "You're not leaving that there, are you?"

Mase rolls his eyes. "No."

Ivy Rose walks in, almost tripping over Mase's backpack.

"*That's* why I told you to pick up your backpack," I add.

"I said I wasn't going to leave it there," he deadpans.

"Masen," I warn.

"Lovely," Ivy answers, walking around Masen as he grabs his backpack to put away.

I holler at him when he's halfway up the stairs. "Mase, what do you need to say to everyone?"

A smirk crosses his face. "I'm sorry for mouthing off and not putting my backpack away. We're still watching *Spider-Man*, right?"

He looks at me, waiting for me to answer before he takes his backpack upstairs. I give him a small smile. "Thank you... and yes, we're still doing a family movie night. Get your homework done before dinner."

"Ok," he says as he rushes into his room. I hear his footsteps to his room and his door shut with an excited "Yes."

Ivy shakes her head and heads to the kitchen, where my mother finishes putting the groceries away. I follow her after fighting with my chair and my body to cooperate with each other. It really sucks having my right leg and right arm in casts. I didn't realize how right dominant I am until trying to push myself up with my left arm, only to land right back in my chair.

I find the two most important women in my life in the kitchen talking. For anyone else, that would be scary, but they've been doing that since I was a kid. Hell, Ivy used to spend every free period in my mom's Spanish classroom. The two of them even used to travel to Latin American countries together, along with my sister Kennedy, after I graduated.

I pull the fridge door open to grab a bottled water when Ivy jumps my shit. "What the hell do you think you're doing?"

"Getting a drink." I take a long swig from the bottle to prove my point.

My mother joins Ivy. "Go sit back down."

"No, I've been in that recliner all day. I need to stretch. I can stand right here and help the two of you prep the veggies or... Wait, did you get the strawberries?"

Mom folds her arms and gives me that annoyed face. "Of course. You are not slicing strawberries left-handed."

Ivy guides me to the island stool. "You could barely hold a pen to sign yourself out of the hospital. Now you think you can use a knife? No."

"I can do things for myself."

Mom pats me on the head and pulls yellow, red, orange, and green bell peppers, along with onions and chicken, out of the fridge. "Ivy, pull the strawberries and start slicing those before he tries to do them himself and we have another trip to the hospital."

"I love the confidence the two of you have in me," I quip.

"Awwwe, did we hurt the little jock's feelings?" Ivy smirks, batting her eyelashes to mock me. Her voice softens. "Grant, you almost died. Let us take care of you." She waves her hands, attempting to shoo me away.

"Little?" I lean toward Ivy Rose. "We both know it's not little." She hasn't called me a jock since she graduated high school. I'm guessing my mother had the same talk with her that she had with me.

Ivy rolls her eyes and looks away, unable to hide the smirk. That shut her up.

Footsteps come thumping down the stairs, and Mase appears with a math book in his hand.

"Dad, I don't know how to do this." He brings his math workbook to me.

"Alright, bring it here." I scoot the other stool beside me, and he climbs up, placing the book down between us.

Ivy pulls out the strawberries and puts them on the island. While the women start working on food, I help Mase with his homework. I sneak strawberries out of the pack when Ivy isn't looking. I can't help myself—it's one of my favorite fruits.

She catches me once and scowls at me.

"Hey! Stop stealing the strawberries."

She tries to smack my fingers, but she's too slow.

"Sweetness, I have no idea what you're talking about." I pass the strawberry slice to Mase, and he almost drops it putting it in his mouth, leaving a red trail on his chin.

Ivy Rose deadpans, "Smooth, real smooth."

I shake my head. "That's your son."

"Oh, *now* he's my son, but when he made a touchdown during foot-ball season, he was *your* son. Is that how it is?" My mom tries to hide her laughter while Ivy Rose has a huge smile that reaches her eyes.

I steal another strawberry slice, pop it in my mouth. "That's *exactly* how it is."

"Oh, really?"

I continue to watch Ivy Rose until Mom tells us dinner is done. Thankfully, our banter continues through dinner as well.

"*Spider-Man* time!" Mase bounces in his seat.

"Which one?" I ask, trying to push myself up from my chair. Ivy Rose comes over and helps me up. "Thanks," I whisper, running my good hand down her arm.

I queue up the movie Mase asked for and sit in the middle of the sofa.

"Mase, sit on the other side so you don't accidentally hurt your dad's arm or leg." Ivy Rose grabs the pillow I was using for my foot from the recliner and sets it under my foot.

Mase curls up on my left side while Ivy Rose sits on my right. I move my arm to the top of the sofa, and a few minutes later, she begins scooting closer to me. By the middle of the movie, Ivy's head rests on my right shoulder and Mase is asleep in my lap. I lie back and rest my eyes, relishing this moment.

Chapter 29

Ivy—Present Day

A PLUS TO HAVING Ali at the house is if I get lost in a project, I can work without worrying about if Mase had dinner, completed his homework, or had a bath. She takes care of everything like he's her blood, even tucking him in to bed like a toddler. And for some reason, he *lets* her!

Stepping in the house is eerily quiet at night. Even when Mase is at school, the sounds of activity outside give life to the neighborhood. At night, it sounds like a crypt.

As I walk down the steps to check on Grant after seeing Ali in the room with Mase, I hear a crash in the kitchen.

"Dammit!" Grant complains.

I find him half lying on the floor trying to pick himself up and a small puddle of milk in front of the fridge. With a sigh, I slip my arm under his broken arm so he can use his good one to pull himself up. Once he's steady, I grab the paper towels to clean up the milk on the floor and cabinets.

He leans against the island, his jaw twitching, indicating his frustration. "I'm sorry. I just wanted some milk."

I clean up the puddle and wipe up the small tear making its way down his leg. After throwing the wet paper towels in the garbage, I turn to him. "Come on, let's get you in the tub so you won't smell like spoiled milk. You're probably overdue for one anyway."

He gives me a small smile. "You saying I smell?"

I press my lips together and "Weeellll... maybe a little." I hold my thumb and index finger slightly apart. He takes the hand I'm holding up between us. "Anytime... Well, *anything* you need help with. Call me."

He pulls me so close that our noses are touching. I'm surprised with his strength, given he just was in the hospital. "Ivy Rose, are you using my own line on me?"

My heart swells at the fact that he remembers the line he used on me. "Let's get you cleaned up."

Before I can pull away, his lips brush my cheek. I can't hide the smile that bubbles up from my chest, and I gently push him away, bending down to grab a trash bag from under the sink. I run my hand across his cheek before heading upstairs.

A few moments later, I hear him hobble up the stairs, but he stops by the bedroom instead of coming to the bathroom where I start running his bath.

"Sorry it took so long; I needed a change of clothes," Grant explains as he drops his fresh clothes on the toilet seat.

I nod, grab the trash bag, and pat the top of the toilet lid with a hand. "Come here. Let me wrap up your leg so you don't get it wet. Sit."

I pull the bag around his calf, trying not to watch him take his shirt off. A shirtless Grant is a sight to behold. Every ridge and curve of his muscles are burned into my memory. I used to spend hours moving my hands up and down his chest and abs. I'm so lost in thought I miss him taking off his athletic shorts.

"Rosebud, help me in the tub." I stand close to him while he eases himself in the tub, then props his leg on the edge. "Glad I can still render you speechless."

I clear my throat. "Anything else you need help with?"

"Washing my hair."

I grab a plastic cup from the kitchen and wet Grant's hair. Grabbing my shampoo, I lather his hair, slightly massaging his scalp the way I know he likes. Our friends-with-benefits situation had quite a few perks to it. He hums his pleasure. I rinse his hair and run my fingers through his longer, thicker strands. I'm surprised he hasn't asked Ali or me to take him to the barber. His bangs are falling across his forehead, and the back touches his neck.

"Grab the soap," he whispers, looking me in the eyes, which makes me melt. I should leave. He doesn't need help washing his body.

I shouldn't pick up his soap or the washcloth or create a lather. Let alone slowly scrubbing his neck down his well-defined arms—well, his toned right arm down to his cast without getting it wet. Arms that qualify as arm porn. And I definitely shouldn't wash his chest with the compass tattoo above his heart.

He releases a long moan. I should be worried about him waking up Ali or Mase, but instead, I continue making large circles from his chest and down his incredible abdomen. Those circles get closer and closer to his waist.

Who am I kidding? My eyes have barely left his dick since he climbed into the tub. I want to lick every inch of him. I want to climb in that tub with him and ride him like I used to. Like I did in my dreams two nights ago.

I move the washcloth to the crease between his leg and his growing cock, then massages his balls and finally move along his shaft.

"Jesus, Rosebud." He grips the side of the tub with his good hand.

My hands need to touch him. Dropping the washcloth, I move my hands along his shaft, stroking him up and down and running my fingers along his shaft and around his head, especially along the underside—a sensitive spot for him. I know it turns him on even more when I touch there. I repeat it two more times.

"Sweetness, I'm going to come if you keep doing that." His voice strains.

I continue to glide my hand up and down his shaft. I missed feeling him and hearing his moans. Grant leans his head back against the wall, his face completely relaxed for the first time in weeks.

I should let him finish his bath in peace. I shouldn't repeat my hand strokes, gripping him tighter and tighter with each downward stroke and rubbing my finger along the top of his head, knowing he's getting closer and closer from how his muscles tighten. His thighs slightly shake, showing me he's restraining himself. I add a small twist to my wrist movement. Once. Twice.

"Fuuuuck…" Strands of white cover my hand. When he's come down from his high, he says, "Christ, don't run from me." With his good hand, he grips my wrist still holding his dick. His lips brush my cheek. "Help me get out."

After he climbs out and wraps a towel around himself, he pulls me to him. He kisses me like I'm his last breath. I can feel every emotion through his lips—love, fear, affection, and passion.

I need to get out of this bathroom before I lose my willpower and my clothes. How did my hands land on his chest, right over the compass tattoo? I pull away from him, roll my lips inward, and leave the bathroom.

What the hell just happened? It's not like I haven't dreamed about touching him every day since I messed up and moreso since the accident. What does this mean? Why do I want to do it again?

Chapter 22

GRANT—PRESENT DAY

"Y**OU HAVE THREE APPOINTMENTS** today, and Jackson said that he's stopping by with a few guys from your team. Do you need a pain pill? You're making a face."

Without waiting for an answer, Mom heads into the kitchen to get my pills that I stopped taking days ago. I'd rather feel the pain than be numb.

"You know I'm not going to take any more pills, right?" I holler at her.

"I know. I need to thank Ivy for helping you with a bath. You smell much better. Let's get going."

"Thanks, Mom. It's fantastic to know that I smelled and no one said a thing." I hobble out to Ivy's car that she left my mom. I gotta admit, it's easier for me to get in and out of than my truck.

"Plus, you're in a better mood. Almost makes me wonder…" She trails off, opens the car door, walks back to the house, and locks it up.

"Mom!"

"Oh, I don't want to know." She returns, helping ease me into the car. "Although if it does—"

"Can we change the subject?"

"I mean, Mase would be ecstatic that his parents are getting along so well." She pulls out and turns left.

"For all that's holy, subject change! Fuck."

She takes a right on Oak. "That's what I'm hoping happened last night, but you're not *that* happy."

"Just fucking shoot me." I stare out the window, praying for a black hole to swallow me.

"I think Ivy's dramatics are rubbing off on you. At least she talks about sex without getting all melodramatic about it."

"I just don't want to talk about my sex life or my relationship with Ivy Rose."

She coolly shifts lanes. "With me, you mean. At least you stopped calling her Ivy, which hurt her feelings, by the way. Maybe you should listen to me on occasion."

"I'll work on that as long as you don't ask me about my sex life."

"If I really wanted to know, I would ask Ivy. She tells me every-thing. I'm pretty sure I can tell you when you started that stupid friends-with-benefits thing. Hand me my purse, or better yet, get my ID out. Make sure you get the right one."

"How do you still have an active dependent ID?" I question, but she rips the card from my hand before I can look at who her sponsor is. My guess is my father. I also question whether they actually got divorced. None of us have seen divorce papers, nor have either of our parents seriously dated.

She hands the gate guard our cards and makes small talk. She stuffs her ID between her legs and drops mine in the center console.

"Not going to have me put your card away?" I ask suspiciously.

"I'm particular about where it goes in my wallet."

"Sure, Ma. Remind me what year you got divorced."

"Grant, you know damn well what year it was. Don't play games with me. Oh, look we're here."

"Yes, how convenient for you. You know, except we're a block from the clinic," I say as my mother rounds the block and pulls into the parking lot. "A block is plenty of time to tell me all about your divorce and why you have an active DOD ID."

"Lookie, we're here. Do you need help getting out?"

I shake my head at my mother's antics as she helps me climb out. As usual, she pulls away to park the car while I hobble my way to the doctor's office. I usually make it to the office door when she catches up to me.

The downside of these appointments is that I hurt like hell. The doc switched my arm cast to a soft splint I can take off at night and to shower. Too bad my leg is an actual break and not a hairline fracture like my arm. I'm still stuck with the walking cast, but I have a cane instead of crutches.

Back in the car, Mom updates me on the family news. "I forgot to tell you; Evie called me. They want Masen to come to Michigan."

"What did you tell her?" The pain in my leg is stronger than usual, but not enough that I'll take anything more than ibuprofen.

"Go to hell. That kid isn't leaving your side. I guess they hired a lawyer. I called Maggie, hoping she could work her mayor magic. She has a way of talking people into doing things. If that doesn't work, your father said he has a lawyer for Ivy."

We exit the main gate and head back to Ivy's.

"You're the only person she allows to call her that," I say, shaking my head slightly with a light chuckle.

"Who? Maggie?"

"Mmhmm. Everyone else has to call her Margaret."

"That's because I'm special."

"You're special all right. That's why we all love you so much."

"I love you too, son." She flashes me a proud smile, and I just shake my head before returning to our previous topic. "You think it will come to that?"

I watch her facial expression so I know whether I should be worried. Her downturned mouth tells me I better talk to Ivy and my father.

"I doubt it, but it's like we always used to say—hope for the best, prepare for the worst." She attempts to be cheery.

Now I know why the guys are coming over—to distract us.

Chapter 23

Ivy—Present Day

TODAY HAS FUCKING SUCKED! I can't remember a day that was worse. No, that's not true. One day was worse. He didn't wake up for three days after we got there. Never want to relive that.

I burned through three copper pipes. Burned straight through them instead of heating them for bending. Those things are not cheap. After the third one, I cleaned up my studio and went to the sales floor.

I paste a fake smile and use my customer service voice to greet Toby and Mira who are both finishing up with customers at the registers. I grab the green basket to reshelve items, leaving the blue one in case Mira and Toby need it.

Toby nods and says, "I bought Misty a new collar. Isn't it adorable?" *Who the fuck is Misty...oh, his cat.* He shows me a picture of a yellow tabby cat with a pink sparkling collar.

"Cool. Very, uh, sparkly," I respond trying to be polite and not show that I don't give a rat's ass about his cat. Damn, my mood is getting worse. I start to put away the basket items by the aisle when a middle-aged guy in jeans asks, "Ivy Hersh?"

"Yes?"

He shoves papers at me. *What the hell?* I open the manila envelope and read. *Motherfucker!* They are suing me for full custody? What the hell? No way can I be polite to customers in this mood. I return the half-empty basket to the registers, where Mira attempts to talk to Toby. He ignores her. Another asshole man. Damn it. That's probably not true.

"Ivy, look at this," Toby says, showing me his phone. It's a video of his cat playing with a toy mouse. How unoriginal—at least get her something cute to play with. I refrain from snapping his damn head off and telling him so.

"A mouse? Maybe a cuter toy." See? Restraint. I must give a face since Mira walks away—quickly.

Toby doesn't notice. He nods and says, "Good idea. She deserves another toy."

Mira drops a picture frame while she's helping a customer. I head over there to make sure everyone is alright and clean up the mess. Mira disappears, again. This time she returns with Cat.

Cat gives her customer service smile even though the pinch of her eyes shows she wants to throttle someone. *I feel ya sista.* "Mira, grab another frame, carefully while Ivy and I finish cleaning this up." Once Mira and the customer are out of earshot, Cat glares at me.

She whisper-shouts at me, "What the hell is wrong with you?"

"I was served with custody papers by tricky Dicky."

"Funny. What do you need?"

"A new fucking life with my kid even though he's still being a little piss-ant to me. He's mine and Dick isn't taking him." I do everything I can to control the tone and volume of my voice.

We pick up the pieces of the frame and deposit them in the trash. Cat grabs the UPC to document the damage. Damn, she remembered and I didn't.

Mira drops a mirror she's scanning at the register. Cat dashes two aisles away to grab another for the customer and takes a picture of the UPC on the customer's mirror for another damage. I glare at Mira.

Cat pushes me and orders, "Office, now."

I make the mistake of walking by the registers, where Toby asks, "What do you think about this toy? The pink teaser stick?"

"Oh, glad you told me what it was. I thought it was—"

"Ok, let's go. Toby, buy it. It's cute. Ivy and I need to talk. Excuse us." She pushes me to my office and closes the door.

"What the hell?"

"It was for everyone's benefit. The snarly look on your face, I'm surprised we have customers left. Do you have a lawyer?"

I drop into my chair and bury my head in my hands. "No, and Dick will make shit up to win. This is why my mother sent me away. She knew he would pull some sketchy bullshit. I hate admitting when she's right. Don't tell her."

Cat gives me a *yeah right* look. "Get real. Though she might be able to help you get a lawyer."

"I'll get one. I can but can't afford it. Dick will drag this shit out so I'm paying through the nose in lawyer fees. I'll do it cause Mase is my entire world. I love that angry little guy."

Cat pulls me into a hug. "Go home. Maybe talk to Grant. He's good at making plans, maybe he can help you create a plan of attack. In case you didn't notice, I'm telling you to go home. Call me later."

"The hell, hag? You're kicking me out of my own store?"

"Yes, wench. Talk to your man and make a plan to get rid of this." She grabs the papers. "Then I don't know, maybe tell him your feelings."

"I'm going, but this is bullshit." She gives me another hug and pushes me to the door.

There's a shit ton of cars in my drive and in front of my house. Who the hell is here? I walk in and see the guy who drove Grant and Jax to my house all those weeks ago—Cash, I think? Four other guys sit in my living room, chatting with Jax and Grant.

The smiles and laughter stop the moment I walk in. It doesn't help that I slam the door and probably have a bad look on my face.

Grant hollers, "Rosebud, come here."

"Grant, I'm not in the greatest mood," I say, throwing my hands up, still clutching the court papers. Mase sits on Jax's lap, watching football with all the guys.

"Don't make me come get you."

"Yeah, that'll take a while," I snap, knowing I'm being a bitch, but a few steps into the living room, Grant stands. "You got your arm cast off."

He smiles. "I still have a splint to keep it immobile, but I can use my hand now. Tell me what happened."

I hand him the documents. I feel the tears forming, knowing I'll either be forced to cave to their demands or sell my store to pay for a lawyer. "I don't know what to do." My voice cracks, and he pulls me into his arms.

When we separate, he pecks me on the cheek. "Take those to Mom. She'll fix it."

"How can you be so calm? They're asking for custody." Tears begin to fall.

"Are you a bad mother?"

I shake my head since I'm not sure if I can talk without crying.

"Is there any legal reason why your son shouldn't remain right where he is?"

Again, I shake my head.

"Then they have no reason to take him from you." Grant grabs the papers. "This is a scare tactic to force you to give them visitation, which you don't have to do since they live in another state."

"How do you know that?" I fidget with my fingers. Grant notices and takes my hands into his.

"C'mon, you know the Sumners. Do you really think I didn't predict they would do this? I had Dad look into this the moment Jax told me they wanted to see Masen. We already have a lawyer lined up. They have no grounds unless you're an addict or harming Mase, which doesn't apply." He cups my face, and his gaze never leaves mine.

My fucking hero. If those people weren't in the living room right now...

"Where's your phone?" I ask.

"By the recliner."

I steal his phone to call Mitch. I have Ali and Kennedy's numbers but not the rest of his family. The need to hear this from either Mitch or from the lawyer he hired nearly overwhelms me.

By the end of the night, both Mitch and the lawyer, Beau Clemson, reassured me that the Sumners have no grounds. Clemson even told me he hired a PI to dig up dirt on me and only found I had a *relationship* with the Senator's son. That's the worst he could find. I mean, was it really a relationship?

Now the PI is trying to find something on the Sumners. I don't agree with his tactics, but I'm not paying him, either. That's what Mitch told him to do. Part of me wants to tell Mitch not to be a politician about this, but momma bear needs to protect and keep her cub.

Chapter 24

GRANT—PRESENT DAY

I**T'S NICE BEING HERE** with Mase, my mom, and Ivy Rose, but there's a downside to all this quality time with them. I want this to be permanent. Right now, I feel like if the docs cleared me, Ivy Rose would kick my ass back out. Shit, there are too many ifs and what-ifs.

"Dad!" Mase hollers from the front door, his voice filled with fear.

"Kitchen, buddy," I answer, trying to keep my weight balanced on my left leg while I chop bell peppers for the stir fry. It's nice to have partial use of my arm and complete use of my right hand.

Mase tackle hugs me, almost knocking me down and causing me to grab the countertop with my left hand. "Careful. What's wrong?" I ask, running my hand across his back. Ivy walks in, surprised when she sees me.

"I thought since Mimi didn't pick me up that you left," Mase whines into my chest. He has yet to let go of me.

"I'm guessing you thought the same thing?" I glance over at Ivy Rose.

She grants me a small smile. "Perhaps. It *did* throw me off when your mom called. She didn't explain anything, just said she couldn't get Mase." Ivy Rose leans against the island. "So, what's she up to?"

"I have no idea. She told me she was running errands... and that was seven hours ago." Mase finally releases me. "I do have to go back to work on Monday, though."

"Buuut you can't drive?"

I pick up the knife to start slicing the green pepper. "That's where Jackson comes in. His bit—I can carpool with him."

"But Jax lives on base, so does that mean you're... leaving?" Worry lines Ivy Rose's face.

"Do you want me to leave?" I stop chopping and worry that Ivy will tell me to get the hell out.

Mase jumps in. "Hell no."

"Masen!" Ivy and I reprimand him at the same time.

"What? I-I..."

"Room, *now*! I've told you about that language." Ivy points up to Mase's room.

With a frustrated sigh, Mase stomps out of the kitchen. "I'm not taking back what I said!" he hollers on his way up the stairs.

Now alone, I look at Ivy Rose. She rolls her lips inward, indicating she wants to say something but is keeping it to herself. That's not like her, especially around me. "Part of me wants to go address that"—she points upstairs—"but..."

Grabbing a yellow bell pepper, I resume chopping. "Let it go."

Ivy nods with a sigh and comes to lean on the opposite side of the island. After a moment, she runs her finger along the edge, avoiding eye contact with me. "Should I also let go that you implied you're going back to your townhouse when you're still healing?"

Part of me wants to cheer, jump for joy, or at least smile, but I keep a straight face. "Jax and I haven't discussed whether he's willing to pick me up here or there. Besides, I figure you're probably tired of me."

Her voice is soft, almost like she's in pain. "Like I could ever get tired of you. Seriously, Grant. Besides, you can barely take care of yourself and you... you're just going to leave?"

I pause chopping long enough to see the concerned look she gives me, complete with worried eyes.

Ivy Rose throws her hands up. "Really? How are you going to feed yourself?"

"Sweetie, I'm cooking for you tonight. I'm good on that." I wink at her.

"How are you going to bathe yourself?" she demands, drumming her fingers beside my prep bowl holding the peppers.

I shrug, pretending like it doesn't matter. I need a new tactic if I want my family back with Ivy Rose and Masen. My mother's advice might be the answer—go back to how it all started. Back to playing games. Without looking at her, I answer. "Perhaps I should take care of that myself."

"All by yourself?" Her voice heavy with innuendo since she's given me a hand job every time she helps me bathe.

Scrapping the last chopped bell peppers into the bowl, our gazes lock. "Yeah, have been since around thirteen. Besides, I have full use of my hands in the shower... well, bath. Oh, and when I sleep" I hold my wrist brace up—"this isn't going to stop me from anything. I figure in a week or so, it will be gone."

"Aren't you a bit cocky for someone still in a foot cast?" A concerned look crosses her face until she looks at me smiling. A small smirk appears at the corner of her mouth. She remembers our game.

"Hmm, definitely won't be able to pick up any chicks with it. Kinda contradicts my whole badass Special Forces thing I got going." I pick up the mushrooms, slicing them while trying to watch the glimmer in her eye.

"True. Though I don't think you should try to take a bath with your foot still like that. You might still need some help. Can't have you slipping in your shower. Maybe Jax can drive over here… at least for a few days, just to make sure you're healing."

I paint a disgusted look on my face. Inside, I feel the opposite. My sweet Rosebud wants me to stay. "I don't know if he'll go for it," I say with hesitancy even though I want to do the opposite.

How did I not notice her slowly moving toward me? Her hands still mine, forcing me to stop slicing the mushrooms. "You know, if you ask him, Jax will do whatever you want." Those beautiful fingers begin moving up my arm, then across my chest.

"Ivy! What's Ali making for dinner?" My best friend bursts into the living room. I hear Mase's footsteps down the stairs like a bunch of wrestlers.

Ivy whispers in my ears, "Ask him, please."

She plants a lingering kiss on my cheek before she welcomes her brother. I feel a small smile cross my face over how she just attempted to manipulate me. Of course, I'm going to let her think I'm doing it because of what she said.

Chapter 25

Ivy—Present Day

THE SMALL RANCH-STYLE HOME with a perfectly landscaped flowerbed circling the small front porch isn't what I expected when Cat told me she and Brax were renting a house off-post instead of living on base. There are three cars parked in the driveway on the left side of the house—Cat's Kia, Brax's black Silverado truck, and Lizzy's Mercedes-Benz her grandparents gave her as a graduation gift.

The white front door opens before I can knock. Cat tilts her head with a pitcher of an orange slushie. My guess is some form of frozen margarita since she and Lizzy love them so much.

"It's about time you got here. C'mon!" She pulls me into the house and takes the bottles of wine from me. "Were your ears ringing? We were just talking about you and wondering how things are going with Grant."

248

The living room and dining room are connected with an archway. The navy-blue sofa sits adjacent to the large picture window with two overstuffed chairs on each side of the room. Small baskets of pencils and sketchbooks are under the blonde wood coffee table. Looking through the dining room, she has a medium-sized table and six chairs closer to the archway. In the right corner of the dining room near the floor-to-ceiling window is an easel. I bet the large storage box along the right wall is filled with paints, brushes, and palettes.

"Is that Ivy? She better get her butt in here so we can hear all about her and Mr. Sexy," Dee hollers from somewhere in the house.

Cat leads the way to the other two girls. "Lizzy has started the margaritas. This time she's making pineapple mango. I hate how delicious they are."

We find Lizzy chopping mangos, then putting the fruit in Ziploc bags for when she's too drunk to use a knife. She will have everything prepped so all she has to do is throw the ingredients into the blender. Lizzy nods when we enter the kitchen. Dee stands on the opposite side of the room, making the queso dip.

Dee snaps her fingers at me without turning around. "So, we need an update."

"He goes back to work on Monday." I open the fridge to grab the ingredients to make the chicken nachos.

Dee stops stirring the cheese sauce on the stove, and Lizzy freezes with her knife inches from the mango she was slicing. Cat, well she's behind me, so I can't see her reaction, but I bet it matches the other two.

"So, what does that mean for the two of you? Is he going to keep staying with you, or is he going back to his place? How's he going to drive? There's so many questions..." Cat trails off so she can figure out what type of support I need from her.

I'm not the easiest person to read. I'm sure it's a bit of a guessing game for my friends, though I have been trying to be a better friend and let people get closer to me. Other than Grant, Cat is the only person I've let get this close. Cat comes with Dee and Lizzy, so my circle went from two to five, not counting their significant others.

"Grant is carpooling with Jax since he still can't drive. And I might've bullied my brother into picking Grant up from my house instead of Grant's townhouse." I stare at Cat, who gives me the *yeah right* look. "The man can barely bathe himself."

I grab a glass and pour myself a margarita, even though I know I should eat first. I regale them with how Grant cooked us dinner and how I talked my brother into picking Grant up from my house instead of Grant's place.

Lizzy drops into one of the chairs. "So, will you ask him to stay? What's your next step?"

"You should seduce him," Dee says like it's no big deal.

I'm about to say how stupid that is when Lizzy jumps in. "That's a great idea!"

"Couldn't hurt, but Ivy, you need to talk to him. Tell him how you feel." Cat sips her margarita.

I look at my three girlfriends, waving my drink in the air. "And how am I going to start that convo? *Come here, lemme give you a blowie. By the way, don't move out*," I snip, taking a drink.

The girls erupt in laughter.

"No," Lizzy says. "But I'm sure he wouldn't say no. Talk to him when neither of you are naked."

"I don't know. Michael and I had our big talk right after I screwed his brains out," Dee says, grabbing a few mini quesadillas from the platter.

"Eeewwww, that's my brother." Cat fake gags. "I wish I could say differently, but Brax and I did the same thing." Cat rolls her eyes.

"Seduce him, then have a life-changing discussion when he can't even think straight." I laugh. "Sounds like a *solid* plan. Are their brains even functioning at that point? I need honest answers from him."

"Tomorrow night, have Ali watch Mase and make him a nice dinner and talk," Lizzy says.

"I mean, technically we've talked."

Cat gives me a look of disbelief. "Not the deep, life-altering talk you just said. You guys have just scratched the surface. Have you told him your deepest fear?"

I look away and shake my head. Dee licks the cheese off her finger. "Do you know what his dreams are? The future of his military career or at least what he envisions it to be? What does he want out of life?"

Shit, shit, shit. I don't know any of that about him. I'm such a horrible friend. How can I know the man for over twenty years and not know his hopes and dreams? He knows every damn thing about me, from the freckle under my left breast to how I refuse to touch messy foods.

"Honey, why are you crying?" Lizzy asks, coming around the island. I didn't realize I was crying until she said something. I touch my face and feel the tears.

I try to come up with a reason, but there's no hiding this one. I stutter and just let it out. "I... How can I know him for the majority of my life but not know the basics about him? I can tell you what his favorite color is, how he eats his steaks, the way he likes his coffee, and his favorite sports teams." I wipe my blurry eyes and continue. "But I don't know his hopes and dreams, let alone his future plans and all that really important shit. I mean... *he* should've ran from *me*!" I should stop here, but do I? Hell no.

"He knows everything about me! He helped me open my dream. Picked out the paint, took the day off work to help me on opening day! You know he was five cars away from me when I lost my virginity? So, in a way, he was there for that too! He was who I had in the delivery room with me. Yet I don't know where he sees himself in five years!"

Dee says, "He doesn't know *everything* about you."

I freeze and stare at her like... like she broke my welder or set fire to my store. "What do you mean?"

"Does he know why you ran from him? Why you refuse to be in a real relationship with him?" She pauses. "Do *you* know why?"

"I told him."

Cat raises her finger at me. "No. You said you apologized for running and not coming to talk to him. You didn't say anything about explaining the *why*. He probably needs that. I would if it was me, but then again, he has the patience of a damn saint."

Lizzy softly repeats Dee's question. "Do *you* know why?"

"Eli," I say with a nod even though I'm not sure if that's true, either.

All three of them laugh. Dee's the first to comment. "That's a load of bullshit. You didn't even love him."

Lizzy's next. "You're hiding behind Eli's ghost."

Cat just stares at me—stares straight into my soul like she can see the truth. She knows things no one else does. I'm not sure if I'm ready to admit what the truth is yet. I'm scared. What if it messes things up even more? But then again... if I don't, I might lose Grant, again. This time for good. Fuck, I've been selfish.

Cat takes a long sip of her margarita and says, "She knows the truth. Tell him what's in your heart. Don't filter it or candy coat anything. Do your Ivy thing and word vomit it all over him, and he'll take it all."

I feel the tears prickling at my eyes. I blink numerous times to keep them at bay because I want to get this out. "What if he doesn't?"

Cat pulls me into a hug. "He will. I have complete confidence in him."

I hope she's right. I'm scared shitless about what I will find, let alone how he will react.

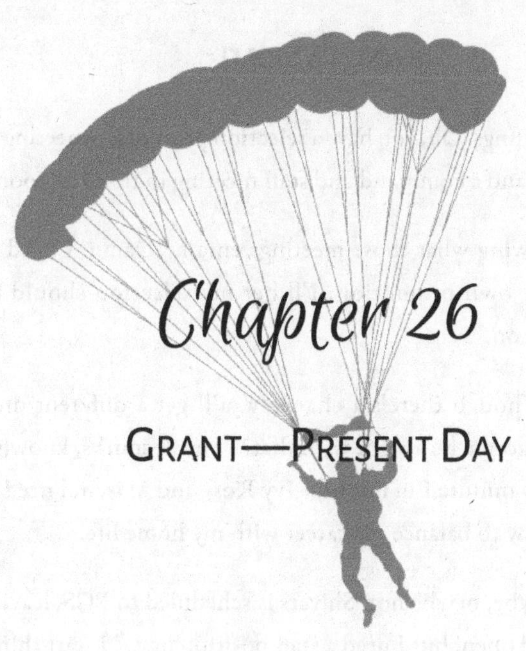

Chapter 26

GRANT—PRESENT DAY

I T'S WEIRD WALKING IN the office after being off duty for so long. Thankfully, I don't have to leave my office the entire day. The rest of my body is stiff from leaning over my desk and working through the small mountain of paperwork waiting for me. All day, my mind drifts back to Ivy Rose and Masen. I wonder what life would be like if I didn't renew my contract.

"How was your first day back?" Hersh sits in the chair in front of my desk.

"Boring as hell. Where's my team?" I toss the pen on the desk.

Hersh leans back in his chair. "We were trying to be scarce in case you were pissed about all that paperwork. FYI... that stack started a few days ago. I kept up with it until last Wednesday when I was pulled into four briefings. Oh, you have a selection promotion meeting in the morning and a command and staff meeting in the afternoon."

I groan, knowing what those meetings entail. "Damn. I need to check on my own promotion. I'll bet my selection should be coming up soon."

"Probably. Though there's a chance you'll get a different duty station. You gonna be alright with that?" Hersh smirks, knowing I'll hate every minute I'm not near Ivy Rose and Masen. I need to figure out how to balance my career with my home life.

"Hmm... maybe, maybe not. Shivers is scheduled to PCS, leaving his command open, but I need a staff position first." I start thinking aloud about how I can make this work since I still have three years left on my contract.

"True, but that only buys you a year, maybe two."

"I don't know. Maybe I'll take it one year at a time."

Hersh nods. "You ready to get out of here? I'm hoping your mom will make her infamous chicken tortellini."

I release a full-belly laugh. "You know, she thinks her best dish is the chicken enchiladas recipe she got from her host family's abuela. I've never had the heart to tell her that we all hate it." I grab my cover and cane.

Hersh makes a gagging face. "Really? I hate that crap. Even the cheese doesn't taste right. How do you screw up *cheese*, the most delicious thing on Earth?"

"She infuses it with red chili pepper three days before she cooks it. It doesn't help that my dad used to rave about that dish. He loves spicy food, but damn, that dish is *only* spice."

Thirty minutes later, we walk through Ivy Rose's door to the smell of garlic, cheese, oregano, thyme, and rosemary.

Mase appears at the top of the stairs, yelling like the world is coming to an end, "Dad! I need your help with my math."

No matter how many times he calls me Dad, it never gets old, and it always puts a smile on my face. "Bring it down and I'll help you," I tell him.

"That kid cracks me up." Jax chuckles, heading to the kitchen. "No hi or nothin'. Straight to the point."

"True. He's definitely Rosebud's kid," I say, hobbling behind Jax to see who's here with Mase.

I question why my mother is still here. I figured she would've gone home after a few days, but maybe she's bored with retirement. Nah, she's here for Mase and to spend more time with him. I know my mother loves me, but she adores that sweet seven-year-old.

Shimmery red hair is the first thing I see when we round the corner. Ivy Rose stirs the white sauce. I want to walk up to her... kiss the hell out of her. But it's still too soon for that; I need to be patient and remember the long game. Even though Ivy Rose has been giving me a hand in the shower, she has yet to kiss me. Instead, I keep my distance and park my ass on the bar stool.

Jax struts up to his sister. "Whatcha making?"

"What's it look like?" she says like he's an idiot.

"Tortellini. Where's Momma Brandt? I need advice on a little señorita." He leans his hip against the countertop and folds his arms.

"No idea. She came into the store and started talking it up with Stephen."

"Who's Stephen" I ask.

Ivy gives me a mischievous smile. "The new director of the Fayetteville and Cumberland County Arts Council. She even told me to pick Mase up cause her lunch with Stephen might run late. And here it is almost six and no Ali." Ivy Rose turns around and points her finger at me. "Do *you* know where she is?"

Like my retired Spanish teacher mother is a helpless, frail woman who needs Ivy Rose to take care of her.

"I've been at work all day," I say. "How would I know where she is when you were the last one to see her?"

"Oh, I don't know. Maybe cause she's your mother and she came here to take care of you." Ivy Rose speaks slowly like I'm the idiot now.

"Really? Yeah, I had tons of time to keep tabs on my mother while completing a desk full of paperwork. Good call, sweetness. I'll work that in tomorrow, along with this Stephen guy's background check," I snark, trying to keep my voice light.

I want to laugh at this whole situation, especially since I suspect my mother is secretly dating, evidently, this Stephen guy. Perhaps I should be concerned, yet oddly, I'm not. My mother doesn't date anyone for more than a few months. I suspect it's because she's still in love with my dad. The same is true for him. Neither of them has made it more than four months with someone else.

"But you've been taking care of me. Does that mean I should know where *you* are all the time? Although, I'm doing just fine since the hand brace is completely gone. I was even able to take a shower without any issues. I was thinking of heading back to the base in the next few days." I know that will rile her up since she talked Jax into picking me up from here instead of my townhouse that's three doors down from his.

Ivy Rose's mouth hangs open for a few seconds before she begins. "W-well—"

"Dad!" Mase runs and jumps on me.

"Masen! Be careful. He's still hurt." Ivy Rose heads over to us, making sure Mase and his whole eighty-five pounds didn't hurt me.

I wave her off and adjust Mase to my left leg. "Relax, he's fine." I turn my attention to my son. "How was school?"

"Fine. How was work? Did you do anything dangerous?"

Both Jax and I laugh. "No, bud. I'm on desk duty for quite some time. I'll probably be transferred soon to another unit."

Mase quietly asks, "Why?"

"I've been with this unit for too long, it's time for me to do something else."

Worry fills my little guy's face. "Where will that be? Do I need to pack?"

"Pack?" I ask, looking at Ivy Rose.

"Yeah, if you move. I have to pack my stuff cause we'll go with you," Mase explains with a determined look.

I glance at Ivy Rose and tell him, "I don't get much of a say. I'm trying to stay close, though. When I find out, we'll make a plan."

"Mase, let him figure some things out, then we'll talk about what to do next," Ivy Rose says in a quiet voice.

I add, "No matter where they send me, it changes nothing for us. Ok?" I hope he believes the bullshit because if I have to PCS to another base, it will change everything—including my hopes for putting our little family back together.

"But I just got you back." Tears fill my little guy's eyes, and that completely breaks my heart. I had every intention of going back to my place when Jax leaves for his. Being this close to Ivy Rose just about kills my soul, but how can I say no when my son is crying for me to stay?

"I think we need to have a long conversation about our little family," I explain.

"We're not a real family." Those tear-filled eyes shift to anger.

"Says who?" Jax jumps in, coming closer to Mase and me.

Ivy Rose shuts the burner off and comes over to run her fingers across Mase's forehead. Her gaze bounces between Jax and I while she explains, "That little punk Jordan has been going around saying that everyone whose parents aren't married isn't a real family. Is he doing that again?" she asks Mase, pulling him into her arms. She says quietly, "That little shit is only saying that because his parents just got remarried. He's wrong. Family is—"

"Us. We are and always will be your family. No matter what happens." I cup his freckled face resting above his mother's arms to ensure he looks me in the eyes.

"Anna says dads always leave." His gaze moves from me to his mother.

"Oh, my sweet boy, that's what you've been worried about?" Ivy runs her fingers through his messy hair.

He nods and returns his focus to me. "You left once, and now you're going back to the base a-a-and leaving Fayetteville?"

I sigh. "First, I didn't handle things very well before. I screwed up by staying away like I did." I open my mouth to continue, but Ivy Rose runs her fingers through the back of my hair. My body remembers her touch, but thankfully it also realizes Mase is on my lap.

"We both made mistakes." She offers me a small smile. Hopefully that means she wants the same thing I do—being together.

"Second and the most important one. You are the most important person in my life. I love you more than..." I trail off to keep my voice from cracking.

"Football?" Mase offers eagerly.

I chuckle along with Jax and Ivy Rose. "Definitely more than football." I begin with the saying Ivy Rose used to say to him since he was old enough to talk. "More than the moon, the stars, and—"

"The entire solar system," Mase finishes. He circles his arms to show how much love we have. "Uncle Jax, you wanna play Madden with me?"

"Sure, buddy." Mase gingerly climbs off my lap and runs to his room like a herd of elephants instead of a seven-year-old.

Ivy Rose returns to preparing dinner by pushing the sauce to the back burner and filling a pot with water.

With her back still to me, she says, "We should talk about your possible PCS."

"Nothing to talk about right now since I have no idea if or where they might send me. I'm amazed I've been here for as long as I have. I need to do one year in a staff position and a year in command. I'm missing both. I'm trying to find one here, but..." I trail off and lift one shoulder. "Sweetie, I was informed of all this today. I don't even know all the details yet. Gimme time to formulate a plan. I'm trying to figure out how to stay here since there are officers who spend their entire career on the same base, so I know it's doable."

She turns around, and tears fill those gorgeous eyes. "Y-you... I... Mase needs you." Her voice breaks toward the end of the sentence.

Grabbing the bottom of her T-shirt, I pull her close to me. "Is it just Mase that needs me?" I stand and wrap my arm around her, only our clothes separating our bodies. I hover my mouth over hers. "Tell me, sweetie, do you need me too?"

The kitchen timer buzzes as she slips out of my grasp to return her attention to cooking. She adds the tortellini to the boiling water, pops the garlic bread into the oven, and resets the timer all in fluid movement.

"I don't need you. You've been gone before, you know, when you were deployed for two years when Mase was one, and when you went to West Point, and—"

I slink my lips onto hers, at first desperate and hard like she holds my entire life, which she does, and my sweet Rose wraps her arms around my neck, bringing me closer to her. I slow our kiss down since I want this to last, massaging her tongue with mine in a slow dance. Everything disappears but how she feels in my arms. I finish with a few small pecks before I step back, remembering our son is upstairs.

"Wow." Ivy Rose touches her lips. "You've—"

"Maybe Jax needs to take me home."

She runs her hand up my chest. "Oh, hell no he's not. You're staying tonight. Besides, we need to talk instead of playing the bullshit games we always do."

"Thought you liked playing those games?" I brush a stray hair off her cheek.

"That was before."

I pause, waiting for her to tell me what's on her mind. She doesn't. She rarely does. "Before what?"

She hesitates, then looks up into my eyes. I've never seen the look she gives me. Her throat bobs before she continues. "Before I knew that I wanted a forever."

Before I can respond, Mase stomps down the stairs, hollering, "Dad! I beat Jax on COD!! Can you believe it?"

"That kid's timing is impeccable," I whisper before he enters the kitchen.

Ivy Rose turns back to the stove, checking the pasta and pretending like our moment never happened.

"Dad, did you hear me? I beat Jax!" Mase bounces excitedly from foot to foot.

Jax struts in as Ivy Rose informs us that dinner is done. I look at Jax. "He beat you?"

He gives me a *yeah, right* look. "You know how hard it is to lose that badly?" Not waiting for my response, he continues. "Harder than winning against McKlowski on his favorite game. Little Bear sucks on COD."

"Thought you were playing Madden?" I ask.

Jax whispers so Mase can't hear him. "He sucks at that more than CoD. I was trying to find a game he could beat me at." He glances at Ivy, who's avoiding eye contact with me and whispers to me, "How'd it go?"

Instead of answering, I give him a knowing smile, hoping he understands me because I can't explain anything to him until our drive. Tomorrow.

Chapter 27

Ivy—Present Day

WISH I COULD SAY I wasn't disappointed when Grant said he was going to bed early since he had such a busy day. He was falling asleep during the movie. I'm surprised he made it to Mase's bedtime. Logically, he should be tired. I should be understanding of that, especially since I begged him to stay just so I can have him for one more night.

I'm pacing the length of the living room, trying to figure out my next move. *Shit, why am I pacing? I never pace. Grant paces. I fidget. What the hell is wrong with me?*

I plop myself onto the sofa when Ali walks in with a smile bigger than the toothpaste commercials. Flipping it on Ali, I use the mom voice and tone she used on us as kids. "Where have you been, young lady?"

She tilts her head. "None of your business. I will be available tomorrow to spend some time with my grandson. Good night." She prances upstairs, leaving me speechless. I decide now I *have to* get to the bottom of this and figure out where the hell she's been going.

I would call Cat, but Brax just came home from a long training mission, meaning she's out of contact for a few days. Dee has been crazy busy between her new married life, baby, and graduate school. That leaves Lizzy. It's 11:04pm. She should still be up. But Lizzy is so rational. She'll tell me to go to bed and talk to him tomorrow. She'll talk me out of the plan formulating in my brain. Dee would say go for it. Cat would ask me what's best for me and Mase, then ask if this plan would benefit all involved. Then tell me to be careful, knowing I'm not going to listen. Why do I need anyone to tell me my plan is good, bad, or well... anything?

Instead of initiating my plan, I take a shower, brush my teeth and hair, and moisturize my body. Anything but going back downstairs. Maybe reading the new indie mafia novel will take my mind off the man sleeping downstairs or that kiss he gave me earlier.

Jesus, I forgot what an incredible kisser he is. Heading over to my side of the bed—yes, I still only sleep on my side as if he's—No, book on the stand. Shit, I took it downstairs last night to read while I listened to Grant sleep. Oh, that sounded slightly creepy, but it did help me sleep.

Creeping downstairs so I don't wake up Ali, Mase, or Grant, I pick up my throw blanket from the sofa and my book from the end table and snuggle into Grant's recliner to read... and listen to him sleep. Except...

I don't hear anything. I tiptoe to the guestroom/den and slowly push the door open.

I take in the walnut desk and leather computer chair, the bookshelves on each side of the desk filled with my books and a few of Mase's. The two armchairs are normally across from each other but are pushed against the wall for the pull-out bed. Grant's body is curled up on the left side of the bed, facing the door.

He used to argue with me about how he needs the side of the bed closest to the door to protect us better. He would have a faster reaction time if an intruder broke in. After a few restless nights for me, he switched back without a word. He does sleep facing the door—lucky for me, that meant he was also facing me.

My feet move to him without my permission. He's sleeping peacefully. I should go back to my book, but my body isn't listening to my brain. I lift the yellow comforter as I slide beside him.

He mumbles my name. I'm uncertain whether he's sleeping, dreaming, or if he knows I'm beside him. He wraps his arms around me and whispers in my ear, "My sweet rose." He's never called me that before. It's always been Rosebud or variations of sweet, mostly "Sweetie," which I've always thought was hilarious since I *don't* have a sweet personality.

Grant buries his face between my neck and shoulder, and I relish how it feels to be in his arms. This is what I've been missing. The softness of his skin. The slight scruff along his jawline rubbing on my neck. The way his biceps slightly bulge while he holds me.

Gently moving the tips of my fingers down the length of his arm from his shoulder down to his wrist, I can't help but kiss his shoulder and then kiss down his bicep. Slow, feather-like kisses. Halfway down his bicep, I switch to his chest, knowing how much he loves it when I play with his chest and nipples. When he hums, I swirl my tongue around his nipple.

His voice is deep from sleep. "Rosebud, please tell me I'm dreaming." He rolls me on top and attacks my lips with his. Rough, demanding, with a hint of desperation. Twining my arms around his neck, I pull him closer. His hands glide up my body, our bodies synchronizing to each other. My hips move on their own accord, drawing a moan from Grant. The thin athletic shorts he's still wearing do nothing to hide his erection.

Slipping his hands under my nightshirt and tossing it off, he whispers, "God, you're so fucking sexy." I answer him with a searing kiss I can feel in my soul. Grant matches my every movement. Part of me melts with each swipe of his tongue, yet it's still not enough. I need him. All of him.

I claw at his shorts, trying to push them off. He lifts his hips, allowing me to pull them off. My heart races thinking about all the things I want to do with him, but that seed of doubt creeps in... until Grant clutches the back of my neck, pulling my lips to his, reassuring me how much he wants this—and me.

Part of me wants to relish every moment. Slow it down. It's been months since we've been together. My patience is almost to the breaking point. I want to feel him and watch him lose control.

Grant greedily kisses down my neck to my cleavage, but instead of letting him ravage my breasts, I slide my hand between us to slip him inside me. I'm too impatient to let him tease me. I need him.

A quiet curse is whispered before he kisses and nibbles along my cleavage. He pulls the right nipple into his mouth. I love being on top—controlling the pace and tempo. The way his hands move up and down my body makes me feel like a sex goddess. Grant rolls his hip up, hitting that perfect spot, creating the beginnings of those delicious warm spasms. His talented tongue moves to my left nipple—the sensitive side. A hip roll and a few flicks of his tongue are all it takes. Grant follows me a few minutes later.

I fall on his chest panting, trying to catch my breath and pull myself together. He gently runs his fingers through my hair, then kisses the top of my head.

"Jesus," Grant pants.

I lay my head on his chest. "Is that a good Jesus?"

"Definitely. Short, but so damn good. No more walking on eggshells with each other."

Lifting my head so I can look in his eyes, I'm thankful for the light streaming in from the solar lighting on the wood fence Grant installed last summer streams in from the window. "We should probably talk about this and..." I trail off, afraid to verbalize what I'm thinking. How do I make it up to him for running from him all those months ago and for being a selfish bitch?

"Not tonight. I just want to hold you." He yawns.

"Ok," I say, still worrying.

He shifts us like how we used to sleep with him spooning me and facing the door. "Sleep, sweetness. Stop thinking, just... be here with me."

I scoot farther into him until I feel him along my entire back. Grant pulls my leg between his and tightens his arms around me. I want to watch him sleep, but his arms grip me too tight to move. I drift off listening to him sleep.

Chapter 28

GRANT—PRESENT DAY

IT TOOK EVERYTHING IN me to climb out of bed this morning. I swore I was dreaming last night when Ivy Rose climbed in bed with me. Waking up with her wrapped around me and having her red hair spread out across my pillows wasn't a dream. I should be exhausted from the lack of sleep and pulling a long day at work, but I feel like I could run a marathon if I didn't have a broken leg.

My day is filled with back-to-back meetings, including two that might help me find a staff position I need for my next promotion. Bonus, those positions will keep me at Bragg for another year, maybe two. Before I know it, the day's over.

Do I have Jax take me to Ivy's or to my townhouse? I don't want to fall into the same pattern with Ivy. If I'm being honest with myself, something I rarely am when it comes to her, we have been playing these games for over fifteen years... hell, maybe since we met.

Even though things were fantastic last night, I'm still thinking about returning to my townhouse at the end of the week. Maybe sooner, if possible. I had a plan, and that plan didn't include screwing Ivy three ways from Sunday, no matter how much we both enjoyed it. She won't let me in her heart through sex. Been there, done that.

"Hey, man. You ready to get the hell outta here?" Jax asks, looking just as weary as I feel. My entire leg is stiff from sitting at my desk for so many hours.

I stretch my entire body. "Yeah."

"Are we leaving base for that? Or..." He trails off, hoping I'll finish his sentence.

Running my hand across my face, I have no idea how to answer him. I want to be there every waking moment with Masen... and Ivy. But I know in a few days, she's going to realize how serious shit is getting and she'll run—again.

"I have no fucking clue." My phone rings before I can explain my dilemma to Jax.

It's Masen. "Dad, Mom told me to call you. You coming home soon? Can you bring food, cause Mom's in the garage studio and forgot that I need food. I need you to get me some food," Masen says in one long breath.

"Hold on, buddy. Slow down. Mom told you to call me, why?" This kid makes it sound like he never eats when the opposite is true.

Little Bear sighs. "I told you. Mom's been in her studio and forgot about me."

I give him my warning tone. "Masen. She didn't forget about you. I bet you were upstairs playing video games until a few minutes ago."

Moments like this, he's definitely Ivy's son with his dramatics. He mumbles incoherently. I look over at Jax, who has made himself comfortable in the chair across from my desk, shaking his head, knowing how over the top my kid is.

"What do you want to eat?"

"Fooood."

"No shit. Get your mom." My focus shifts to Jax while Masen takes the phone to Ivy, "We're leaving base and stopping for takeout since Little Bear is *starving*." I exaggerate the last word. Jax nods and we head out.

"Hey, Grant. Can you pick up some takeout? I lost track of time and—" Her voice muffles like she pulls the phone away and talks to our son. "Sorry, someone is being impatient."

"We're just leaving the office. It will take a couple minutes before we're home. By the way, where's my mom? Or did she disappear with her boyfriend again?"

Ivy laughs. "Yeah, about that. I don't think she's dating Stephen. But she's definitely dating someone. I spotted her car at the Marriott."

I cringe, climbing in Jax's car, not wanting to admit why my mother is at a hotel. Let alone wanting to know who she's with. "Subject change."

She huffs her frustration since she wants to analyze and figure out what and who my mother is with. "Fine. I'll call Kennedy later."

"Good call. What are you in the mood for?"

"You."

"Food, sweetness. What am I picking up?"

"Chicken sounds good."

We spend the evening eating and watching Disney movies together. Jax leaves before we start on the movies. I relish having my son on one side and my girl on the other. I don't let Mase fall asleep on me like I normally do since I can't carry him upstairs. After the movie, Mase and I head upstairs to start his bedtime routine.

I barely make it down the stairs when Ivy says, "We still need to talk."

I nod. "That we do." I sit at the end of the sofa, propping my foot up on the ottoman.

Ivy Rose sits beside me, turning her entire body to face me. I can see the turmoil and worry on her face. She says quietly, "I'm sorry for running away from you instead of talking about what bothered me."

"You've already apologized—twice. Tell me what bothered you that night."

Ivy takes a deep breath. "Well... I thought it was because—"

"No, that night, what was going through your head when you literally ran from my arms? Not later when you analyzed the hell out of it with your girls. The moment you left me. What was in your pretty little head?" I say as gently as possible. If I'm going to prevent her from running from me, I need to understand why.

"Because..." Ivy Rose flicks her pinky against her thumb, showing how nervous she is. "If you love me, you'll die a-and..." Her voice breaks. "If I leave, you won't—I know how stupid and irrational it sounds now. I just... I panicked." She throws her hands in the air, and her face crumbles with tears streaming down her gorgeous face. "Everything was so fucking perfect that night... hell, that whole week. When I finally stopped, I cried. I know how bad I fucked up. I was going to apologize, but you left and... I... A-an-nd you were pissed when I got home. I-I had no idea how to fix it. Sorry just didn't seem to be enough."

"Sweetness—" I start, but she raises her hand.

"I know how ridiculous that sounds. You should've heard Dee jump my shit, not to mention Cat and Lizzy. They also called bullshit about Eli being the reason, which... they're partially right. He was just the excuse I used that night." She twists her fingers around each other, an indication of how upset and nervous she is.

I hobble over to her and wrap my arm around her. I want to help her eliminate the fear that's obviously still there. I don't want to diminish it, and I want her to keep talking through this. "I'm right here." I pause, lifting her chin and gazing into her eyes. "Eli had nothing to do with your fears. Now your dad's death, that I would understand. I need you to keep talking to me. And I'll do the same."

"How're we going to do that when you're at a different base?" Ivy's voice breaks toward the end, and she stares at something over my shoulder.

I pull her into my arms because I need to hold her—reassure her that I'm going to be right here whenever I can. "If it makes you feel better, I'm trying to move to an engineering unit. I mean, some of those guys are complete idiots. Look at McKlowski...and Bly. The Army gives them C4 to just play with. That's some scary shit," I joke, trying to lighten the mood and make her at least smile at me.

"True. Josh loves to blow things up a bit too much." She looks up at me and gives me a small smile.

"Sorry would've helped. It did help. What about now? What do you want?"

She sniffles. "A lot of things. First, I need to know your dreams."

I give her a confused look. "My dreams? Like, at night?"

She shakes her head. "Like what you want to accomplish in life. You've helped me achieve mine, but... hell, I don't even know what yours are. I want to help you too."

I give her a huge smile. I rarely see the tender side to my Rosebud. Gotta admit, I like it. Do I tell her that my dream is getting my family back. Her eyes plead with me to answer her. "Promise me you won't run from me."

"Promise, promise. No running."

I smirk, remembering how we used to use that phrase when we were kids. "I want my family back—you and Mase, but this time, you're mine." I pause to gauge her reaction. A pleasing smile crosses her gorgeous face, so I continue. "I want to get married and have more kids someday."

"I think we should work on *your* dreams. I'm sorry if I was selfish… and didn't take your feelings into consideration. The girls… Well, they kicked my ass. I might've deserved it. I like… no, love your dream. What about your career?" She pulls me closer and gives me a tight squeeze.

Part of me wants to ask what the hell is going on. I don't disagree with anything she's saying. If this helps me get my girl and kid back, I'm going to take it. The icing is that she's not running from me. She's coming to me.

"Isn't that the million-dollar question. I want to stay here at Bragg. If I can't…" I shake my head because I'm not sure what I'll do if I can't stay here.

"We'll figure it out together. I want to be equal, not like before when you always took care of me. We need to take care of each other. I don't think you can do that in your townhouse…you know, cause what if your family needs you?"

"Oh, that's low, sweetness. Using our son against me?"

She shrugs. "If I need to. I would even have him beg you."

"You would use Mase against me?"

She shrugs and pecks me on the lips.

"Tell me, am I sleeping in our bed or on that lumpy ass pull-out?" I ask. I'm exhausted from very little sleep last night and the amount of energy it took to get through the day. I don't have anything left in me. "I don't have the energy to make it back up the stairs."

"Another night on the shitty pull-out." Ivy Rose swings her hips, knowing I'm watching that ass walk away from me.

Lord, help me with this woman. I love her so damn much, but she needs to realize how much she needs me just as much as I need her.

Chapter 29

Ivy—Present Day

D EE PULLS LASAGNA OUT of the oven when I walk into her kitchen. Cat sits at the table feeding Cristian, and Lizzy stands in the corner of the living room arguing with someone on the phone. My guess is Josh, but something is going on with her sister. She hasn't shared a lot about it, but Dee said that Sami is a beauty queen who wants to quit and their mom won't let her. Lizzy is pretty lipped about what's going on.

I hand three bottles of wine to Dee, who sets them in the fridge. "Where are all the guys?"

Cat and Dee answer simultaneously. "Training."

"Oh."

Dee smirks at me. "Tell us how it's going. For the love of all that's holy, tell us you talked to him."

I roll my eyes. "It's going. I'm concerned about Ali, his mom. She's been disappearing, and for a while, I thought she was dating Stephen, the director of Fayetteville Arts Council. But—"

Dee interrupts me as Cat and Lizzy laugh from the dining room. "I don't give a rat's patootie about Ali and her puck boy."

"Puck boy?" I bust out laughing at her version of rated G talk and coding things up since Cristian is nearby.

"You know exactly what I mean, so spill it. Did you talk to him? I do hope Ali is getting a good pucking."

Cat pops the garlic bread into the oven, and we help her bring the food into the dining room. I say, "I talked to Grant. Like, really talked. I know his dreams, and I'm going to help him reach them."

"So, my bestie wench... Really? What are his hopes and dreams?" Cat asks, bringing plates out.

"Damn it, I forgot to ask about his hopes." I grab my phone so I can text him. I need to know everything about him—again.

Cat rests her hand on my wrist. "It's fine, ask him later. You're talking about important stuff, that's fantastic. Better than someone." Cat nods to Lizzy, who's still in a hushed argument on the phone. Yeah, she's definitely talking to Josh. He's the only person to get her riled up like that.

Dee sits down by Cristian and asks, "So do you want to share about his dreams, or do you want to keep it to yourself? We understand if you don't want to share. There are some things that are so special you want to keep them in your heart."

Lizzy finally joins us. "And other times you want to slit his throat."

A few minutes later, Cat pulls the garlic bread out and drops them in the bread basket. I don't have to ask Lizzy why she wants to murder her boyfriend. She's wanted to marry him for years, although Josh being a commitment phobe marriage is unlikely to happen.

Instead, I change the subject. "So, about Ali, I need some sleuthing skills. I found out the other day that Stephen is gay. He's not who she's meeting up with at the Marriott."

"That eliminates him from your pucking suspect list. Plus, why would they go to a hotel? He lives here. Wouldn't they just go to his place?" Dee says, cutting the lasagna.

I continue. "True, but I still don't know who. Her car has been at the Marriott for the last three days. She's hooking up with someone. I want to figure out who the hell he is. Grant told me to leave her be. If she's happy, that's all that matters. But I'm not ok with that."

"I agree with Grant." Cat picks up Cristian's fork from his feeding tray and places it back in his hand. "You're changing the subject."

Dee snaps her fingers, wanting everyone to start making their plates. "Girls, let's eat. I'm glad Ali is getting some pucking time in. Why does it matter who she's doing? And I need my marshmallow to spill about her and Josh, and I need an update about what the heck Sami's going to do."

I continue to focus on Ali since it keeps me from overanalyzing my relationship with Grant. "She's my second mom, I have to protect her even if Grant thinks this is a phase like when I wore nothing but black for a year. That's not a good look on this flawless skin."

Cat responds without her gaze leaving Cristian. "Let. It. Go. Ali can take care of herself, especially if her son isn't the least bit concerned. We all know you're focusing on her to avoid talking or thinking about Grant. I'm proud of you for having a grown-up talk with him."

Lizzy moans from the delicious food. "Did Cat make this? Oh, my lord. This is delicious."

Dee playfully slaps Lizzy's arm and looks at Cristian and whispers so Cristian can't hear her. "Bitch, you know I made this. Cat gave me her recipe." Dee looks at Cat. "Thanks for helping me learn to cook."

"Ugh, I'm so sorry."

We all turn at the new voice of someone who just entered the room. A blonde with hazel eyes, wearing jeans and a V-neck shirt, stands in the dining room with an armful of books and three white bags.

"I found this adorable bookstore with a huge fantasy section. You know how I love my fantasy and sci-fi, Liz. I lost track of time." It almost sounds more like a whine.
A few of the girls look at each other. Dee looks back at the girl.

"Ummm... who are you?"

Lizzy rolls her eyes. "This is my sister, Sami, who probably bought way too many books. Sami, Ivy and Cat." Lizzy points to each of us.

Sami gives a shocked look. "What? For one, there's no such thing as too many books. Two, nice to finally meet everyone in person."

"Do you have any other bullet points or just the two?" Lizzy teases.

Sami drops the three white bags along the wall. "Just those. It smells amazing in here. I take it one of you cooked?" Sami's gaze bounces between Cat and me.

Dee glares at Sami while Lizzy bust out in laughter.

Cat answers. "Dee made it from my family recipe."

"Holy shit! Dee can cook?! Seriously? I gotta try this. Wait, sis, will I die from it or wish I was dead like her brownies my freshmen year?"

"Ok, biotches. Stop busting my balls and eat," Dee calls from the kitchen.

"Dee!" Cat and Lizzy say at the same time.

"What? Eat. So I can hear about why Sami is actually here instead of in school. Ivy, do you want to share more about your man? If so, we're all ears." Dee heads to Cristian, who is slapping the tray of his highchair.

Cat shifts her focus from Cristian to me. "So, is Grant still living in your home office, or did you move him back to your room?"

"He won't leave the office, even though that pull-out sofa mattress is uncomfortable as all get up. I haven't asked for him to come back to our room since we talked almost two weeks ago. I don't get why he wants to sleep on that lumpy thing when we have a perfectly soft bed upstairs. They changed his cast to a shorter one with his boot, that's why he wanted to leave. I mean, he hasn't mentioned going back to his townhouse since we talked. I talked him into staying one more night, where I screwed his brains out. It's kinda been like that since."

Lizzy drops her fork. "Are you kidding me? You're just doing the same thing you did before. Learn from your mistakes. Try this... Talk to him!"

"Sure, pot. I'll get right on that. Have you told Josh you're in love with him? And we *did* talk, and he told me that being a family is his dream. And that he wants to get married and have more kids. You know how badly I wanted to run away from him? I almost had a panic attack until I realized I want that too. The tightness in my chest left. Poof. Freaking gone. Like magic."

"Oh snap," Sami says between bites. "Hold up, I want to make sure I understand this correctly. Grant is your childhood crush who is in love with you, and you won't admit you love him too, right?"

Cat pours another glass of red wine. "Sounds about right."

"Hag! Whose side are you on?" Instead of answering me, Cat takes a huge gulp of her wine.

Dee chokes on her wine and answers the previous question. "Lizzy broke up with Josh, and he's been texting and calling her when he has free time."

"Brax said Josh is unbearable." Cat wipes Cristian's face and hands, peppering his adorable face with kisses.

"So, Ivy, how are you going to change things?" Lizzy quietly asks. "Kudos for talking. Now, it's time for action. Maybe that's why he's staying in the den?"

"I don't know. Except for his leg, things feel like they did before Cat's wedding. No, it's better. Dinners, movies, game nights, family stuff... and it's nice." I take another bite of my food. "I'm scared." I blink multiple times to keep the sudden tears from showing.

Thankfully the girls don't push more, but Lizzy and Cat give me a reassuring hug. I hate them, especially my hag of a bestie, for knowing the moment I need a hug from her.

Dee looks across the table to Sami. "Ok, little one. Spill. Why are you here? I need to know the situation so we know how to help."

Sami wipes her mouth and lays her napkin in her lap. "I quit school. If I'm not enrolled in college, I can't compete in those damn pageants."

Lizzy drops her fork and her face drops. "What the hell? You were only a semester away from graduating!"

Sami shrugs like it's no big deal. Dee has a smirk on her face. Cat continues to keep Cristian occupied.

"Ok, I didn't quit. I just wanted to see Lizzy's face when I said that. I graduated early, but you know in Momma's eyes that's like quitting since I can't do those pageants anymore." Sami shrugs like she didn't just drop a bomb on everyone. I just met the girl and I like her flare. She continues. "I have money saved. Plus, Grams said I can work for her if need be. Well, I guess it would be for Aunt Ginny, but you know what I mean. Though, I don't really want that. I'm lining up a clinical by the beach house, so I'm staying with you, sis."

Cat turns around. "What do *you* want?"

A huge commercial smile crosses Sami's face. "I love helping people."

"I figured It would be cosplay since you're so good at dressing up like aliens, superheroes, and Star Trek characters," Lizzy says.

Sami waves her manicured hand. "That's a really fun hobby. Plus, nerds are the best lovers. So attentive and sweet." She spaces out like she's reliving a memory.

"Ok. So, Sami is a hot mess who has a nerd fetish," I jump in, hoping we don't circle back to me like Dee did earlier.

I know I need to have another conversation with Grant and get to the bottom of why he's staying in the den instead of our room. I need to figure out why he's staying in that damn den instead of our bedroom.

Why does it bother me so damn much?

Chapter 30

GRANT—PRESENT DAY

SATURDAYS ARE MY FAVORITE. I sleep in until nine, when Mase comes in wanting me to cook him breakfast. Rosebud and I can stay curled up together until he marches in. Saturday is also her late day at work. She teaches a metalsmithing class in the late afternoon and evening.

Jesus, she smells like roses and... sex. I rarely wake her up early. I can't get enough of her. Hell, I don't think I was like this when we started our friends-with-benefits deal. I nibble and place light kisses on the back of her neck and slowly move my hands down her delicious curves.

"Wake up, my sweet Rose," I whisper in her ear as a smile crosses her face. Thankfully, we're both still naked from last night.

She hums, turns around, and drapes her leg around me.

"Wake up, sweetness. I'm not going to give you what you want unless you tell me I can."

She slips her hand between us to stroke my growing dick. "You can fuck me whenever and however you want. You always have permission."

I roll us over so I can pepper kisses down her neck to her beautiful tits, kissing down her sternum and licking and nibbling around each breast before pulling her puckered nipple into my mouth. She wraps her legs around my waist, pulling me closer and aligning our bodies.

"Grant, please." I grip her ass, pulling her against me, releasing a moan from both of us. Her hands skim down my back, straight to my dick. She rolls us over, running her hands down my body before sliding onto me.

"Oh, Jesus," I moan, losing all train of thought but how incredible she feels. Her warmth completely surrounds me. I look in her dilated brown eyes as she gifts me a small smirk. Her hips swivel, hands moving up my chest, flicking my nipples. If she keeps doing that, I'm going to finish before I can satisfy her.

I caress her lips with mine, soft, loving—a way to show her how much she means to me. My sweet Rose grips my shoulders while I grip her perfect ass. I let her set the pace even though I want to slow down and relish every moment. Every thrust and hip roll eases the ache that's been plaguing me since she walked into my hospital room. Hell, since she ran from me in Pennsylvania. I need this. Her.

She bites her bottom lip to prevent her from screaming. Her pussy starts tightening, and those sexy little groans tell me she's close. Rolling my hip and dragging a nipple into my mouth pushes her over.

Ivy grinds her hips into mine, increasing the pressure and causing my balls to tighten. Her nails dig into my back, those quiet little sighs along with her entire body tenses, indicating her quiet orgasm.

All the blood rushes. My focus is on the fiery goddess riding me. A chill runs down my spine straight to my sac. Her velvet walls grip me, milking every last drop.

Ivy Rose collapses on me, both of us sweaty and panting. I can barely feel my body. She kisses my chest. "We should probably get moving. I'm sure Mase will be up soon."

"A few more minutes won't hurt," I say, rolling us over and massaging her lips with mine, trying to convince her for round two, even though I doubt we have enough time.

Ivy's arms twine around my neck. "Hmmm, show me."

The moment my lips touch hers, the sound of an elephant stampede echoes throughout the house. I reach beside me for the covers in case Ivy didn't lock the door.

The knob turns. "Dad! The door's locked. Can we make waffles instead of pancakes?" The knob wiggles again, and there's frantic knocking.

"I'll be right there, bud."

Ivy nibbles on my ear and whispers, "I told you so." She smacks my ass, an indication for me to move.

Climbing to the right, I start to rise from the bed. "I would comment on how much I like that... but we can't finish..." I trail off as I pull on my boxer briefs and athletic shorts. I purposefully keep my back to Ivy Rose while she dresses. If not, we wouldn't make it out of this room, and we have a very unhappy seven-year-old already.

"Do you realize we haven't used any condoms or that my birth control isn't working because of the antibiotics I was taking for my sinus infection I had last week? If we're going to keep..." She stops when she looks at me. I like that she's planning for this to continue, but I worry about falling back into friends with benefits. The benefits are nice, but I want everything with her and Mase. "So, there's a chance I can get pregnant... Wear a condom?"

I laugh. I'm not sure if it's because she ended her speech as a question or that she's worried about me knocking her up. Like I would complain about that. Actually, I like the idea. Seeing her carry my baby.

I shrug. "I'm ok with that."

"Good, so are you going to start sleeping upstairs with me... where the condoms are?"

"No." I head to the kitchen where Mase is waiting.

"Morning, Little Bear. Oh, hey, Mom! Nice for you to come home. Have a good time with Dad?" I throw the last part out, trying to figure out who her mystery guy is. The last few times she snuck around like this was with my father. Plus, Dad hasn't been dodging our calls or straight up not answering—something that's not like him, except when he's with Mom. For some reason, he answers on the first ring when he's with her instead of just calling us back later.

"So, this is home now?" she questions instead of answering mine. She is eyeing me like she's trying to figure out how much I truly know.

That's when Ivy's voice carries into the kitchen from the living room. "What do you mean *no*? No to wearing a helmet or to benefits?" She's not really stomping, more like quietly brewing since she noticed Mase is in the room. I'm thankful she coded everything up. I mean, she usually does, but still.

Mase pulls the eggs from the fridge while I get the flour and other dry ingredients. I'm in a fantastic mood, but I need answers from both of them. I can't openly say what I want since little ears are in the room. I'm going to fuck with both of them.

I answer my mother first. "Of course, it is. My son is here." I make a funny face at Mase when he brings the milk to the counter. "And the firecracker... who knows I'm not going to wear a helmet to get benefits." I glance at my mom but focus on Ivy.

Mom sees through the code. "Grant, I don't want to know!" Mom sets her coffee cup down on the island, attempting to hide her grin.

"Dad! Are you playing football without me? If so, you should always wear your helmet," my son lectures with a serious look on his face. Everyone but him laughs, which changes his serious look into confusion.

"Yes, Grant. Listen to your son," Ivy pops off, still smiling from Mase's comment.

I pull the bowl from the cabinet and begin dumping the Mase measured ingredients into the bowl. "Now he's my son instead of our son? Good to know."

"Just reminding you what can happen if you enjoy your benefits without your helmet." Ivy points her eyes at Mase like I wouldn't want another child. As if. I would fucking love that.

Instead of answering Ivy, I poke at my mom some more. "When will Dad be over? In a few hours or days?"

"Son, I'm curious about these benefits without a helmet. Mase, are you going to add chocolate chips?" Mom attempts to change the subject. Nice try. Besides, knowing my father, he won't be able to stay away from his grandson for too long.

"Nope, just blackberries and whipped cream." Mase adds the milk while I'm stirring. I used to use the stand mixer, but it's easier for Masen to help when I do it by hand.

A car pulls into the drive. "Pops is here!" Mase yells. *It took ya long enough, kid.* I thought Mase was just picking up on our conversation, but my father walks into the house, confirming my suspicions. Mase runs to the entryway and leaps into my father's arms, practically knocking the old man over.

I look at my mother, who has a guilty look painted across her face. *Busted.* "So, how long has that been going on?" My finger moves between her and him.

"How long have you been going helmetless? And it's none of your business." She calmly sits down at the island and sips her coffee.

I lean over so my voice doesn't carry into the living room where Mase and my father are. "Are you seriously complaining about my lack of a helmet since that would mean another grandbaby?"

She tilts her head back and forth. "True. Continue on. Sorry, Ivy, I gotta side with my son on this one."

Ivy Rose rolls her eyes and pours another cup of coffee for herself. I cage her in with my arms and whisper in her ear, "Don't be surprised if the rest of your pills disappear. I really like the idea of you carrying my baby."

"Seriously?" she chokes out.

"Hell yeah." I peck her on the cheek and grab a large spoon from the drawer beside her.

"What if the benefits are gone?"

I pour the batter into the preheated iron. "You won't do that. Besides, you want me to move back upstairs. Isn't that counterproductive?"

My sweet Rose crosses her arms in a vain attempt to outsmart me. "No. Not if we're trying to build something more."

I turn around to watch every move she makes. The subtle eye twitch tells me she's nervous, and how she's constantly swallowing is an indicator she's censoring herself. I'm not the only one evaluating facial expressions—she watches my every expression as well. I wonder how much my face tells her. I'm more expressive to her than I am at work.

My voice lowers almost to a whisper. "Do you want more?"

"Dad! What's that smell?"

Smoke billows from the waffle iron. I grab the tongs and toss the hard black waffle to the plate sitting beside the iron.

"Damn," I mutter. The fire alarm goes off from all the smoke. Everyone rushes around, opening windows, doors, and turning on the ceiling fan. Mase climbs on one of the stools with my dad right beside him, laughing.

"Still want waffles?" Of course, the little shit nods.

This is not how I imagined my morning going.

Chapter 31

IVY—PRESENT DAY

MY ENTIRE WEEKEND IS jam-packed. By the time I get home from Ephemera, it's almost 11:00 p.m. and everyone is asleep. Sunday isn't much better since Mitch decides to take the entire family to the aquarium. I shouldn't complain, it's a great idea.

Mase bounces between Mitch and Grant's side. The three of them together melt my heart. Mitch completes every activity with his grandson, even the ones Mase deemed "too baby-ish."

Grant calls his parents out and tells his mom to go home with his dad.

I'm grateful for Monday. I can sleep in and relax when I get home. No afterschool activities.

Oddly, my brother has disappeared. I haven't seen or heard from him since Friday night. I didn't really realize it until just now, and my fears are immediately alleviated when Jax struts through the door with Grant.

"Hey, what's wrong?" He must see the concern on my face.

I playfully slap him. "I was worried about you this weekend. No dinner. No stopping by. Not even a phone call or a simple text."

Grant pecks me on the head as he passes by. "He was in blackout."

I have to stop and remember what that means… and how a blackout is when the soldiers are not allowed to have communication with anyone outside of their squad or unit. Sometimes it's a security issue. Other times it's because another soldier in the unit or close to the unit was hurt or injured.

"Why were you not part of the blackout? I mean, not that I'm complaining."

"I'm being officially transferred, so I don't belong to that unit anymore. In four days, I belong to 20th Engineering Brigade." Grant hobbles to the den to change out of his uniform.

I look at Jax. "I don't understand. A few weeks ago, he said he was leaving Bragg. What happened?"

Jax smiles. "He put in for a different position so he can stay close to you and Mase. He bought himself at least two more years at Bragg. Maybe more if he can find a command position here too, which shouldn't be too difficult."

"No more Special Forces?" I ask.

Jax shakes his head.

"No more frequent deployments?"

Another headshake from Jax.

"He's staying? For sure, for sure?"

Jax shrugs. "As far as anyone knows. He's in a brigade that just returned from deployment, so their rotation is complete—for now."

I squeal like a teenager and rush into Grant's arms, knocking him onto the bed. Grant only managed to get his uniform jacket, pants, and a boot off before I burst in.

Grant chuckles. "What's this all about?"

"I didn't realize..." I pause, trying to figure out how to explain my thoughts, fears, and worst nightmares.

"What is it?" He cups my face, concern etched across his.

I can't fully verbalize the relief I feel knowing he's going to be home more. I mean, he can still get deployed, but this new position is less dangerous. I know if he works in a brigade, he's basically a paper pusher at a higher level. I'm completely ok with that. Better than ok. I feel the tears leak from my eyes, and Grant brushes them away.

His voice is gentle and comforting. "Oh, sweetness. What's wrong?"

"No more Special Forces?" My voice cracks.

A small smile that doesn't quite reach his eyes. "No. No more SF teams. I should be home every night by 1700… eerr—5:00. That alright with you?"

I nod, still unable to speak or stop crying. He uses one finger to lift my chin, forcing me to look into his eyes. "Did my accident scare you that much, or did this remind you of Eli?"

I'm honestly not sure. Maybe both? "I don't want to lose you." My voice shakes and breaks at the end. He envelopes me in his arms, rocking us slightly, then kisses my forehead numerous times.

Taking a slow, steady breath, he says, "I'm going to say something, and I don't want you to freak out or run from me. Can you promise me you will keep talking and not run?"

I feel stupid for running out during Cat's wedding reception, but I've been doing better and talking through things instead of running. I didn't realize how much I love him or how deeply ingrained in my life he is until he ghosted us. Grant is in my soul. If I'm being honest, he's probably always been.

"I love you almost more than anything. Right behind *our* son. I've worked my tail off for the last two weeks to ensure I stay at Bragg with you and Mase. I want to build a life with you. I miss the days when I used to wake up every morning in our bed together. But I'm not coming back to our room until you're ready to build a life with me. That's why I've stayed in the den. Honestly, I should've gone back to the townhouse, but someone is very persuasive." He gives me a pointed look, and I give him a pleased and proud look. It's not easy to manipulate him.

"I'm glad you didn't." I point at the hide-a-bed, "That needs a new mattress."

He wipes the last few tears from my face as his lips crush mine. A kiss that shows how much and how deeply our love is. He slows us down, which is slightly disappointing.

He pulls away. "You let me know when you're ready for me to return to our room. Don't ask if you're scared of losing me or lonely or horny. You can come to the den for that or to the townhouse." I'm sure he can see the worry written all over my face.

In a quiet voice that's completely unlike me, I reply, "What about Mase?" I want to push him on the bed and seduce him, talk him into staying, but the determined look on his face tells me only one thing will change his mind.

He releases a regretful sigh that I actually learned he got from his father. "I'm not breaking my promise to him. My ortho appointment is Tuesday. I should get the boot off and use my foot again."

"So, you're going back to the townhouse?" My voice breaks, but I'm trying to keep my tears at bay.

He lifts my chin so I can look into his gorgeous blue eyes. "I don't want to"—he closes his eyes—"but I should. We can't build our relationship doing what we've always done. It didn't work then... It won't work now." His voice breaks at the end like this is breaking his heart too.

I throw myself into his chest because even though he's the one breaking my heart, he's also the only person who can comfort me.

He kisses my forehead. "Stay for dinner so we can talk to Mase."

"Until I get settled in my new position, I'll have a lot of late nights anyway. But after that, I should have relatively normal hours." He wipes the damned tears from my cheek and continues. "What are you doing Friday night?"

Swiping the last of the tears that won't stop, I give him a small smile. Only Grant would make a joke at a time like this. "Washing my hair."

He shakes his head. "No, seriously. We've done everything but go on an actual date. I want to take you out."

Pausing my racing heart and mind to watch him, I realize I need to... be rational. His eyes begging. His mouth turns down in worry. "Ok."

A bashful smile appears, a smile I haven't seen from him since we were teenagers.

"Let's go feed Jax and Mase." He pecks the top of my head.

Chapter 32

Grant—Present Day

I'VE HAD TO RESCHEDULE my date with Ivy twice! The first time was because Mase was sick. I spent the weekend with him, helping Ivy so she could still work on Saturday. Then Ivy caught the flu bug Mase had. Instead of eating at a fancy restaurant, I'm having frozen pizza with Mase and playing Call of Duty while my sweet Rose sleeps. I am getting concerned since she's been sick longer than Mase was.

I hear Ivy's default ringtone go off in the bedroom. A few minutes later, the shower runs. Hopefully, that means she's feeling better.

"Dad, watch it!"

That reminds me we are in the middle of a game. A sniper almost killed me. I guide my character to the upper deck of the yacht for a better vantage point and give Mase advice on how to hide, then shoot the enemies as we tell each other to watch out. I lose track of how long we play until Ivy Rose clears her throat.

She's standing in the doorway of Mase's bedroom, leaning against the door jamb wearing black yoga pants and a purple T-shirt. Her damp hair hangs loose. Her cheeks are still flush since she always uses scalding hot water. "Grant, can I steal you for a quick minute?"

"Can we finish this level, Mom?" Mase asks as his character is shot. "Nevermind, that was my last guy."

I hand him my controller so he can finish off the game.

Oddly, she takes us to our bedroom. Part of me wants to celebrate that, but it *is* the closest room. "Thank you for helping me this week."

I give her a look like she's crazy. "Why wouldn't I? I've always been there for you."

"I know." She takes a deep breath. "I wasn't entirely sure if I was sick because of the flu since I'm late."

My heart stops. "You're pregnant?" *Fuck, yeah. This is the best news ever.*

She shakes her head, handing me a white stick saying *Not Pregnant*. My excitement drops into my stomach. I also want to throw her over my shoulder and fuck her senseless so I can *get* her pregnant. Ivy Rose has barely looked at me since we started this conversation, which makes me wonder if she's relieved. Probably since she said she doesn't want more kids.

Her gaze meets mine. "You would think I'd be ecstatic since we're in this limbo with each other. I mean, we're together, but we're not. But... I cried. I also waited three days to take the test, even though all the girls kept telling me to take it sooner. I convinced myself that's what's going on with my body and not that stupid little virus Mase brought home. For those three days, I saw our little family back together like it was before. You talking to my belly and..." Tears fill her eyes, but she blinks to keep them at bay.

"I know things were not perfect before and... Jesus, I don't think I'm saying this shit right."

I smile. "There were moments that our life was pretty fantastic, but we never talked about *us*... or our future."

"I know. I didn't see a future. I didn't see beyond those moments. But you taught me how to plan for the future, first through Ephemera, and helped me achieve my dream job. Then by being a dad without being asked, you just did it because he's a part of me. That was your way of telling me how much you love me without saying it cause you know me. You knew I would run from you... since, well... that's what I fucking do."

She gathers herself and continues. "I know I already apologized numerous times about what happened at Cat's reception, and we've talked about a lot of our issues."

"That we have." I smile at her, hoping she can see how I feel about her.

"It doesn't matter when I would've admitted I'm in love with you, you would've ran."

"You're right. I wouldn't know what life is like without your support, friendship, or love. I needed... Without you walking away, I don't think I'd realize how important you are. There isn't an us without you." She fidgets with her fingers, showing me how nervous she is.

I move my head slightly, trying to figure out what she's trying to tell me. I start to say "What are—" but Mase runs in.

"Dad, I finally did it! I beat the flag all by myself!"

I smile down at a grinning Little Bear, who's bouncing on his heels. "Let me finish talking with your mom, and we'll move on to the next location, ok?"

Mase nods, hollering that he's going to own the snipers in that level too.

We both begin to talk at the same time. "Go ahead," I say. Ivy quietly laughs, relaxing her fingers and not playing with them. *Here goes nothing*, I think.

"I love you," she says, then pauses.

"I know," I tell her, trying to keep from smiling. I want to jump and yell it from the windows for everyone to hear, but I keep my poker face and let her finish.

She shakes her head. "No, I'm in love with you and—"

"I know." I feel the smile escape, even though I'm trying to keep a straight face. She is the only person who has ever broken my poker face.

I can see how frustrated she's getting, but I don't want to say much so she'll get everything off her chest. "I-I want all the things I dreamed about when I thought I was pregnant. I want an us. Us the way you... the way I think you pictured us."

I use the soothing quiet voice that calms Mase and move closer to her so my mouth brushes against hers. Briefly. I whisper against her lips, "Tell me. I need you to say it."

Gripping the bottom of my shirt, she says, "Come back to our room. Help me make the rest of your dreams come true."

I close my eyes, relishing the words I've been waiting to hear.

I have to touch her. My lips descend on hers. This kiss is demanding, desperate, and filled with every ounce of love. It doesn't take long to forget everything but the gentle swipe of her tongue, the softness of her lips. I'm sure she can feel me against her stomach.

I break the kiss, trailing feather-light pecks along her jaw. "We need to stop. I promise to finish this tonight. But our son..."

I definitely hate stopping this kiss, but hearing Mase playing in the other room is the splash of cold water on my brain, reminding me I can't strip her down and show her exactly how much I love her right now.

The determined, lust-filled look in her eyes makes me excited for tonight, though I do want family time too. I don't want Mase or Ivy anywhere but with me.

"Don't even think about it," I growl. "He's staying with us. Besides, you owe me a date."

"Is he coming with us? You want to go on our first date with Mase?"

I give her a look like she's lost her mind. Why wouldn't I want to spend the evening with my family? "Well, yeah. What better way to start? Together as a family." I pull her back into my arms and whispers in her ear, "Later, we can work on changing the results of that pregnancy test."

"You want a baby now?"

She releases me, and I head back to Mase's room.

I shrug when I reach Mase's door. "I don't care when we start—today, tomorrow, next week."

"Those are..." Mase interrupts her when he drags me into his room.

I'm sure she wants to talk about babies and everything I just dropped on her. Throwing out her pills is crossing my mind. I would do it if I knew she wouldn't rip my balls off for it. Though if she throws them out... that's a whole other thing. One I would love to happen. Just thinking about having a baby with the woman I've loved for over twenty years makes me the happiest man on Earth.

Chapter 33

Ivy—Present Day

I check on my two boys a few minutes later. Mase barely notices I'm in the room until Grant says, "Thought you were getting ready for our date?"

"I didn't think you meant tonight," I say. "Where are we going?"

"We're not telling," Little Bear pipes up as he goes on a killing spree against zombies. "Watch it!" He moves his black controller like he would move his body.

"How do I know what to wear?"

He replies without his eyes leaving the screen. "Casual." The corner of his mouth turns up.

I know he's thinking something seductive. "Do I want to ask about that little thought you just had?"

"Wear a V-neck shirt or tank top," he adds.

"But not more revealing than that?"

"No, we are going to a family friendly place. Plus, I'm the only one who gets to see more than that."

"Possessive, now?"

Grant stops shooting zombie to face me. "It was no accident that guys dumped you after dating you for a few days. I couldn't stand the thought of anyone touching you—even then, but I was too stupid to realize what that meant." He turns back to the game. "And someone always chased my dates off too, right... babe?"

He calls me that just to emphasize his point. I did wreck every date, girlfriend, and anyone who was interested in him. I even told them he loved to be called babe and baby. Boy, did they. That's why he started to call me various nicknames with the word sweet in it like sweetcakes, sweet buns, sweetie pie, and the one he still prefers, sweetie.

I sigh. "Fine."

I leave them to finish their zombie-killing spree while I try to figure out what to wear. I do want to tease him without putting the girls on display too much since he did say it will be family friendly. I call Cat. Even though I've been around Grant for years and have done the whole friends-with-benefits thing with him, I'm... nervous. We've never dated.

"Did you take the test?" Cat answers.

I roll my eyes at her abruptness. "Someone eager? Dee is abrupt, not you. My question is why?"

"Didn't answer my question. Is that a no?"

I sigh. "I took it. Just the flu." A thought hits me on why she's being so bossy—Brax is home. He was gone for six weeks.

"Hmmm... bummer. Did you talk to him like everyone's been telling you?"

"Yes, Mother. Told him everything and that I love him. We're going on a date tonight. How's Brax?"

"He was a bit late coming home, didn't strut in until two hours ago. Need a sitter?" Her voice gets mumbled like she pulls the phone away while talking to Brax. "Who cares... Deal. So, bestie... do you need a sitter?"

I laugh and mentally give myself a pat on the back for knowing my friend so well, something that hasn't always been true. "I take it Brax doesn't like his evening being disrupted by a seven-year-old? That would also explain why you were a bit bossy earlier... Very Dee-like."

"Aww, cute. Like I would make Braxton wait... Ok, or I wouldn't jump his sexy ass the moment he walked in, which I've already done twice. So, not that I mind, but why are you calling, then?" There's my sweet friend. Brax must've left, not that he's made her change or is mean. She's so enamored with him that she still gets flustered when he's around.

I bust out laughing at her, knowing that Brax is begging for more sexy times with my bestie.

"Nope, and if he doesn't stop bitching, he's going to watch Cristian alone tomorrow night while my brother has date night with Dee." I imagine her shooting daggers at her husband. "Love you too," she says to Brax, then turns her attention back to me. "I adore him, but damn, he's been home like five minutes. You'd think having sex against the door and two more times would make him happy... Ok, it did. But I just need a moment to check in on my hot-mess bestie before I disappear with him."

"Let him know that his evening is still intact, so he still gets his sexy times with his wife. Grant wants to take Mase with us. It sounds like they planned the date together, which is adorable. But I, uh... What should I wear? I want to tease him but not show off too much since he said the place is family friendly. Help me?"

Cat answers as if she's been waiting for this moment. "Grab your lilac tank top and pair it with the white silk top with giant purple, lilac, and pink lilies. That top slings off the shoulder giving a peek at your cleavage. Your boobs look great in it, especially if you pair it with that lacy push-up bra you bought when we went to the lingerie store. Has he seen that set yet?"

"He hasn't seen any of the new sets."

"Maybe tonight, then?"

"There's no maybe about it. He's coming to our room tonight, and I'm screwing his brains out. Thanks for the advice. I need to get ready." We send our love with promises of seeing each other at work. I turn around when I hear Grant clearing his throat.

"I'm just checking on you." He runs his nose along my neck, smiles, and walks back to Mase's room. I was hoping for a kiss, a peck, something more than that. That smile tells me he heard the last part of my conversation. I bet Grant plans to tease me all night. Two can play that game.

I grab the pale pink push-up bra Cat was talking about along with the rest of the outfit she recommended and my favorite jeans. The only makeup I add is a little bit of mascara and lip gloss. Standing outside Mase's bedroom door, the television and gaming system are off.

Mase giggles. "I don't know."

Grant whispers to Mase from the blue bean bag he's relaxing in. His legs are spread out with his foot crossed over an ankle. Mase bounces on his heels, that adorable face filled with joy. Whatever the two of them are planning for tonight, I won't forget how happy this makes my little boy.

Our gaze meets, and a brilliant smile appears that reaches his eyes. "Ready to go, sweetheart?"

We arrive at Scene 55, an arcade with an indoor roller coaster, laser tag, go-carts, bowling, billiards, a small mini-golf course, and a full restaurant housed in an old automotive factory that spans almost two blocks. Flashing lights, beeping, money clinging, theme music, and kids screaming—it's complete chaos. Controlled chaos, but my little boy's face lights up as his gaze bounces from the arcade machines to the talking host encouraging players or leading customers through the game. That's not counting the smells of pizza, sizzling steaks, and stale beer greet us. Because even though this is a family entertainment center, it wouldn't be complete without a full bar.

I grip Mase's shoulder, worried I'm going to lose him in such a large place. Mase remains beside Grant with wide eyes, taking everything in. Grant steps up to a teen girl wearing a bright red uniform and name tag. He pays the girl, and she hands him a red card with the company logo that looks like a credit card.

Grant leads us off to the side. "Little Bear, remember what we discussed. You need to stay right beside either me or your mom, ok?"

"Got it." He gives a thumbs up. "Where are we starting?" Mase bounces on his heels, trying to contain his excitement. I gotta admit, this place is pretty amazing, and I'm kinda stoked about this.

Mase eyes a shooting game that I'm not sure is age-appropriate for him.

Grant notices. "You want to start on the arcade games?"

The biggest smile lights up his face. Grant looks at the game Mase was eyeballing and continues. "Let's try to find games your mom will play with us, ok?"

Mase hops on a Mario Cart game. "Come on, Mom. I know you like this game."

Grant swipes the card reader by Mase's knees, then swipes the two machines beside Mase for Grant and me. I pick out my character, Princess Daisy, a redhead like myself with a yellow dress. We play three games—Mase wins two and I win one. I think the two of them let me win.

The next game is air hockey, where Mase plays against me, with Grant helping him. Every time Mase scores, Grant winks at me. The next game is another two-player game. Grant stands behind me, wrapping his arms around me and placing his hands over mine.

He whispers in my ear, "Little Bear is vicious with this game and super competitive."

"Oh, well I can watch you guys play."

"Hell no! And miss the chance to get my hands on you?" He pecks the side of my neck.

Mase attacks me the moment the number one disappears. I squeal like a teenage girl for how badly my son starts beating me, but Grant moves the buttons over my fingers. We continue to play like that for another hour, until we deplete the credits on the card. Grant takes every opportunity to touch me, wink, and even give me the occasional kiss.

"Alright, how about we cash in these tickets, then go bowling? Do you want to eat while we bowl or after?" Grant's gaze shifts from me to Mase.

"Can we get pizza?" Mase asked.

"Sure." Grant pays for our bowling and places our food order while I help Mase pick something out with his tickets. Of course, he picks out a handful of candy and a small bouncy ball.

We join Grant at lane seven as he finishes punching in our names. I forget the sweet little things Grant does for me and Mase, like picking up our bowling shoes and setting them at the end of the cushioned bench. There's a pitcher of soda with three cups sitting on the table. It doesn't take long to pick out our bowling balls and slip the special shoes on. I'm about to say something to Grant about helping Mase when Mase grabs his ball and steps up to the lane like he's done this before.

Grant leans back, pulling me into him, and nods his head at Mase. Little Bear tosses the ball, but it veers to the left, only hitting the back two pins.

I look at Grant, then back to Mase, who has a perturbed look on his face. "He knows how to bowl?"

Mase's gaze shifts from the thing the ball comes from to me. "Duh. Dad and Uncle Jax used to take me every Saturday night while you were teaching." Mase throws his second ball, knocking down five more pins.

"Your turn, sweetie." Grant gently nudges me with the tips of his fingers.

I get up but turn around. "But I thought the two of you were taking turns with Mase while the other went out."

Instead of answering me, Grant nods his head to the lane. I throw the ball straight into the gutter. At least the next ball hits a singular pin.

I hook my finger into the bottom of Grant's T-shirt. "You didn't answer my question."

A sly smirk touches the corners of his mouth. "Sweetheart, why would I want anyone else when I have you?" He pecks me on the cheek and grabs his ball. Of course, the ass gets a strike. He coaches Little Bear, "Mase, aim the ball to the right a little bit." Then he turns to me.

"Rosebud, come sit with me and watch how to actually bowl. Maybe you'll pick up some tips from him," Grant teases, winking as he pours drinks for each of us.

"That is so not right." I playfully slap him and sit beside him, where he pulls me closer so my head can rest in the crook of his neck. Grant continues to give Mase directions on how to improve while he teases me about how horrific I am. We stop playing when our pizza arrives. The rest of the evening is filled with teasing, flirting, and laughter.

When we get home, Mase is so tired he practically drags himself upstairs, but stops in the middle of the staircase. "Mom, did you enjoy your date?"

I can't help but give him a small smile. "Of course I did. I take it you helped plan tonight?"

A proud smile crosses his tired face. "Yeah. I wasn't sure if you'd like it cause that's the kind of stuff I do with Dad and Jax. But Dad said you would love it just cause I planned it." He rushes back down the stairs and practically tackles me in a bear hug. "Love you, Momma." This kid melts my heart. Mase hugs Grant, then slowly walks upstairs again.

Grant slides his arm around me. "Time for the after party. I heard someone say she was going to screw my brains out tonight, or did you get too tired losing to a seven-year-old?"

I skim my hands up his arms. "Excuse me, sir. What kind of woman do you think I am that I would sleep with you on the first date?"

His lips devour mine, reminding me exactly how he feels about me. He grabs my ass with one hand, and the other pulls me to him so I can feel his hard length against my stomach.

He slows us down and whispers, "You are anything but easy. Come to bed with me and let me love you."

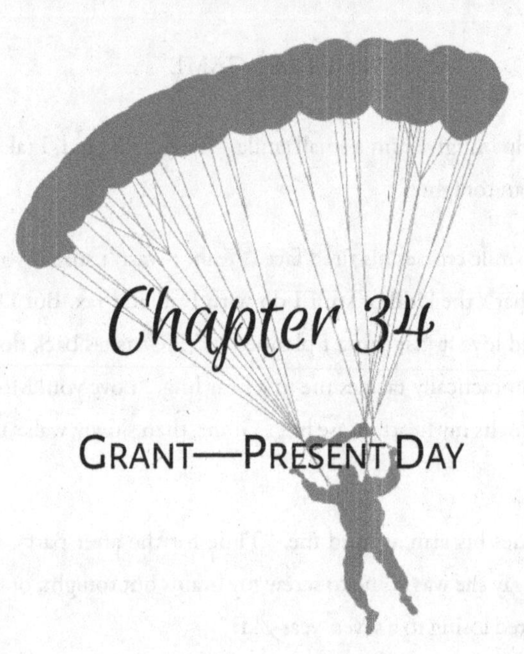

Chapter 34

GRANT—PRESENT DAY

"**D**AD! MOM WON'T SIGN my basketball form. Can you sign it?"

This shouldn't be the first thing I hear when walking in from a late night at work.

"Little Bear, let me change, then I'll talk to your mom. Where is she?" I look up to see Ivy Rose with her arms crossed, along with an irritated look on her face.

"Masen, we discussed this. Go to your room." She points to the stairs with that death stare. Mase stomps up two stairs. "Quit the stomping or I'll stomp on you!" Ivy hollers.

I cross the room, pulling her into my arms as her phone rings. She holds her phone up so I can see who it is—Charlie. I cringe, praying Charlie's family doesn't completely ruin our evening.

"Hey, Charlie." Thankfully, Ivy keeps her phone volume loud so I can hear both sides of the conversation.

"Not much. Just wondering if Masen plays other sports or has any other things coming up."

Ivy's voice drops showing her irritation. "Now why would I tell you that?"

"Umm... so we—well, really me, can have an excuse to come see him. Did I catch you at a bad time?"

I mouth that Charlie may not know.

"Have you spoken with your parents lately?"

Charlie's tone drops. "What did they do?"

"Sue me for custody. At first, it was for full custody and now it's for grandparent visitations."

"Oh, Jesus. I'm so sorry. There's no excuse for what a control freak my dad is." Charlie sighs. "I'm guessing there's no chance of me seeing Masen, then?"

Ivy gazes into my eyes, having a silent conversation without saying a word. I shrug.

Ivy explains to Charlie, "Part of me wants to let you come down since I know you don't have much to do with your family. But another part is hesitant. And what if you're helping your family take my son away?"

Charlie speaks quietly. "I get your reluctance since my family... well, my father... is a complete control freak."

"Let me call my lawyer and see what he says. I can't make any promises or know what to do since your parents... I have to protect my boy."

"I understand. I will do whatever the lawyer says. I will even do a visit at a lawyer's office, no matter how weird that will be. I don't want to lose my last connection, ya know?"

"Alright, I'll call you in a few days, then."

I take her phone and place it on the end table close to us. "Sounds like you're having a pretty fucked-up day." I dig my hands into her hair and place feather-light kisses along her jaw toward her mouth. Our kisses remain soft, slow, almost sensual.

"Yuck! You're kissing again. You're supposed to talk to her about basketball." Mase walks past us to the kitchen.

"Your son is a heathen today. His mouth is going to get him buried in the backyard," Ivy warns.

"I'll talk to him, but tell me why he can't sign up for basketball." One last taste to tide me over until bedtime, when I can properly cherish every inch of her body and help her relax.

Ivy rests her forehead on my shoulder. "I just thought we could have a season off from sports. It's tiring. He always joins multiple teams, and with the traveling teams on top of the regular club team... that means practice every day with games twice a week. That's early mornings and losing our Saturdays. I really love our Saturday morning routine."

I come up with a compromise. "He can play on the regular club team, but no traveling team since they tend to be over three hours away for games. I'm home more now, so I can help you with practices and shuttling him to and from games." I struggle trying to figure out why she would want him to take a season off from sports. Sports are a way to release all that energy.

"Fine—only club playing. I don't agree with this, but you're home more so you can deal with the parent drama." Ivy practically snatches the paper on the kitchen table and signs it. "Also, educate the child on his mouth. I need to finish dinner."

"Mase! We need to talk."

"What? Are you leaving again?" he sasses, leaving the kitchen.

"No. Knock off the backtalk or you're doing push-ups. Go apologize to your mother while I change, then come to my room."

I don't need to talk to Mase about his behavior cause being called out about it will put a stop to it. What Ivy Rose doesn't realize is that Mase deeply cares what she and I think about him.

Mase joins me in my room when I pull a shirt on. "Tell me what's with all this attitude toward your mom."

"She wouldn't sign the paper. You know how much I love playing."

"You know better than to treat her like that. You gave her an apology, right? If not, get down there and do it with a genuine hug."

"I forgot the hug." Mase turns back to the door.

"What're you doing?"

"Giving her the hug."

"Do it when we go down. Remember our talk about making us an official family?" Mase nods. "I think it's time to do that. You still want to help me?"

Mase grins and nods.

"Alright. Remember what we talked about."

Chapter 35

Ivy—Present Day

TALKING WITH MY LAWYER for most of the day isn't how I imagined it going, but I have answers and a plan. I feel better about the whole situation, especially since Clemson reminded me that the Sumners really don't have a case. They can push for grandparent visitation, but they can't force me to take him to Michigan for that. They have to come to us. And allowing Charlie to come here to visit with Mase will help our case since it shows I'm willing to work with them.

Charlie answers on the first ring, and instead of the customary small talk, I jump right into why I called. "When do you want to come see him? The lawyer said it's fine as long as you don't leave the state with him."

Her voice lowers like when she's angry. "I only want to watch him play sports and spend time with him. Unlike my family, I don't want to disrupt his life. He's happy. Jax is the fun uncle... and I want to be that awesome aunt for him."

I nod even though she can't see it. "Basketball has a weird schedule since the holidays break it up a bit. Practice begins next week, but games don't start until after New Year's. We haven't made plans for the holidays yet. Sometimes we go to Michigan, and other times everyone comes here. If you want to see him before that, just tell me when and we can plan something fun to do."

"Thank you... I appreciate it." Charlie's voice is watery and broken. "I'll check my work schedule and let you know when I can come down."

Spending the rest of my day in the metalsmithing studio tops off my day. I make three necklaces, finish off a pair of earrings, and start working on a wall design using bronze and steel. The annoying alarm on my phone tells me it's time to pick Mase up from school.

Mase bounces into the car with a huge grin on his face. "Did you have a good day at school?" I ask.

"It was ok. Is Dad home yet?" He's practically bursting with excitement about something. Grant normally isn't at home this early in the day.

"No, he'll be home later." I look at him through the rearview. "Masen, what's going on? Everything ok?" I give him the mom voice, so he'll tell me.

His little brows pinch together. "Yeah, Dad said he was going to be home early today."

"Okaaay... Anything *else* I need to know?"

At this point, Masen stops bouncing, and his eyes jump around before he looks out the window. "Well..."

"Masen..."

Masen sighs. "I had to stay inside cause you forgot to sign my permission slip."

We stop at a stoplight and my eyes slide closed. *Shit.* "Oh, Masen, I'm so sorry."

"It's ok. I didn't really wanna do it anyway, but my teacher made two of the dads sign it this morning. Dad said he would sign, but they said he couldn't do it. Only a parent could."

At the green light, we turn on Oak. "Oh... you're upset that Grant isn't legally your dad?"

He slowly nods.

"Let me think about how to make that happen, ok?"

We sit in silence for the next few blocks so I can figure out how I want to bring this up to Grant. The easiest solution would be to marry him, then Grant adopts Mase. Oddly, that thought warms my heart instead of scaring the shit outta me.

"Mase, I think I have a solution, but I want your help. Can you do that?"

He nods and points to our driveway, where a black GMC truck sits. "Told you he would be home." A pleased smile spreads on his face.

A dozen peach roses with one white rosebud sit on the kitchen island with a note leaning against it. Mase runs upstairs to put his backpack away. My curiosity is getting to me. A quick inhale of these gorgeous flowers and I read the note.

A rosebud remains closed to the world to protect itself.
It begins to slowly bloom for more sunshine and water.
For twenty years, you've been my rosebud, hiding the most
beautiful parts of yourself—to protect your heart.
These past few months, the more love and tenacity
I gave you, the more you opened up to me.
Thank you for allowing me to see you bloom—our love to
  bloom.
I love you, my sweet rose.

Taking deep breaths, I hold the note to my chest. I need to find Grant—tell him how sweet and... perfect this is.

"Come here." Grant pulls me into his arms, smelling like his sandalwood body wash.

"You scared the crap out of me," I playfully slap his back.

My left hand continues to press the note against my chest while the other grips the side of his shirt. Grant wraps his arms around me, securing him to me. Burying my face in his chest to be as close as possible to him, I barely notice the wet spots I'm leaving on his shirt. Hopefully, he's not wearing a white shirt since I put mascara and eyeliner on this morning. He kisses the top of my head.

"Sweetie, the poem can't be that bad."

I shake my head. "It was perfect. Did you pick peach cause it's my favorite?"

Grant pulls away just enough to cup my face. "Yes and no. Peach also symbolizes sweetness, which you are... Well, you are to me. And gratitude—I'm grateful for everything you've given me."

"Does the white rosebud have meaning too? I mean, other than my nickname." Unable to wait any longer, my lips gently mesh with his. He doesn't deepen the kiss.

"Of course. White symbolizes a new love and unity. I lucked out that the florist had a white rosebud."

I throw my arms around him "It's perfect."

Our kiss changes from gentle to demanding and desperate in seconds. Grant sets me on the countertop, almost knocking over my roses. I wrap my legs around him, pulling him closer.

He moves his lips down my neck. "I love you so fucking much."

Bringing his lips back to mine, he says, "I love you too."

"Eeeewww, not again."

Grant rests his head in the crook of my neck, taking calming breaths as he chuckles. "It's time, Mase."

"But we were going to do that together." A look of confusion passes over his face, then he grins before rushing back toward the den.

I can't help but feel a little annoyed. "What are the two of you up to?" I ask.

He gives me a quick peck on the lips before helping me off the counter. Mase returns with a small felt jewelry box—it's too big to be a ring box but too small for a necklace.

Grant encourages Mase. "Go ahead, bud."

"Mom." He pauses to gather himself since his little chest slightly shakes, showing how nervous he is. "This is something you made for someone to show the love between two people." He pauses, looking at Grant for support, who nods for him to continue. Mase whispers to Grant, "I forgot what else I'm supposed to say."

Grant chuckles and ruffles Mase's hair. "It's ok. Just open it."

I gasp when I see the rose-gold infinity engagement ring I made last month. Mase delicately picks up the ring and points to the smaller sapphires along the front of the ring, "My birthstone is here, see? I told Dad to add his too, but he said I'm more important than him."

Grant takes the ring from the box, and my nose starts to sting as the tears come. *Is this really happening right now?*

"The diamond is from my grandmother's wedding ring," Grant says. "She gave it to my dad for my mom, but he had already bought one and proposed beforehand. So, he gave it to me."

He kneels down next to Mase, and both of them look up at me. My eyes get flooded with tears, blurring my vision. I can't help the layered gasp and the quiver in my jaw. My heart is practically beating out of my chest. I feel hot and scared and numb and...

... And then Grant, the love of my life, the best man I could have ever wished for, the only man I've ever truly loved, says the words I never thought I'd hear come out of his mouth.

"Rosebud, will you marry me?"

I swallow. Hard. My first instinct is to run. At least, it would have been about a year ago.

But after I ran, I was brought face to face with my life without him. With my son without him. With waking up every day without him. I hated it. I hated myself for running, but I was too damn proud to admit it. And instead, I took it out on Grant.

Now... looking down at the two boys who mean more to me than anything else, there's only one thing that makes any sense.

I nod as the tears flood down my cheeks. My voice comes out in hardly a whisper. "Yes..." I swallow again and repeat myself. "Yes, yes, yes."

Falling to my knees, I put my arms around both of them. The sobs completely take my body over. I close my eyes and just give in. For the first time in my life, I give in to my emotions.

The three of us hold each other for who knows how long. Grant releases me to wipe the last few tears and pulls me into a kiss that I never want to end.

"Does this mean Dad can sign my papers now?"

Grant and I laugh. "Not yet, but we can call Pop's lawyer to have him draw up adoption papers that will make him officially your dad. If you want, you can even call Pops yourself to ask," I explain, swiping the few rogue tears from Mase's cheeks.

His entire face lights up. "I can?"

Grant hands Mase his phone. Mase animatedly talks to his grandfather while pacing the length of the kitchen.

Grant pulls me into his arms. "Who do you want to tell first?"

"I'm not sure. I'm torn between calling Jax to pick up our son so I can make love to my future husband or ordering takeout and watching a movie together," I say, running my hands across his chest.

"I love both ideas. I'd rather celebrate together—as a family. After our son is asleep, we can—" I cut him off with a soft kiss.

"Dad! Pops wants to talk to you," Mase hollers, even though he's less than five feet away.

"Ok. Help your mom figure out what to eat." He grabs the phone. "Hey, Dad…"

We spend the next thirty minutes figuring out where to order from and what movie to watch while Grant talks to his dad. I should call my family and at least Cat, but I want tonight for just us. Tomorrow, I'll announce it to everyone else.

Mase grabs his fluffy blanket and cuddles up on the sofa while I cue up the movie he picked. Shocking, another superhero movie. Grant drops in the space between us after grabbing the pizza when it arrives. Mase lays his football pillow on Grant's lap while I curl into Grant's arms.

Nothing better than being here with my boys. Life is pretty damn perfect.

Epilogue

SAMI

I NEEDED THIS. I'VE spent the past few weeks cleaning out my college apartment and letting my pageant coach know that I'm not continuing with the pageant circuit this year, even though I could compete for another year. My mother is lucky I've done it for this long. I hated every moment of it. The way we are criticized and critiqued just added to my own insecurities. Being the people pleaser I am, I felt like I was letting my coach down for not competing. I also felt a sense of relief. I can focus on finishing my PhD in psychology and figuring out my life post-college.

I haven't had a lot of time for my secret pleasure—cosplay. I adore attending Comic Cons and fantasy conventions. Nothing's better than pretending to be someone or something else for a few days. Sometimes, I'll even make up elaborate stories about myself for the weekend. You know, to match the outfit. Like when I dressed up in the white Princess Padma combat outfit, my name was Madison from Wisconsin. Or Charlotte from South Carolina. I'm not a very good liar. I seriously wonder how these people don't realize how full of crap I am.

Dressing up and attending these conventions always lifts my spirits; today is no different. I might even use my real name if asked. I have nothing to hide anymore. Who cares if they figure out I'm a *former* beauty queen? I don't have to worry about the judges or my coach finding out I'm cosplaying, even though I think it makes me more personable. Lance, my pageant coach, and I completely disagreed on my cosplay proclivities.

I arrived in Charlotte last night for this Comic Con. I'll fly farther south to my sister in a small town near the coast. Usually, I go all out for my costumes, but I packed most of them up. All I had within reach was my elf costume, which, according to the three nerdy guys, looks a lot like Zelda, or so I was told. I'm not a big gamer, but I have heard of the character. I also know Link is her love interest. He's also an elf who wears green with brown tights or brown pants.

After spending an hour searching, I finally find my favorite fantasy author situated between a comic bookstore and an artisan jeweler specializing in Celtic pieces. Stepping up to the author's table, I remind myself to not fangirl all over this woman. Buy the book, get a signature, and thank her for the beautiful worlds and characters she creates. Deep breath.

Thankfully, I do exactly as I mentally practiced. Walking away, I'm staring at her message with my name and her signature. She wrote my name! She said hi and thanked me for buying her book. Did I mention she said *my name*! In my excitement, I trip over my long dress, sending my precious book and my bag of other books flying. I knew this dress was a mistake...

"Are you ok?" a dark-haired guy asks, wearing a green elf costume... No... he's dressed as Link from that Zelda game! He's picking up my books, watching my reaction.

"I'm fine. I forgot I need to be careful with this dress since I'm not wearing the right shoes with it. Normally, I have higher heels, but those are still packed. I'm... I'm sorry. I doubt you want to hear about my costume issues. Thanks," I say as he hands my books back to me. I try to hide how frantic I am about my newly acquired *House of Beating Wings*.

"Is this the one you're looking for, Princess?" A smirk crosses his handsome face. I tend to lean toward nerdy guys. They are my kryptonite. My pageant coach always sets me up with athletic or business types of guys. Not my type. Too arrogant, too used to getting their way. This guy's not built, but he's not scrawny. There could be a few reasons why he called me that. Only one is acceptable.

"Princess?" I situate my bookbag before taking the most precious book from his slender fingers. I wonder what kind of job he has with those kinds of hands.

"Princess Zelda. The purple and white dress is the one she wore in *The Twilight Princess*," he answers with a kind smile.

I feel the smile cross my face, knowing this guy is like me, but with video games. "I never know which video game her costumes come from, but I can tell you which graphic novel it came from."

"Well, the games follow the graphic novels fairly accurately. The games always come before the books. Do you only read fantasy or do you venture into sci-fi?"

I tilt my head back and forth. "It depends. It has to have a good storyline. I'll DNF that crap without it or strong characters! I can forgive a slight lack of world-building, but not by much. Honestly, is it really fantasy without a strong world? It's meant to be an escape. An escape from reality. It's the author's job to create something special."

He nods. "I get it. The level of artistry needs to be there."

"Exactly," I say, snapping my fingers.

"Do you mind if I walk around with you?" he asks, stepping to the left so a family of four has enough room to walk by without the little Captain America's shield hitting his leg as they pass.

"It depends on if I'm right about your costume."

The smile falls from his face. "What, Zelda doesn't recognize her boyfriend and soulmate? If she doesn't, then we can't hang out." A smile returns, making his dimples pop and his eyes light up.

I slip my arm around his. "Come on, Link. What do you want to see next?"

We walk around the convention, shopping through Artist Alley, then enter the celebrity and photo op area. We spend the entire day and evening taking photos with has-been celebrities, voice actors, and attending panel discussions. We don't realize how late it is until the convention center begins to thin out, indicating it's almost closing time.

"Please tell me you have a weekend pass?" I ask, holding his hand while we make our way to the exit.

"My, my, my, Princess, are you eager to see me again?" That sexy smile appears again.

"I'll take that as a yes. Where are you staying? I'm across the street." Thankfully, he doesn't know I talk faster when I'm nervous. Why am I nervous with him? We've spent the whole day together. It was fun and so easy to talk to him.

"Down the street. Come on, I'll walk you back to your room so you don't have to carry all this stuff." He waves at a guy who compliments his costume.

"Are you saying I bought too much?" I tease with a small smile.

"Hell no. My mom taught me better than to judge a woman's shopping. Besides, this is Comic Con. There are things here you can't get anywhere else." He holds up his bag, which isn't even half full.

Thankfully, the spring Charlotte air is slightly warmer than it was this morning. Our short walk to my hotel is nice, so nice I wish it wasn't so close. I don't want our time to end.

We step into my room and situate everything on the small table by the window. "Thank you."

I mean to kiss him on the cheek, but he turns his head at the exact moment my lips touch his. Though, I can't complain about the way his soft lips feel against mine. He cups my cheek and deepens the kiss. Our mouths fuse together in harmony as he pulls me closer, and a satisfying hum from him lets me know he's enjoying this just as much as I am. I run my fingers through his hair, knocking his green cap off while he grips my ass, bringing our bodies so close that only our clothes separate us.

Is this how the heroines in books feel? Too bad I can't freeze time or cast some other magical spell to make this moment last longer.

He breaks our kiss to place open-mouth kisses along my jaw and down my neck, causing me to moan in satisfaction. "Princess, you taste so fucking good, but if you don't want—"

I kick my heels off. "Get me out of this dress."

He spins me around so fast the room spins, and before I can get my bearings, the dress falls to the floor, leaving me in my white lace bra and matching panties. No way am I admitting that I picked those out hoping someone would see them tonight. The look on my Link's face makes it well worth it—a combination of awe and lust.

His voice cracks. "You are so gorgeous." A wide smile crosses his face.

I slip my fingers under the two leather straps crossing his chest to lift them over his head, followed by the last two belts around his waist.

I can't wait a moment longer to touch those lips. This kiss is all lips, tongue, and some slight biting. I would moan his name for how he's making me feel, but I don't know his real name. Why didn't I ask before now? How did I spend the entire day with the man and not know his name? God, his arms feel good around me.

His magical lips travel down my neck, sucking on a spot right below my pulse point that drives me absolutely wild. "Oh, Link, that feels..." I trail off from losing my ever-loving mind as he drops small kisses and love bites along my chest and cleavage before wrapping his mouth around my nipple through the lace. A sensation that almost makes me orgasm on the spot.

He chuckles, sending a vibration from my left nipple straight to my pussy. "If you want to moan my name, call out my actual name. Joel." *So, that's his name. Very fitting.*

"You have too many clothes on." I moan and attempt to pull his tunic off, but I'm only able to grab the lower edge of the shirt since he tosses me on the king-size bed. I almost miss his quick striptease of tossing his boots over his shoulder, ripping his shirt over his head, and pulling off his tights, which he almost falls on the floor doing.

"How the fuck do women wear those all the damn time?" He gives me a panty-melting smile before he devours my mouth again, ending the kiss quickly as his hands go around my bra to my back. "This needs to go." He unsnaps my bra and tosses it... I have no idea where it lands since his lips on mine again are a complete distraction.

I weave my fingers into his hair, pulling it while his hands get acquainted with my breasts, followed by his mouth. Jesus, that mouth. I moan his name.

"Good girl," he says, sliding my panties off. "Princess, these are soaked." He gives me an evil grin that makes his green eyes sparkle.

"Someone is doing waaaay too much talking," I attempt to match his smirk with one of my own.

"Oh, Princess. I'm going to blow your fucking mind tonight." He places feather-like kisses from my breasts down to my thigh, but not touching where I want him the most. He runs his nose up and down my thigh and into the soft skin where my thigh and hip meet. A soft wisp of air hits my clitoris, causing my entire body to jump.

His tongue finally touches me... light like he's testing the best place for his tongue. Once he finds the spot he's looking for, he sucks and flicks. I wish I could say it takes a while for my orgasm to build so I can truly enjoy the things his tongue and mouth are doing, but it only takes mere moments before I see spots and explode in the biggest orgasm I've ever had.

When I'm finally able to lift my head, he's rolling the condom on. A soft tentative kiss is what we share before he asks, "Princess, do you still want this?" Part of my brain is questioning what he means by *this*, and the other part melts for the fact he's making sure I still want to have sex with him. No way would I ever say no, not after that mind-blowing orgasm. My mouth is physically unable to formulate words, so I merely nod.

Joel slowly slides himself in. I moan while he says, "Jesus, you feel fucking amazing."

"Then move." I slap his ass.

He chuckles, but he doesn't move as quickly as I expect. His response is a slow, languid kiss where his hips keep pace with our lips. It doesn't take long before I feel the tingle of another orgasm forming.

Gripping my ass and shifting my hips forces him deeper. "Oh my god, Joel. Right there." His lips dive into mine, and the orgasm sends me to the sky once again. His pace quickens, making me lose my damn mind in euphoria and bliss as he follows me shortly after.

He gives me a quick peck on the lips before he discards the condom in the bathroom, then drops beside me on the bed.

"Be right back," I say as I spring up and dash into the bathroom to pee.

I didn't fully appreciate this man's body. I have to admit, I tend to be attracted to a man's brain. The smart guys I've dated did not have much muscle... at all. But Joel has a four-pack with soft lines for the last two abdominal muscles to complete that six. He's not super muscular, but very toned. He has a lot of muscle definition. He *does* have that sexy scruff—the few days of growth but not quite a beard.

Joel lifts his arm from across his forehead. "You going to keep staring at me, or are you going to get in bed?"

"Maybe I just want to ogle you."

"I would say get over here so I can fuck you again, but I only had one condom." His eyebrows raise and lower.

Reaching into my bag, I grab a small box of condoms. "Good thing I brought my own," I say, tossing the box beside him.

"I would give you shit about expecting tonight to happen, but since I'm reaping the benefits..." Another sexy smirk. "Get your ass over here so I can give you more orgasms. We'll probably be late getting to the convention tomorrow."

"How late? Because there's—" I squeak as he jumps from the bed and tosses me over his shoulder. We land on the bed together.

He brushes a tendril of hair out of my eyes. "Tell me, how much can I dirty up my princess?"

"I did wait an entire century for you," I explain, remembering the storyline from one of the graphic novels.

"That you did. It's hot as hell you know that." We spend the rest of the night using half the box of condoms.

Two months later, I'm relaxing with my new group of girls—Lizzy, Dee, Cat, and Ivy—with their significant others at my aunt's beach house. I take another drink but almost choke when I see who walks up—Joel, my Link. Mr. Comic Con.

What the hell is he doing here? He's sexier than I remember, with water dripping down his defined chest to his abs, those toned arms... It's suddenly very hot out here. He drops that panty-melting smile, and I'm sure my jaw drops into the sand.

What the hell is he doing here?

Acknowledgements

First, my husband, who many times I've wanted to strangle—in the murder mystery way, not the kinky erotica way. You have been my sounding board and constant support for half my life. I wouldn't have the strength or courage to put myself or my writing out into the world without you. Second, the spawn normal people call children. I love all four—well, five counting our adopted neighbor girl, Victoria. Thank you for pushing, teasing, and encouraging me when my writing and life got the better of me. Alex and Mathew for helping me ensure my male voices are true to their occupation by letting me pick your Army brains or looking the information up for me. Alex, you listened to each bad sentence and helped me breathe life into this story. Mathew, you get another sentence just because you've been complaining that you don't have your own shout-out and living up to the stereotypical middle child. Thank you for the quirky metaphors you say and I steal for my characters. My sweet twins for the hugs and for making me laugh when I wanted to curl up in a ball. Victoria, you've listened to my whining, complaints, and celebrations. You are no longer the little neighbor girl or the beanpole's girlfriend—you are the fifth child. My aunt Rebecca, who has always encouraged me to follow my dreams from the first reading of Cinderella to yesterday when I complained about marketing.

Nay, you have been more than my editor. You've listened to my weird freak-outs, my meltdowns, and my odd notes and messages. Like the trooper you are... you laugh and tell me to get back to work. And you get my off-the-wall sarcasm and jokes. I hope we have many more books together.

My author friends—the saying is it takes a village to raise a child. I've heard this adapted for books. It is a labor of love, and all of you have embraced this newbie—crap, I guess three books, I'm not a newbie anymore—amateur writer.

Finally, the reader... this book wouldn't be possible without you buying, praising, and talking up books. Thank you for purchasing this book and supporting indie authors. Happy reading!

About the author

Randa Knight was born and raised in a small town on the Ohio/Indiana border. Her love of reading began with her grandmother reading to her every weekend. She has been an avid reader and blogger for the past few years. She studied Literature with a Creative Writing minor at Indiana University (Go Hoosiers!) where she fell in love with writing. The idea for the Boys of Bragg series began during a creative writing course and has evolved over the years.

When she's not writing, you can find her obsessing over her Mustang or at the dirt track not far from her house. You can find her on:

Website: www.randaknightbooks.com

Tik Tok: www.tiktok.com/randaknight

Instagram: www.instagram.com/randaknight

Facebook: https://www.facebook.com/groups/711841902510339

Twitter: www.twitter.com/randaknight

Also by Randa Knight

The Boys of Bragg series

A Change of Heart

The Art of Love

Read on to see where it began with Dee and Michael....

Dee

"NO, NO, NO, NO," I repeat, staring at the white stick I peed on five minutes ago. This cannot be happening. I had a plan. Until recently, I never planned anything. One of the numerous effects Michael has had on my life. He's a planner. Me, I'm a fly-by-the-seat-of-my-pants type of gal. These stupid things can be wrong, right? False positives and all that. Yeah, I don't believe myself either. No way can that little stick be right.

Great, just fucking great. I broke up with the man two weeks ago. Now I gotta call the sexy stud to tell him he's going to be a father. Never mind he's the love of my life. That's not what I'm focusing on right now. What I'm thinking about is that I'll have to see the smug look on that gorgeous face. I can't do it. I can't. I can't face those sparkling blue eyes, high cheekbones, silky jet-black hair, oh and how can I forget his sculpted body? The man works out every damn day and it shows. If I call him, he'll come over and I gotta face all that sexiness. I'll cave to him. I always do. That's why I had to break up with him. He makes me weak—everywhere. Oddly, he didn't fight me.

I pick myself up off the cold bathroom floor where I've been wallowing and grab my cell. The phone rings several times. "Hey, I need you to come here like STAT. It's..." I pull the phone away from my ear to see the person I need to speak with—Lizzy. What? I'm not making life-changing decisions without consulting my person. Lizzy has been my rock, my soulmate, since freshmen year at University of Nebraska where we were neighbors and later roommies.

"What's up? I have about ten minutes before I head in to help Aunt Ginny with her next meeting. Talk fast," she says, the exhaustion evident in the tone of her voice.

"Ten minutes won't do. I need you here now. I was just leaving you a voicemail. This is epic. Life-changing. I-I..." I trail off. I will myself not to cry.

Lizzy cuts me off. "Ok, you know I can't just hop in my car and run over to you. It's a two-hour plane ride or a ten-hour drive from New York to the beach house. I don't have time for this today. Please give me the cliff notes version of your latest meltdown. What, did Mike show up and sweep you off your feet... oh no...did he propose even though you broke his heart...again?" she questions. Her voice oozes with disappointment, and judginess is evident with the last part.

My voice cracks. "N-no. I-I just really need you," I say as I feel the tears trickling down my face. What makes it worse is that I can tell she's having a craptastic day too since she's rarely this blunt or terse with me. And she has level-five sarcasm going on, which only I usually do. Not sweet Lizzy. She's channeling her inner Dee. I knew someday I would rub off on her. Too bad it's me she's doing it to. Karma is a fickle bitch I've been served with twice today.

She sighs. "I'm sorry. I'm having a really, really bad day. I hate that I can't just drive to you. It makes me mad. Let me call you back in a few. I'll try to clear my schedule to come down for at least a long weekend." She whispers, "God, I hate this place. Love ya." Click. She doesn't wait for my response. That is so not like Lizzy. She's the sweet, considerate friend who puts up with my dramatics. I'm the selfish party girl who attempts to corrupt her. I really don't want to call Michael.

And I don't. Instead, I head to the local box home improvement store for some supplies. I need to dig my hands into the ground. Breathe life into something through my hands.

Four bags of fertilizer, two bags of potting soil, plants, a new trowel, an extra hand cultivator, and some seeds. I'm missing something. I continue to walk down each aisle trying to figure out what I'm missing when my cart abruptly stops. Chad. My co-worker at the Green Creek Community Center. Chad looks in my cart, raises his eyebrows.

"What happened?"

"I have no idea what you're talking about," I respond and smile innocently.

A full belly laugh escapes his lips. "Nice try, suga'," he replies with his deep southern accent. "Tell me what has you upset. You only do that," he says, pointing to my cart, "when you're upset about something, you know like every time something happens with you and..." Chad is interrupted by a short blonde, who wraps her arms protectively around his waist. That's his cue and he follows her. "This conversation isn't over," he says. Why couldn't I be attracted to that hunk of a man?

Great, something to look forward to on Monday. It won't just be Chad; he's got a big mouth. The gossipy little bitch will tell Bessie and Maggie. All three of them will gang up on me to spill my guts. I love my co-workers, but sometimes they annoy the hell out of me.

I lug the bags into the trunk of my car when Lizzy texts me her flight info. Guess I'm not gardening tonight.

Six hours and two pints of Rocky Road later, Lizzy whines, "Not that I'm complaining, but why are we only eating ice cream? This is not the norm—ice cream, pizza, and copious amounts of booze are. Annnd, you still haven't told me why I hopped on a plane to North Carolina." She licks her spoon clean.

I walk into my in-suite bathroom, grab the stick, toss it at her... and wait for her reaction.

Oddly, the klutz actually catches it. Her eyes bug out. "Ewww, gross. You peed on that? Holy shit! The two lines mean? Oh crap! Have you...?" I shake my head. I wait for her to process it so she can help me. It still hasn't sunk in. She takes a few deep breaths, looks me dead in the eyes, and adds, "What have you done so far?"

I shrug and murmur, "Peed on the stick... and called you... oh and went to the store." I plop down beside her to finish off the Cherry Chunk pint on the coffee table.

She squints her eyes, puckers her lips, and tilts her head toward the sliding glass doors that lead to the back deck. This is her thinking look. I need Lizzy to help me. "Call the doctor?" I shake my head. "Only me?" I nod. "Ok, so you're still freaking out?" I refuse to look at her.

She continues. "Of course, you are. That's why you called me here. Gardening supplies?"

"In the trunk," I reply.

"Where?"

"The beach house four doors down is empty." I lean back on the sofa, prop my feet on the coffee table, and a deep sigh escapes my lungs.

"How many of the neighbors are around?"

"Not many, one or two for the whole street. It's still off-season."

She disappears into her room, returning wearing faded jeans, a t-shirt, and a hoodie. One would think we're planning a crime instead of illegally landscaping my neighbor's yard.

"I'm presuming we're doing this tonight. Why are you still sitting there?" she questions. I love that she knows exactly what I need. I change so we can head out. This isn't the first covert gardening project we've tackled.

We unload half of my trunk into the neighbor's grassy area before I tackle it with the hand cultivator. Lizzy does the same a few feet from me.

"Do you remember when we came here right after graduation?" She rolls back on her knees, her eyes starry with a huge grin on her face. That was the greatest summer. It was also when we met Michael and his best friend, Josh.

Buy *A Change of Heart* from your favorite retailer.